STEELE-FACED

A Daggers & Steele Mystery

ALEX P. BERG

BATDOG PRESS
KNOXVILLE, TN

Batdog Press
www.batdogpress.com

Publisher's Note: This is a work of fiction. Names, characters, places, and incidents portrayed in this novel are a product of the author's imagination.

Cover Art: Damon Za
Book Layout: ©2013 BookDesignTemplates.com

Steele-Faced / Alex P. Berg — 1st ed.
ISBN 978-1-942274-17-9

1

I stood at the foot of a castle, five stories tall with sides of solid granite, worn and smoothed from age but capable of brushing off an ogre attack or catapult barrage with little more than a shrug. The high walls blotted out the sun and cast me into chill darkness, made worse by the snickering whistle of an evil breeze. Wrought iron gates, black as night and cool to the touch, barred entrance into the castle's depths, and I stood, rooted in place by the enormity of the task of breaking in.

Then again, maybe it wasn't a castle. Maybe it was just a five story apartment building with unusually thick walls and a bit of a pedigree. Maybe the looming shadow it cast over me had more to do with the angle of the morning sun than its gargantuan size. Maybe the gates were nothing more than doors and they'd open at the touch of my fingers, and maybe, *just maybe,* it wasn't the difficulty of entering that rooted me in place but my own indecision.

Either way, I was fairly sure a princess lurked behind those walls—although if history was any indication, she was in no need of saving.

The breeze blew again, a bitter gust that proved winter had well and truly arrived, providing me with the impetus I needed to pry my feet from the ground. I pulled on the wrought iron doors, cast my gaze around the lobby within, and found the stairwell.

Without even so much as a grimace, I launched myself up the steps. I fairly flew up to the fourth floor landing, or at least it felt that way to me. I'd recently broken the two hundred pound threshold, down twenty-five from my heaviest, and should a roving female hand find itself over my biceps or abdomen, it would find a bulge of muscle and no bulge at all, respectively. Through sheer force of will, as well as diet and exercise, I'd turned back the hands of time, although unfortunately no one had informed my hair about the temporal anomaly. It was all still there, thankfully, but the internal regulation system responsible for the slow loss of pigmentation from my crop of umber seemed oblivious to my new physical prowess. This morning, I'd counted a whopping twenty-seven grey hairs in the mirror. Twenty-seven!

In unrelated news, despite my exercise regimen, I still had way too much free time on my hands.

I crossed to apartment four fifteen. There, I adjusted the ratty piece of cowhide on my back, combed my hair a bit with my fingers, took a deep breath, and knocked.

I must've waited about a minute, though it felt longer. I fought the temptation to knock again. Once was enough.

The door cracked open.

"Well. Hello there, stranger."

A beautiful half-elf stood on the other side of the frame, tall and slender with piercing azure eyes, arched eyebrows, and a slim nose. Her long chocolate brown hair had been drawn into a loose braid at the front and swept over to the side, where it disappeared among the loose locks that tumbled over her shoulders. A cream-colored cowl neck sweater caressed her neck and hugged her torso, and a pair of dark brown trousers, single-pleated, pressed tight against her thighs before flaring out over her calves.

I spent five or six days a week in Steele's presence, from the crack of nine-thirty in the morning to sundown. It wasn't nearly enough.

She leaned against the door frame. "So what brings you to these parts?"

I cleared my throat and snapped the hem of my coat. "Hi. My name's Jake Daggers, and I'm selling these fine leather jackets..."

"*Fine* leather?" said Steele.

"Oh yes," I said. "Sturdy. Dependable. Warm, safe, and comforting. Capable of a tender, gentle caress."

Shay gave me a demure smile. "We *are* talking about jackets, aren't we?"

"Of course," I said. "What else would we be talking about?"

"What else, indeed?" Shay sniffed and turned the corner of her lip down. "Well, I don't know. The jacket looks pretty ratty to me."

"Don't be fooled," I said, running my hand across the exterior. "This is the display model. The real thing is much better."

"Is it, now?" said Steele. "So it's cleaner and fresher? The leather firmer and more supple? Stronger, perhaps lighter weight, and a little more fashion forward? Not something I'd be embarrassed to be seen around town with?"

I narrowed an eye. "We *are* still talking about jackets, aren't we?"

Shay smiled. "Of course. What else would we be talking about?"

"I can think of a few things, but I've been told I have an overactive imagination."

Shay stepped back from the frame and waved me in. "Come on in, Daggers. I'll be ready to go in a few minutes."

She didn't have to ask me twice. I'd been waiting for months for her to ask me into her apartment. Of course, I hadn't envisioned the first time to be as I waited for her to finish getting ready for work in the morning, but I'd accomplish the feat any way I could.

Steele hooked a right into the kitchen as I closed the door behind me. Instead of following her, I headed straight into what I assumed would be her living room.

A jungle had overtaken it.

Greenery sprouted from a hundred different pots, some on shelves, others on tables, and more still on the floor. Bushes and saplings, flowers and shrubs, bonsais, cactuses, and succulents. Annuals and perennials of all shapes and sizes. Enough bark, fronds, and petals to brew a thousand pots of tea.

Sunlight streamed in through a large east-facing window, bringing with it warmth and the fuel of life. A rich, earthy scent filled my nose, that of damp soil and the perspiration of leaves, kissed with a touch of sweetness from the half-dozen plants who'd flowered despite the season.

I ran a finger across the thick, ridged leaf of a four foot-tall shrub and called out to Shay. "If you'd have warned me, I would've brought my machete."

Her voice trailed over from the kitchen. "And risk having you cited for possession? Better to leave you unawares."

It was a felony offense in New Welwic to carry around a weapon with a blade longer than six inches, even for police officers. For keeping the peace, I made do with my nightstick, Daisy, which I continued to refer to by name despite Shay's protests. Her steel-weighted efforts were better served against skulls than trunks and branches, though.

A small, leafy plant with bright purple flowers caught my eye. I found a path through the underbrush and crossed over to it.

"You like that one?"

I'd just knelt when Steele's voice brought me back to my feet. She stood at the edge of the plants, resting her elbows on the edge of one of her sofa chairs.

"This is the plant you brought with you on the first day of work," I said. "What is it? A tulip of some sort?"

Shay smiled and snorted, as if she were on the edge of a chuckle.

"What?" I said. "You're surprised I remember? You're not the only one with superior observational skills. Or am I totally wrong about this thing's genus?"

Steele picked her elbows off the chair and joined me by the flower. "No, you're right. It's a dwarf tulip. Pulchella variant. And you were right about the pit, too."

I'd warned her at the time there wasn't near enough natural light by our desks to support life. I'm not even sure how *we* survived, to be honest. Copious amounts of coffee, probably.

"Well, it sure perked up, didn't it?" I said.

"It just needed light and love." Steele stroked one of the petals with a perfect fingernail.

"And here I thought you weren't into horticulture."

"What gave you that idea?"

"On one of our cases," I said. "I mentioned something about you being close to the trees because of your elven heritage, and you countered by saying you grew up in an apartment downtown."

"Midtown. And that doesn't mean I don't like plants. Obviously." She waved her hand around the room. "New Welwic is sorely lacking in greenery. At least here, I can keep the chill out, and every once in a while, if I'm lucky, I get a flower. Even in winter."

"Do you have a favorite nursery?" I asked.

"Honestly? I got most of these from my aunt. She's a botanist. She tells me how much water they need and when to prune them. If it were up to me, half of these would probably be dead."

"So your aunt's a botanist. Dad's a chemist," I said. "Science runs in your blood, doesn't it?"

"It's better than high cholesterol." Shay smiled. "Be right back."

She stepped around the foliage and disappeared into the kitchen.

I inspected another plant, one with thick, fleshy leaves. "Speaking of your folks, how are they?"

"Good," she called back. "As much as I hate being forced away from work, it was nice spending a few days with them. I got to see both of my brothers."

I'd warned Steele after our last case, in which she'd been kidnapped and imprisoned, that likelier than not the Captain would force her to take time off to rest and recuperate. Never mind she'd been imprisoned for a grand total of four hours. It was about avoiding 'mental fatigue,' something the Captain was keen on—in other people. I'd never seen the bulldog take a day off in his life.

Perhaps that's why I'd been so nervous standing outside Shay's apartment building. The Captain had banished her from the precinct mere hours after the resolution of our last case, and rather than sit around, mope, and read dopey mystery novels like I would've—and in fact *did* during my own administrative leave—she immediately departed to see her folks, all of which meant I hadn't had a chance to spend time with her since the arrest of our killer. Or since our passionate kiss.

I remembered it well. Sitting there in the dark, our sight nullified but other senses heightened from danger and anticipation. The press of her body against mine. The faint hint of her lilac perfume. The sweet taste of her lips and the brush of her hair against my face. I'd frozen the moment in my mind. Names, I might forget. Birthdays, too. Childhood friend's faces? You bet. But that? Never. The hint of honeysuckle on her breath, and the scent of—

"Coffee?"

I blinked and looked up from the succulent. Steele had returned, and in her outstretched arms she offered me a thermos.

I accepted it and took a sniff. "Where'd you get this?" Steele wasn't a coffee person, except for the occasional cappuccino.

"I had it on hand."

"But why?"

"Because I figured you'd be over here sooner or later, and I know you enjoy it."

I took a sip. Warm, bold flavors exploded across my tongue, containing hints of nuttiness and smokiness and a smooth chocolate aftertaste. Steele hadn't just made me coffee. She'd made me *the best* coffee.

I moaned a little. "That's it. I'm in love."

Shay's eyes widened. *"Pardon?"*

"What? No. I mean with the coffee. *The coffee.* That is... I, uh...like it? A lot. So...thanks." I cleared my throat and inspected the ceiling.

The smile returned to Shay's face. "Well, I'm glad you enjoy it. I can share where I bought it, if you like, but it's a bit of a hike. Let me grab my coat and we'll head out."

Steele turned, and I wiped my free hand across my forehead. I'd avoided that crisis with my usual deft flair, but my slip of the tongue brought to mind bigger questions. How *did* I feel about Shay? I couldn't be in love.

We weren't even dating. Well, perhaps we were, even if we hadn't gone on a date since the conclusion of our last murder. And then there was the coffee situation. I tended to drink throughout the day, but I absolutely *needed* the rich brew in the mornings after waking up. Shay knew that. Which could only mean...

I glanced toward her bedroom. Could she be sending me a message?

I sighed. If only women were as easy to solve as murders.

2

Morning sunlight glinted off the seal of justice over the entrance to the 5th Street Precinct. Despite the chill, beat cops milled outside the broad double doors, chatting and smoking and shuffling their feet, as did young runners with hopes of earning coin in exchange for their services. My old pal Tolek, proprietor of a mobile pastry cart, purveyor of fried goods, and preyer on unsuspecting detectives' stomachs, waved at me, trying to get me to come over and purchase one of his delicious apricot kolaches. I waved and smiled in return, but I didn't reach for my coin purse.

I turned to Shay, who'd bundled herself in a shearling jacket, scarf, and gloves, and spoke under my breath. "I wish Tolek would stop hanging around the precinct entrance. It's awkward seeing him every morning and not buying anything."

"You make it sound like you're ex-lovers," she said.

"You jest, but those looks he gives me? I gave my ex-wife Nicole much the same for the first year or two of our breakup."

"So go over there and buy something if you feel so bad," said Shay. "Doesn't even have to be for you. Think how happy you'd make the rest of the station if you sprung for a couple dozen donuts."

"And risk a citation from the Captain for willfully fattening members of the force?" I snorted. "You know how he is about our healthcare premiums. Besides, I don't think it would be a good idea. It would only make Tolek pine for me that much harder. Look at him. He's devastated."

He kept smiling and waving.

I shook my head. "Poor sap."

Steele snickered. "You're a heartbreaker, Daggers. Get the door for me?"

I did, and we waltzed into the precinct, past the welcome desk, and into the dimly-lit heart of misery, gloom, and despair we lovingly referred to as the pit.

In truth, it wasn't so bad. It was austerely furnished, thanks to the city legislators' belt tightening efforts, and gloomy to be sure—the only natural light we got was what trickled through the windows in the Captain's office—but hidden behind the heavy, not-quite antique desks and the ever-present musty odor hid a bit of rustic charm. Or so I'd convinced myself, anyway. It was possible I'd been around the precinct long enough that, like a kidnappee, I suffered from severe capture-bonding.

I followed Steele as she snaked through the cubicles toward our own desks on the far side. We weren't more than twenty paces from our thrones when a big, rumbling voice cut across our path.

"Hey, Steele. Welcome back."

Like a hill giant surging from underneath a layer of dried leaves and detritus, Quinto rose from his desk and lumbered over to join us. Standing roughly six feet, seven inches tall and weighing over three hundred pounds, he in many ways resembled a giant, but the grayish tinge to his skin hinted at a different heritage, one with a little less giant and a little more troll.

Not that I knew for sure, of course. No one at the precinct did, unless our resident coroner and Quinto's girlfriend, Cairny, had been successful in liberating the information. Regardless, we all knew better than to press the issue. Quinto was sensitive about his lineage and not because of his mismatched buckteeth, brick outhouse-like stature, or looks only a mother could love. Rather, Quinto hated the stigma of weak-mindedness society attached to the so-called lesser races: orcs, ogres, and trolls. He prided himself on being as clever, observant, and astute as the rest of us. Ten years of working at his side had proven he was far better than most.

"Glad to *be* back, Quinto," said Steele. "And I'm happy to see the precinct hasn't descended into anarchy and chaos in my absence."

"Anarchy and chaos?" Quinto smiled and snorted. "That's a bit much. Although a churning morass of sloth and inactivity...?"

Steele lifted an eyebrow. "It's been that bad?"

"Are you kidding?" said Quinto. "For one thing, we haven't had a murder since you left, which alone makes for dull times. But then you add your absence to the equation, and, well...you know Daggers."

I puffed out my chest. "I was a model of inefficiency. A coffee-swilling, light banter-slinging, rib-elbowing machine. A primo chatter, eavesdropper, and nose sticker-intoer. I died and was reborn as an anthropomorphic sloth."

"His chatty nature negatively impacted us all," said Quinto. "I barely got any work done."

"Work?" I said. "What work? You admitted we didn't have any murders to investigate."

"Since she's the analytical sort, I present to Detective Steele the evidence." Quinto leveled a thick finger at his desk, pointing out a stack of unfinished paperwork, then shifted the finger to Shay's and my own desks, upon which languished much larger stacks of paperwork.

"Oh. *That.*" I shot Shay a smile. "Well, I couldn't very well deny my partner the sheer *joy* of filing past-due forms."

Shay rolled her eyes. "Yeah, it's boring moments at your desk where you really form those lifelong bonds, you know?"

"Precisely," I said. "Who needs passion and adventure when you can dive into a good T99 or 1053B?"

"Or a P96." Rodgers, bright eyed and bushy tailed as ever, arrived and slapped a sheet of paper against my chest.

I furrowed my brows at my blonde-haired, blue-eyed, unfairly handsome pal. "P96?" I glanced at the sheet. "What the heck is this?"

"A requisition sheet from the folks in accounting," said Rodgers. "Apparently they took your three day saunter around the station as evidence you don't have anything to do, so they're letting us conduct our own inventory on office supplies." Rodgers turned to Steele. "You heard, right?"

"I heard."

I shook my head. "I should've seen this coming. The Captain's not the only one with a mean streak. Speaking of which, where is the old jarhead?" I glanced at the bulldog's office, but I didn't spot him through the windows.

Quinto glanced at the empty office, too. "Apparently he's meeting with the chief of police and the DA. Fallout from the Wyverns case."

I chewed on my lip. During our last investigation, the Captain had revealed to me information about a former smuggling ring which we'd eventually brought down. As it turned out, the Captain had known one of the major players in said ring. At one point, they'd had a cordial relationship. While I believed the Captain had never taken hush money or acted against the best interests of the department, he might look less than sympathetic in the eyes of the public, especially once the prime suspect in the case was forced to testify. The Captain had assured me he'd get through the mess unscathed, but I wasn't so sure.

I forced my eyes away from the office. "So I'm guessing there haven't been any new murders this morning?"

"Not that we know of," said Quinto.

I pumped my fist.

Shay unleashed her upturned eyebrows on me. "You do realize this means we need to wade through that stack of paperwork?"

My face fell. "Oh. Right."

Rodgers lifted a finger. "Actually...that's going to have to wait. The Captain left instructions for the two of you before he left for his meeting this morning."

That was different. "Go on."

"He said you should talk to a Detective Steck in vice, on the third floor," said Quinto.

"What about?" I said.

The big guy shrugged. "How should I know? He didn't elaborate as he stormed out the front doors. Just made sure we knew to tell you your cooperation with Steck wasn't voluntary. Whatever he says goes."

I scratched my head. "Well, I'm not sure how much I know about vice crime, but it if gets me away from a T99, who am I to complain?"

"But you don't need passion or adventure if you've got forms." Steele made her eyebrows dance at me.

"You really need to stop using my own words against me," I said. "It's eminently fair and reasonable, and I can't stand it."

"Then maybe you should stop stretching the truth all the time," said Steele.

"And ruin the aura of carefree indifference I've toiled for years to create? In your dreams."

Shay leaned in. "As if you knew what I dreamed about..."

She pulled away, and I took a long draught of my coffee, more as a way of preventing speech than anything else. It wasn't really a question, but for my own well-being, I didn't trust myself to provide an answer.

3

We found the indicated desk on the third floor by the bronze placard on it that read 'G. Steck.' Luckily for us, a man sat in the chair behind hit, his head buried in a notebook and a pencil twirling between his fingers.

"Excuse me," said Steele. "Detective Steck?"

The man lowered the notebook, revealing a face so smooth I was surprised his nose hadn't slid right off. I would've pegged him as having barely celebrated his twentieth birthday if not for the dangerous lack of hair at the corners of his temples. Short, golden brown stubble covered the rest of his head, and a prominent mole on the top of his left cheek provided a point of reference in an otherwise featureless face.

He smiled. "Ah. Detectives Steele and Daggers, am I right?"

I eyed the mole. It wasn't hairy, thank the gods, which meant I could probably force myself to ignore it. "Guilty as charged. I'm Jake, and this is Shay."

"Glenn. Nice to meet you." We all shook hands. "Pull up some chairs. I'll be right back."

Steck stood and rounded a corner, calling out as he did so. "Munn? Hey, Munn! They're here."

Steele and I grabbed chairs from a pair of empty desks and plopped them in front of Steck's workspace. Steck returned and seated himself, as did we. A moment later, a stocky middle-aged woman with a bouffant haircut and a maroon pantsuit appeared.

She extended her hand. "Detective Summer Munn. Fraud. Nice to meet you."

Steele stood and shook the woman's hand. "Detective Munn. How is it we haven't met yet? I thought I'd sought out all the women in this precinct by now."

"There aren't many, are there?" She shook my hand in a perfunctory manner. "But you didn't miss me. The Grant Street Precinct is my home base. I've only been here a couple weeks collaborating with Steck on our case."

"About that," I said. "I'm afraid you have us at a disadvantage. We arrived after the Captain left this morning, so all we know is you wanted to speak with us."

Steck launched into a spiel as Munn left in search of another chair. "Right. Sorry. This all developed so quickly. Well, not really. It's been in the works for two weeks now, but it all went to hell overnight, and the Captain thought the two of you would give us as good a shot of success as anyone in the precinct."

I shared a glance with Steele.

"Why don't you start at the beginning?" said Shay.

"Of course," said Steck. "As I suspect you know, I'm in the vice division. I mostly work on gambling cases. I can't tell you how many underground dice parlors I've shut down. Actually, I *can* tell you. Thirty-seven. I tend to obsessively count things. And share too much personal information, which is neither here nor there, but you're going to figure it out yourselves, so I might as well warn you."

Munn returned with a chair. "What he means is he has a hard time shutting up."

Steele snickered. "Don't worry. Daggers suffers from a similar ailment. I call it foot in mouth disease."

"Anyway," said Steck, "as Munn already let you know, she's in fraud. Now you might be wondering why fraud and vice are collaborating, but it's quite simple. You see—"

"Somebody's running a gambling con?" I said.

Steck deflated like an old balloon. "Um...yes."

I felt bad for stealing the guy's thunder. "Sorry. I should've let you finish. Like my partner said, foot in mouth."

"No, it's good," said Steck. "You're thinking. You're on your toes. We'll need that for later. But yes, we're investigating a *potential* gambling con, one involving three well-known players: Johann Preiss, Orrin Wyvernjaw, and Ghorza Skeez. We're not entirely sure *how* the con is going to go down, but we've heard enough rumors from contacts in the underworld to know something is afoot, and we have a very good idea of *when* and *where* it's going to happen."

"Well, if you know when and where the illegal gambling event is going to take place," said Steele, "then it should be easy to take down. You can stop it before it starts."

"If it were that simple," said Munn, "then Detective Steck wouldn't have needed to collaborate with me."

"So what's the problem?" I asked.

"The problem is the purported con isn't supposed to occur at an illegal gambling event. The event we're tracking is one hundred percent legal. Have either of you heard of the *Prodigious*?"

"The prodigious what?" I said.

"It's not an adjective," said Steele. "It's a noun. A ship's name. She's the enormous new steam ship whose construction recently finished, isn't she?"

"Correct," said Munn.

I eyed Steele over the length of my nose. *"Steam ship?"*

She responded in kind. "Yes, Daggers. Get with the program. You remember when we went to the World's Wonders fair, right? And we saw that Bock Industries steam engine and generator? I told you steam technology was old hat. The impressive part of Bock's design was getting it into such a small package. But the *Prodigious* has been making headlines for the exact opposite reason. It's, well...*huge,* to use a synonym. Every part of it. Including the steam engines."

"To be specific," said Munn, "the *Prodigious* isn't simply a steam ship. She's an ocean liner. A 'pleasure vessel' as the press is calling her. She has a ballroom and a theater, an indoor pool, a massage parlor, and exercise quarters, among other things. And the main draw is its casino."

"They can have that on the ship legally?" I said.

"As long as they only operate it while over international waters, yes," said Steck. "And to celebrate the

Prodigious's maiden voyage, the ship is hosting a high stakes poker tournament in one of its private rooms. So now you know why we can't shut down the event which is supposedly being targeted."

I stroked my chin. "I see. How high a stakes are we talking about?"

"Twenty thousand crown buy in," said Steck.

I tried to whistle and failed. I'm a horrible whistler.

Steele took up my slack. "Wow."

"Exactly," said Detective Munn. "Not only is this tournament going to be a huge money maker for the ship's owners, but they hope the publicity it generates will attract other high rollers, both domestic and international, to its tables. So you can imagine they haven't been particularly receptive to our suggestion they shut the tournament down until we can get a bead on the con we've heard rumors about."

"The ship's top brass won't less us shutter it unless we come to them with definitive evidence showing who's going to commit the fraud and how it's going to be committed," said Steck. "Unfortunately, we don't have that yet, and given the ship departs *tonight,* it's simply not going to happen."

"I could see how that's problematic," said Steele.

"The good thing," said Steck, "is the ship's owners *are* concerned about publicity, and they realize how detrimental news of a botched poker tournament would be to their public perception. So they've agreed to—nay, *demanded*—a police presence onboard. They want officers with eyes on the table at all times. But they don't want square-shouldered thugs loitering around, intimidating their patrons and stinking up the joint. Neither would we. If the parties involved found out we knew what they were up to, they surely wouldn't try anything, or they'd drop out entirely. So, in conjunction with the ship's management, we've come up with a solution we think fits everyone's best interests."

"You're putting someone in the poker game?" I said. "Sorry. Sorry. Foot in mouth, again. You tell us."

"Not someone," said Steck. "Two someones."

Suddenly, I knew why the Captain had called on us. "Hold on. You want to insert me and Detective Steele into a high stakes poker tournament on a swanky luxury boat?"

"Oh, we don't *want* to," said Munn. "We'd rather send in Detectives Hawthorne and Reeves who've been training to go undercover on this mission for the past week. But two days ago they started to feel unwell, and last night they both broke out in a full body rash. The doctor says they've come down with a case of the goblin pox. It won't do any lasting harm, but it's highly contagious, and the two of them need to be quarantined for at least ten days."

"And the Captain somehow thought Steele and I would be good at this?" I said. "I'm not sure how much he knows about my private life, but what Quinto, Rodgers, and I used to do on the weekends over beers was purely for fun. We bet pocket change."

"It's not that simple," said Steck. "You don't know them because they hail from Grant Street, but Detectives Hawthorne and Reeves are a husband and wife pair."

I glanced at Steele. "Uh...where are you going with this?"

"We built a profile for them," said Munn. "A young power couple made rich off commodities trading, Thomas and Samantha Waters, who now play fast and loose with their money in search of adventure and excitement. They hail from up the coast in Littleneck Harbor, to keep their identities mysterious. By now all the other players will have heard the rumors. They'll be eager to learn more about their new competitors, and while I doubt they'll bat an eye if your temperaments don't fully match expectations, if nothing else, they *will* be expecting a couple. And unfortunately for me, no two other people on my fraud team fit that bill. Heck, nobody in the whole Grant Street Precinct does."

"When we came to him with the problem, the Captain suggested you," said Steck. "For one, he thought Detective Steele's unique abilities might come in handy, and for another, he assured us you had a very close working relationship."

The first part didn't faze me. Steele was known as the precinct's resident spell-slinger due to her psychic ability—something only I, Quinto, Rodgers, and Cairny knew to be a total load of hogwash. I carried as much psychic power around in my big toe as Shay did in her whole body. But the second part? Was it my imagination, or had Steck had gone out of his way to emphasize the 'working' in working relationship? Did that mean the Captain knew? Steele and I had tried to keep our feelings for one another hidden, but we'd engaged in that one spat in the interrogation room, and Steele had kissed me outside the precinct not less than a week ago. Rumors had a way of travelling.

Steele took it all in better than I did. "So let me make sure I understand this correctly. You need a pair of detectives, one male and one female, who can pose as a couple. A pair with a strong relationship who know each other's strengths and weaknesses, not only because they'll be working together to unearth some as yet unknown gambling fraud, but because they'll need that strong connection to get them through the tournament. And I'm guessing you're also looking for a pair with all the qualities you'd otherwise want in undercover detectives: quick wits, good eyes, and the ability to play a role."

"Don't forget gambling experience," said Munn. "But that might be asking too much."

"Well, I dabbled with card games in college," said Steele. "And I'm quick on the uptake. What do you think, Daggers? We've got this, right?"

No hesitation. I liked that about Steele. She was strong and confident and wasn't prone to false modesty, but there was a lot more to this assignment than wits and gambling prowess. The part where we were supposed to pose as a couple, specifically. And she hadn't hesitated.

"I don't know, Steele," I said. "It's one thing to play a few hands of cards with buddies over brews, but the dynamics change when you raise the stakes. I mean, twenty thousand crowns? *Apiece?* Even accounting for the fact that we're not playing with our own money, we can throw betting and bluffing psychology out the window. Speaking of which, is the department really putting up *forty thousand crowns* on this endeavor?"

"We get it back if either of you win," said Steck. "Or if we catch any of the other competitors in a con. So, uh...no pressure."

"The good news," said Munn, "is the ocean liner's managing corporation is so desperate for positive press from this tournament that even if we lose—and there's no fraud committed—they'll refund us half the buy in. So even the worst case scenario won't be a total loss. But if we go in and fail to uncover anything, you can bet the accountants will never authorize anything of this magnitude again. So, yeah. No pressure."

I glanced at Steele. She raised an inquisitive eyebrow.

"If it makes any difference," said Steck, "I'll be on board the whole time posing as a porter, and I'll be working with the staff behind the scenes, which means even though the two of you will be limited in your authority due to your cover, I'll be able to poke and prod and hopefully give us an advantage over the competition."

I took a deep breath and let it out through my nose.

"Did I mention the trip is all-expenses-paid?" said Steck.

"*Oh.* Well in that case, count me in," I said.

"Please, Detective Daggers," said Munn. "This is serious."

"I know. I'm kidding." I sort of was. "But Detective Steele is right. You can count on us. We'll get the job done."

Steck breathed a sigh of relief. "Oh, thank goodness. Munn, get the files on Preiss, Wyvernjaw, and Skeez. And the dossiers we put together for Hawthorne and

Reeves. We're severely short on time, so you two are going to have to cram. And speaking of time—how are you two on formal attire? Ball gowns and cocktail dresses for you, Steele. And Daggers, you have a tuxedo, I hope?"

I blinked. "Say what now?"

Steck passed his hand over his short hair. "Wonderful. Okay, come with me. We can go over the files while the two of you get fitted. Hopefully the tailors won't charge us an arm and a leg for same day service."

Steck stood to go, but I was still a few paces behind the lead. *Tuxedo?* By the gods, what had I gotten myself into?

4

I stood on a fitting platform in front of a tri-paneled mirror while some old dude in a three-piece suit prodded my junk with a tape measure. It wasn't how I'd envisioned my day going.

I felt a light touch against my goods.

"Thirty-four inch inseam," said the tailor.

"You, uh...leaving enough space for the boys?"

He stood and looped the tape measure around my midsection. "Thirty-six inch waist."

"You sure about that?" I said. "I think I'm a thirty-four. Maybe you should remeasure."

The tailor stepped back and twirled a corner of his handlebar moustache. "Do you know how long I've been crafting suits, *sir*?"

The emphasis he placed on *sir* didn't pass me by, and while I could admit to being less than helpful, it seemed uncalled for. "Don't take it personally. I'm like this to everyone. But I have lost weight recently. Can you tell?"

The tailor responded by clearing his throat and getting back to work. He pressed the tape measure against the length of my arm.

The door chimes sounded, and I turned my head. Steele entered through the shop's front door, still clad in the shearling jacket and pleated brown pants from before. Her arms were empty.

"No luck?" I said.

"On the contrary," she said. "I found a number of gorgeous gowns. Far too many, actually. It's a shame the cruise isn't longer."

"So where are they?" I asked.

"The seamstress is making alterations to make sure they fit me properly. With luck, they'll be ready in time. How are things going here?"

"Beats me," I said. "Ask the bespoke one."

The tailor stretched his tape measure across my shoulders. "Nineteen inches. Well, Mr. Daggers, it would appear you're fairly normally proportioned for your size. I should have some stock that fits you, with minor modifications of course, at least for the suits. The key will be picking a proper tuxedo. Tell me, do you prefer single-breasted or double-breasted?"

"Suits or partners?"

"Pardon, sir?"

My wit was wasted. I furrowed my brow. "Uh...double-breasted is where you have two sets of buttons in front?"

The tailor sighed, but Steele stepped forth before he was forced to explain. "Let's try Daggers in a single-breasted, two-button suit. One with a notched lapel, neither too long nor too short. To about here." Steele gestured to a point on her own sternum.

The tailor was only too happy not to deal with me anymore. "Certainly, miss. Necktie, bowtie, or ascot?"

"Bowtie."

The tailor disappeared behind a curtain leading into the back of his shop. I stepped off the platform and joined Steele by the seating area: a cluster of four leather-upholstered sofa chairs set around a polished oaken coffee table. Mannequins clad in fancy duds dotted the room, displaying the tailor's wares, while cabinets set high in the walls overflowed with bolts of colorful, expensive fabrics, everything from linen to silk to cashmere. Spools of thread packed the space closer to the floor, enough to patch and darn ten thousand holes. The only thing missing was the sewing tables, but I assumed those were kept in back out of the view of discerning eyes.

Steele crossed to one of the sofa chairs and picked up my leather jacket, which I'd draped over the back prior to having my measurements taken. She sniffed. *"Fine leather..."*

I crossed my arms. "Don't for a minute think I'm retiring that. As soon as we finish our stint on the *Prodigious,* I'll be slipping right back into Darla's arms."

"Darla? You gave your jacket a name, too?"

"It's the first thing that came to mind," I said. "But since we're on the subject of Daisy, that's another point in favor of my leather coverall. Where in the world am I going to store my nightstick in a dinner jacket? Even if Jerrold McThimblefingers in back did have time to sew a secret compartment into my suit jackets, I'm pretty sure Daisy's steely frame would poke through."

Shay set the jacket back down on the chair. "You're not really planning on bringing your truncheon with you on the cruise, are you?"

"Are you suggesting I travel without her? Might as well ask me to go naked."

Shay gave me a double eyebrow raise. "Why are you being so difficult? You act as if being forced to acquire a new wardrobe is torture. I might understand if it were coming out of your pocket, but the department's footing the bill. And since they're tailored suits, you'll get to keep them."

"Well, I'll have to store them, at the very least," I said.

"I've been to your apartment. Your closet's not that small."

I snorted.

"Really," said Steele. "What's bugging you? Is it the comfort angle? Or are you afraid you'll like the way you look and won't want to go back to your old style?"

"Pshtt. I am *not* afraid of that."

I was much more afraid *Shay* would like the way I looked.

Shay brushed off my shoulders and straightened my shirt. "Well, whatever it is, let's get your mind off it. Tell me about the prime suspects in the gambling case."

"You want to test me?" I said. "Okay. I'm game. Johann Preiss. Sixty-three years of age. Owns a half-dozen textile mills. Runs a fairly clean business, but has been accused of unfair labor practices in the past. When his employees went on strike in protest of sub-standard wages, he brought in scabs to take their places, and when the scabs started defecting he sicced his pinks on the lot of them. Roughed a lot of people up. Kept his wages low for years, which meant more earnings for Preiss, but it didn't make him many friends. To this day, he keeps his skullcrackers near him at all times for fear of retribution.

"Orrin Wyvernjaw, thirty-three, dwarven, is your more traditional thug. Has been indicted multiple times on money laundering and racketeering charges, but somehow none of them have ever stuck. According to Steck, he's a major player in the underground poker circuit, and he wins more often than he loses. Nobody's ever caught him cheating, but given his day job, nobody would put it past him either. Not sure if anyone would call him out on it if they *did* notice. He has a reputation for short-temperedness and violence."

"And Ghorza Skeez?" asked Steele.

"I was getting to her. Late thirties. A full blooded orc. Old money, though I'm still not sure how an orc family gets to that status. Maybe her ancestors had a thriving business selling the blanched bones of their enemies. Regardless, she's the one we know the least about. She's a gambling fanatic, having taken part in numerous poker tournaments overseas and often doing quite well, but to our knowledge she's never been tempted by New Welwic's underground scene. Purely on the straight and narrow, in that regard. She's got an elven manservant by the name of Vlad who accompanies her just about anywhere she goes, and she has a bit of a drinking problem, though she tries to abstain during tournaments."

Shay nodded. "Very nice. I'm impressed."

"You shouldn't be," I said. "I'm as sharp as a steel tack. A new one. Not one of those old blunted ones we can barely get into the corkboard at the precinct anymore. Now let's see if *you've* been studying. What's higher? A full house or a flush?"

Shay snorted. "Come on. I didn't insult your intelligence, so don't insult mine. The hand order goes high card, one pair, two pair, three of a kind, straight, flush, full house, four of a kind, straight flush, royal flush."

"You're right," I said. "I apologize. That was trivial, so let's talk strategy. We'll be playing no-limit hold'em, and with us included, we'll have a total of nine players. Let's say we're in the pre-flop betting round. You're in the fifth position, and the first two players didn't raise above the blind. The third player folded and the fourth raised. You've got a jack ten, suited. What do you do?"

Shay started doing the math based on the simple betting strategy Steck had related to us. "Jack ten, suited. That would give me eight points for the jack and ten, and another twelve for being the same suit. It has straight potential on four different straights, so add another thirteen points for a total of thirty-three. I'm in a middle position on the table, so I don't add anything to the score, and with a thirty-three, I should call but not raise."

"Nicely done. But from now on you'll have to do all the summations up here." I tapped my head.

"As opposed to doing them in my gall bladder, which is what I did this time," said Steele.

"You know what I mean. No counting out loud. Remember, we're pros. We've been doing this for years."

"Don't worry about me," said Steele. "I know how to play a role. I've still got most of the precinct convinced I can pull clues from the threads of time, remember?"

The clack of a heeled shoe made me turn. McThimblefingers stood behind me holding a trio of glossy black jackets over one arm, a piece of chalk in his hand and a number of pins pressed between his lips.

"Mr. Daggers," he mumbled. "Are you ready to begin the fittings?"

I sighed. "Sure. Might as well get this over with."

5

The barber jacked up my chair and tilted it back to ninety degrees before placing a small hand mirror before me. "What do you think, Mr. Daggers?"

I wasn't sure I needed the mirror. I'd already taken a look after he'd trimmed my hair, and he'd done an excellent job, so I couldn't imagine he'd do any worse on the shave. Besides, the tingling warmth from the hot towels he'd applied to my cheeks and the sharp, lemony scent of the aftershave gave me a good idea of the end result. Nonetheless, I looked.

"Excellent job, my man." I tilted my head back and forth and ran a finger across my cheek. Smooth as a baby's bottom. "Not sure I can remember the last time I didn't have even an ounce of stubble."

"You're probably using a dull blade," said the barber. "Although it could be your shaving soap isn't lathering sufficiently."

I kept looking into the mirror.

"You *do* use a shaving soap, don't you?"

"What? Yes, of course," I said. "I'm not a barbarian."

The barber kept whatever thoughts he had about that to himself as he whipped the protective cape off me.

I stood and dusted off the few hairs that remained stuck to me. "What do I owe you?"

The door chimes sounded.

"Daggers. Don't worry about it. I'll take care of it." Steck backed in through the front door, a garment bag slung over his arm and a duffel bag clutched in his hand.

I accepted the bag as he approached. "I assume this is what I'm wearing tonight?"

Steck nodded, breathing heavily as he reached for his coin purse.

"You doing alright?" I asked.

He nodded again. "Oh, yeah. Fine. Peachy. Just tired is all. Stressed. And excited. But mostly stressed. I've been running all over town trying to get everything ready. Well, taking rickshaws, mostly, but you get my drift. First to the seamstress's, then the tailor's, back to the precinct, then the seamstress's again, and the tailor's again. It's been nuts."

I glanced through the shop's front windows. Based on the light, I'd wager it was midafternoon. "Tell me you at least got some lunch."

"I ate a meat, potato, and onion knish while I was in one of the rickshaws. It's the most I could afford. Time-wise, I mean. We're running out of it." He handed the barber some coppers to cover the cost of my haircut and shave. "And speaking of running, I can't stay. I've picked up the rest of your garments, as well as Detective Steele's dresses and coats, and I need to deliver them to the *Prodigious.* Meanwhile, you need to get dressed. Detective Steele should be here in—" He glanced at a clock against the far wall. "—five minutes, give or take. So get cracking. See you tonight."

Steck rushed out the front door, and the barber showed me to a private room in back where I could change. Once he left, I unzipped the bag and looked inside. No tuxedo, thankfully, but the suit inside was almost as swanky—a cool gray affair with prominent black stitching and a black silk border along the edge of the lapel. In addition to the suit, the bag held a crisp starched shirt, glossy black shoes, socks, a thin leather belt, and an elegant black tie.

I sighed. What a mess.

Piece by piece, I stripped off my clothes and replaced them with the new ones. When finished, I returned to the front of the barber's, the garment bag, now stuffed full of my casual attire, in hand.

The barber shot me a thumbs up. "Looking good, Mr. Daggers. But I don't think I'm the one whose approval you'll be seeking."

He gestured out the windows. Steele stood at the edge of the street, waiting for me beside a rickshaw.

"Thanks." I took a deep breath. "Wish me luck."

"With you looking like that?" said the barber. "You won't need it."

"Oh, I'll need it."

The barber gave me a curious look as I exited through the front, but I didn't expect him to get it.

Steele stepped forward to greet me. A heavy fur coat draped her shoulders, and her hair had been loosely curled. Diamond stud earrings sparkled, though not as brightly as did her eyes. "Well. Hi there, stranger."

"You already used that line today," I said.

"Yeah, but this time I mean it. Who are you and what did you do to Daggers?"

I glanced down at my myself, crisp and clean and looking like a thousand crowns. "I know. I look ridiculous."

"You're not serious, are you?" said Steele.

"Maybe. I'm not sure. *I* can't even tell when I'm joking sometimes." I gave her a nod. "You look nice, though I didn't realize you were into lemming genocide."

Steele glanced at her coat, a plush light brown fur that swathed her from neck to ankles. Pointy heels poked out from underneath the hem, but I couldn't spot even a speck of fabric from her dress. I assumed she was, in fact, wearing one.

"This?" said Steele. "It's mink. And I'm not. Into small animal murder, that is."

"Your attire says otherwise."

"Not *really*," said Steele. "The coat isn't custom, and considering how much it costs, the department is forcing me to return it after the poker tournament. So I'm not actually funneling any crowns into the extinction of our country's natural wildlife. Besides, it's a necessary evil. I've got to look the part, you know?" She shimmied and snuggled further into the depths of the fur, a smile spreading across her face.

"Yeah, I can see you're making a huge sacrifice." I hefted the garment bag. "Any idea what I should do with this?"

"Your old clothes? Pitch them into the back of the rickshaw. The driver can deposit them back at the precinct after he drops us off. Speaking of which, we should be going. I think we've only got a couple hours until the *Prodigious* departs."

I gestured toward the handcart. "Well, in that case. After you, my lady."

I offered my hand. Steele took it and climbed into the rickshaw, and I followed her in. As soon as we'd seated ourselves, our driver took off at a run, propelling us down the streets of New Welwic with a vigor born either from a desire for riches or from an attempt to stay warm. My money was on the latter. A bitter wind blew as we headed east over the bridge spanning the river Earl, carrying with it hints of salt and a cold spray carried from the depths of the Wel Sea, and I started to envy Steele her thick fur coat. As comfortable as my suit was—a fact I would admit to no one, ever, under any circumstances—it failed in its ability to guard against a stiff breeze. Had Steck packed me a topcoat? I'd have to check once we arrived at our quarters.

Thankfully, we weren't exposed to the elements for long. The bridge's bascule portion was down, and traffic was light—at least until we approached the dock district. Then the streets swelled with pedestrians, and not thick-set, lunch pail-carrying, wool cap and sweater-wearing dock hand types either. Rather men in thick, black overcoats, some with fedoras and bowlers and top hats, and women in stylish, fitted jackets that reached to their knees. Rickshaws clattered along the streets, too, but laden with clientele of an even higher class, dressed in suits and furs as Shay and I were. Then, as we crossed out of the shadow of several huge Cornwall Heavy Industries warehouses, I spotted it.

The *Prodigious.*

She was everything her name implied. Massive. Gargantuan. Enormous. At least six or seven hundred feet long and as tall as a five story building, even after accounting for whatever portion of her lurked below water and before adding the protrusion of her smokestacks. I counted three rows of at least fifty portholes in her side, as well as another row of similar size in the above deck portions, and yet, despite her enormity, she was an elegant beast. A jet black coat covered her hull, while everything above deck except for the tips of the smokestacks sparkled a pristine white. The overall effect was to dress the *Prodigious* in her own tuxedo, adding one more reminder of sophistication and elegance to a ship already in possession of an abundance of both.

"She's a marvel, isn't she?" said Steele. "Hard to believe something that big can stay afloat, much less move. And before you throw it in my face, I'm well aware of buoyancy and thrust and all the other factors that make it possible, but it's still hard to wrap your head around."

I forced my jaw shut with an idle hand. "No kidding."

Our rickshaw driver snaked his way around the crowds before stopping near the ship's gangplank. A line wove around the base of it, herded to and fro by a red rope held between gilded posts.

I spotted a uniformed individual armed with a steel hole punch at the head of the line. "Uh oh."

"What is it?" asked Steele.

"Tickets," I said. "Steck never gave them to me."

"Did you check your suit pockets?"

I batted the exterior ones. Nothing there, so I moved to the interior. My fingers met resistance in the pocket over my heart. When I pulled them out, I found between them two index card-sized tickets featuring bold print and embossed with gold leaf.

I smiled at my partner. "I knew I kept you around for a reason."

She lifted an eyebrow. "Sure you're ready for this? Mr. Waters isn't supposed to get flustered."

"And I won't," I said. "I'm leaving all that on land. As soon as the soles of my shoes meet the deck, I'll be smooth, suave, and sophisticated. At least in public."

Steele snorted. "I'll believe it when I see it."

"Fine. I'll start now, then." I offered my arm. "My lady?"

She smiled and took it, and I led her down into the line. Barely had we situated ourselves at its back, though, when a crewman in a crisp navy blue and white uniform and a sailor's cap approached us from the direction of the gangway.

"Excuse me," he said. "Mr. and Mrs. Waters?"

I nodded. "Yes?"

The sailor tipped his cap. "Greetings. I was instructed to keep an eye out for you. Do you have any baggage?"

"We have someone bringing it for us," I said. "It may already be on board."

"Excellent," said the young man with a bob of his head. "If you'd be so kind as to come with me, I can spare you the trouble of waiting in line. The captain himself has requested to meet with you on the bridge." He held out a hand. "Shall we?"

I suppressed a smile. While my clothes rubbed me the wrong way, being treated with effusive kindness and deference was something I could get used to. "Certainly. Lead the way."

6

The sun dipped low over the horizon as we entered the bridge, sending its rays glancing onto the ship's controls, most of them encased in brass and gleaming brightly. There was the ship's wheel, three-quarters as tall as I was, made of solid oak and polished to a glossy finish, and beside that a stand of wood and brass for the ship's compass and inclinometer. A spyglass had been mounted onto a rotating post at the wheel's side, and behind the helm in a glass-faced cabinet, I caught another golden gleam. A sextant, if I knew anything about nautical navigation—which honesty I didn't, but at least I knew sextants only worked outdoors.

A quintet of speaking tubes tipped with tapered cones spread across the front of the room, and I caught a hint of a command from the one farthest left. The helm was empty, but two men stood at the windows—well, one man and one orc-hybrid, if skin tone and size were any indication.

Our escort stepped forward. "Captain Heatherfield? I've brought Mr. and Mrs. Waters, sir."

The captain turned, letting the light illuminate the bronzed creases of his face and brighten his silver-streaked hair. His uniform resembled our escort's navy blue and white ordeal, but his jacket was of a much finer cut, with large golden buttons and fringed epaulettes on the shoulders. A naval insignia hovered over his right breast, an indication of his former service in defense of our nation.

"Excellent," he said, stepping forth. "Thank you. Dismissed."

The crewman bowed his head and exited stage left. The captain extended a hand. "Captain Heatherfield. Welcome aboard the *Prodigious.*"

My partner shook his hand first. "Samantha Waters. It's a pleasure."

"Please," said the Captain. "I'm a crotchety, weathered old coot, and you're a lovely young lady. Trust me when I tell you the pleasure is mine."

I shook his hand next. "Thomas Waters. Nice to meet you—though I'm sure the pleasure of my acquaintance is less than Sam's. I know this is a random question, but... what is that thing?" I pointed at the stand with the compass. "It's not a barnacle. Those are the clam-like buggers who attach themselves to hulls. But it's a similar sound, right? A—"

"Binnacle," said the Captain.

I snapped my fingers. "A binnacle! That's it. It was going to bother me all night if I didn't ask."

"Actually," said Steele. "Barnacles are more closely related to crabs and lobsters than to clams."

I tilted my head at her. "Are they now?"

She nodded. "Barnacles are arthropods. Clams are mollusks."

"I never would've guessed that."

Captain Heatherfield glanced at us, a puzzled expression forcing its way through crinkled eyes and pursed lips.

"Apologies, Captain," I said. "You invited us up to introduce yourself, and we've already derailed the conversation. I am, I confess, a master of the conversational tangent."

"But not of homonyms," said Steele with a sly smile.

The Captain put up his hands. "Don't worry. I like nautical banter as much as the next ship's captain, but I don't want to waste more of your time than absolutely necessary. I'm sure you're eager to engage in the night's festivities, and to prepare yourselves for an exciting few days of entertainment and gaming, but I wanted to let you know that a personal greeting on my part isn't a luxury I've afforded to all of your competitors in the upcoming poker tournament, *if you catch my drift.*" He tilted his head toward us and lifted his brows in emphasis.

"So you're...*aware* of the situation then?" I asked.

"Yes, but most of my staff and crew are not," said Heatherfield. "Olaugh. Come here, please."

The big fellow turned from his post and joined the captain at his side, his wrists clasped behind his back. He stood roughly my height, though his cap afforded him an additional inch, and while he wore the same outfit as the captain, it fit him not nearly as well. His collar hugged his neck tightly, as did the shoulders of his coat, but then again, every aspect of the guy was broad. His nose. His forehead. His eyebrows. Even his mouth, with the protrusion of small tusks from his lips that marked him as an orc, though not necessarily a pure breed if his olive skin was any indication.

"This is Kratt Olaugh, the *Prodigious's* boatswain and head of security," said Captain Heatherfield.

Olaugh nodded, but he kept his arms behind his back. "A pleasure." He spoke in a thick, husky tone.

"He and I are the only ones aware of your true *affiliation,* should we say, other than your own companion, Mr. Steck, who's joining us aboard the *Prodigious* as a porter. None of the other staff or crew know of your purpose here, but be assured that Olaugh and I are fully committed to helping you and Steck. As I think you noticed from my attire, I'm a former navy man, and beyond that I served as a master at arms. I have just as much a spot in my heart for justice and the rule of law as you do. And while we weren't able to inform the staff about your purpose, we did ask them to cater to your every need. They'll be happy to do so. Should you need something they can't provide or you feel you can't ask them for directly, please approach myself or Olaugh for assistance. Understood?"

Steele nodded. "Thank you, Captain. We appreciate the help."

"Not a problem," he replied. "Though with that said, I should emphasize to both of you how important this maiden voyage is for our parent company. The *Prodigious's* managing corporation expects everything about this trip—the service, the entertainment, and the poker tournament, especially—to be a roaring success. I'm not a gambling man, so I don't care as much about the latter, but I value my employment and I look forward to many years as the *Prodigious's* captain. Should you uncover anything untoward, either with regards to your competitors in the tournament or otherwise, I'd ask that you treat the matter discreetly."

"Don't worry, Captain," I said. "We have our own role to play here, and for once, it doesn't involve kicking down any doors or pounding in anyone's head. My partner wouldn't even let me bring my trusty skull thumper along for the ride."

"It's not exactly appropriate for the company we'll be keeping," she said.

I thought about Orrin and Johann's rap sheets and wasn't sure I agreed with that statement, but I nodded anyway.

A voice sounded from one of the speaking tubes, drawing the Captain's attention. "Good," he said with his eyes turned toward the tube. "Well, in that case, I hope you have a lovely time, and for your sakes, a lucrative one. Olaugh? Can you escort our guests to their quarters?"

"Absolutely, Captain," said the orc. "If you'll come with me?"

He cracked the door and held it for us, and I followed Steele back into the evening's chill sea breeze.

7

Boatswain Olaugh turned the key, unlocking the door to our stateroom with a satisfying clack. He plucked it from the keyhole and held it between outstretched fingers, dangling from an oversized oval keychain embossed with the room's number: one fifteen.

I accepted the key. "Thank you, Kratt."

"I prefer Olaugh. Enjoy your stay." He gave Steele and me a curt nod, about-faced, and headed down the corridor.

I glanced at Shay. "Not a particularly chatty fellow, was he?"

"He's probably stressed," said Shay. "I'd be too if I were a commanding officer on a ship of this size. And I'm not even accounting for this being the *Prodigious's* maiden voyage."

"I suppose." I didn't offer the alternative explanation that he was just a jerk. It seemed self evident.

I cranked on the door handle. "After you."

Steele entered. I followed, closing the door behind me. I hadn't taken more than three steps in before I paused, wide-eyed. "Oh, yeah. Jackpot."

The department had sprung for the swankiest of the swanky. A wide sitting room opened up before us, populated by polished cherry wood tables, cabinets with enamel inlays, velvet-upholstered sofas, and armchairs with intricate scrollwork in the legs and backs. Rich purple drapes hung from the windows, pulled back and tied to let in light, while a grandfather clock serenaded us with faint tick tocks. A warm fire blazed in the hearth, a thick fur rug on the floor in front of it and ceramic vases overflowing with carnations on the mantle above it. Doors to our left and right showed hints of bedchambers as lavishly furnished as our current environs.

Shay smiled at me over her shoulder. "A girl could get used to this."

"Even the most jaded old curmudgeon could," I said. "And before you ask, no, I was not talking about myself. I don't consider myself old."

I crossed to a bar on the right-hand wall, lifted a crystal decanter, uncorked it, and took a sniff. The liquor within greeted my nostrils with hints of raisins, vanilla, and oak. "Hmm. Brandy, I think. Well, not everything can be perfect, I guess."

"What were you expecting?" asked Shay. "A decanter full of ale?"

"For your information, I'm a bit of a whiskey aficionado," I said as I replaced the crystal bottle on its shelf. "And by aficionado, I mean I enjoy distillations that don't burn like the searing fires of the underworld going down. Or up."

"An aficionado, eh?" said Steele. "Tell me, then. Do you prefer malted or grain whiskies?"

"Please," I said. "Malted. Rye malt whiskies, specifically. Charred white oak aged, if possible."

Shay whistled. "Well. Color me impressed."

"You know me," I said. "I can't give a straight answer to a question on the first shot. It goes against my nature."

A knock sounded against the door.

I glanced at Steele. "Expecting anyone?"

"My masseuse."

I raised an eyebrow. "Really?"

"No," she said. "Answer it."

I crossed to the front and cracked the door. I opened it wide after I saw who it was. "Ah. Steck. You made it."

The vice detective had changed into black trousers, a crisp white shirt, and a four-button maroon vest—the same outfit I'd seen on the rest of the ship's porters. With his left hand he gripped one of the brass bars of a luggage trolley, one loaded with several bags.

He dipped his head. "Your luggage, *sir*."

His words carried with them a reminder to still my tongue, and he wasn't wrong. Who knew what prying eyes had already turned our way or what ears lurked in the hallway? It was one thing to acknowledge Steck or an element of Steele's and my police training in private, but to do so in public, even at the door of my stateroom, could jeopardize our mission. And if I was being honest with myself, while I'd thus far kept my promise to act more sophisticated in public, I hadn't fully embraced my persona. Specifically, the aspect where Steele and I were a couple, probably because I was concerned with the effects a fake relationship could have on our real one. Had I made the right choice in agreeing to this mission in the first place?

"Sir?" said Steck.

I blinked. "Right. Sorry. Please, come in."

I stepped to the side, and Steck wheeled the trolley into our living room. He kept up appearances until I closed the door.

Steck shook his head as he looked around. "Fifteen years on the force. In fifteen years, this is the first time a case like this has come across my desk, and yet somehow the luxury stateroom falls to the two of you while I get stuck with porter duty. Where did I go wrong?"

"I take it the crew's quarters aren't as nice," said Steele.

Steck gave my partner a long glance. "We're sleeping in bunks, six to a room, one substantially smaller than this sitting area here. It smells like coal and engine grease, not rose water and...is that *raisins?*"

"It's the brandy," I said. "You can have some if you like. It's not really my cup of tea. But don't blame us. You had your chance."

"To do what?" he said.

"To take our place."

He looked taken aback. "How so? I don't have a close relationship with anyone who could go undercover posing as my wife. Or girlfriend. Or, you know, whatever."

"What about Munn?" I said.

Steck broke out in laughter. "*Munn?* Are you kidding me?" He forced out another laugh. "No way we could pull that off. She's at least ten years my senior. Never mind she has kids and obligations at home that would make it difficult. No one would believe us as a couple. She drives me crazy most of the time. She's a total ball-buster."

He glanced at Steele, who regarded him coolly. "I, uh...didn't mean anything by that, you understand. I'm all for workplace diversity. And Munn's deserving of her station. Really good at what she does. It's that sometimes she gets shrill, and bossy, and...I can tell I'm digging myself a hole here, so I'm going to stop."

Steck picked up a pair of bags from the cart and hefted them. "As you can see, we were able to switch out the single bedroom suite we'd initially reserved for a double. Might cause the maids to talk, but they've been instructed to leave your room alone anyway. We don't want anyone prying. Too much on the line. So, who's got which room? Or are we sharing? Actually, forget I ever said that. It's, uh...none of my business. Man, I need to stop talking. Maybe I'll just leave the bags here in the sitting room. Does that work?"

"That'll be fine, Steck," said Steele. "Thank you."

The grandfather clock clicked and whirred, and its chimes sounded. Steck glanced at its face. "Holy harvest. Six already? We'll be casting off any minute now. You two should head to the mixer. All of your competitors should be there. It'll be a good opportunity to feel them out."

"Great minds think alike," said Steele. "Daggers, why don't you change into your tuxedo."

"You're kidding, right?" I drew my hands across my suit. "You're telling me this isn't formal enough?"

"For a mixer, yes," said Steele. "For the grand ball that follows it, no. So please change."

Steele unbuttoned her coat and shrugged out of it, finally revealing what she wore underneath: an off the shoulder mermaid ball gown in a brilliant scarlet satin. The top half hugged her chest and waist and hips tightly while the bottom flared out at the knees, though it had been bundled and pinned just below that to keep from dragging. Apart from the shape of her calves, it left startlingly little to the imagination.

Steele bent over and undid the pins, letting the dress unfurl and cover her toes. When she straightened, she glanced at me, her brows furrowed. "Daggers?"

I tested my jaw. It still worked. "Um. Yes. I'll, uh...be changing into my tux now."

8

stretched my neck as I walked arm in arm with Steele along the interior of the promenade deck. "I still don't know about this bowtie, Shay. Maybe I should've gone with the ascot."

My partner gave me a once over. "The bowtie is classic. I chose it for a reason."

"That reason wouldn't have anything to do with comfort, would it?"

Shay shot me a cool look. "We could trade shoes if you like."

"Point taken. But honestly, how do I look?"

Shay sighed and rolled her eyes. "You know, for someone who puts as little effort into his day to day attire as you do, you sure can be insecure. You don't see me constantly looking for reassurance about *my* dress."

"That's not a fair comparison," I said. "You look amazing."

"Flattery will get you nowhere." Shay's smile said otherwise. "But for the record, you look quite handsome. Like a rich playboy with little regard for expense. So start acting like it. We're almost there."

Ahead of us, one of the ship's crew admitted individuals into the lounge where the mixer was being held. For a moment, I wondered if I'd need a ticket for admission, but apparently our dress was proof enough of our status for the doorman. He immediately let us in with a flourish of his hands and a deep bow.

Inside, the lounge much resembled our own sitting room except for being larger, better lit, and more densely populated. Roughly a hundred people milled around the interior, sipping on drinks, chatting, and smoking pipes or cigarettes. A trio of bartenders at the far side of the room furiously rattled cocktail shakers and poured drinks, while waiters and waitresses in black jackets and slacks roamed the room bearing trays of deviled eggs, smoked salmon and dill crostini, and shrimp half-submerged in shot glasses of cocktail sauce.

Steele and I drifted toward the center of the room. I eyed the line at the bar, but before I could make a decision on whether or not to dive into the fray, a waiter approached with a tray of tall flutes.

"Champagne?"

"Why yes, thank you," said Steele as she took one.

I'd made my distaste of wine known to Shay on multiple occasions, but the dry nature of champagne made it a slightly different beast. I lifted a flute off the tray by the stem and nodded my thanks to the waiter.

I took a sip, wrinkling my nose as the bubbles hit my tongue, and glanced around the room. "Well...this is a little more crowded than I expected."

"It's for all of first class," said Steele. "You didn't think this would only be for the poker players, did you?"

I shook my head. "Of course not."

Steele kept her eyes on me.

"Yes. Yes, I did. But that's neither here nor there. The question is, what to do now?"

"Mingle, chat, and enjoy ourselves," said Steele. "Though the latter should probably take a backseat to the former. Scouting the opposition and all that. And on that note, I think I have a good idea of where we could start."

She nodded toward the room's left-hand corner. I followed her gaze to a group of five partiers, among them a man in an exquisite three-piece black pinstripe suit holding a black cane topped with a silver dragon's head. Numerous wrinkles creased his forehead, a forehead that reached the crown of his skull before encountering any of his salt-and-pepper hair. He could've been any well-off man of advanced middle age, but the trio of toughs who stood behind him eyeing the crowd gave me some idea as to his identity.

"Johann, you think?" I asked.

Shay nodded.

"Well, we could introduce ourselves. Or..."

I nodded to the other corner of the room where an overweight orc woman sat in one of the room's many sofa chairs. Black hair cascaded down the sides of her face, past her thick tusks, before falling upon the pleated folds of her long-sleeved copper-colored evening gown. Several large warts protruded from various parts of her, a prominent one from her nose and another from her jaw, making her face even harder to love than it already was, but her less than sterling appearance didn't seem to bother her manservant in the least. A tall handsome elf dressed in black and white tails dabbed at the corner of her lip with a white kerchief.

"And I would assume that's Ghorza," said Steele.

"As would I," I said.

"So who would you rather talk to first?"

I scratched my chin. "Well, I—"

"Excuse me," said a friendly, high-pitched voice. "Mr. and Mrs. Waters, I presume?"

I turned to find a gnome standing behind me, perhaps three and a half feet tall and wearing a simple brown vest over a light blue dress shirt, the sleeves of which had been rolled up to his elbows. He held a tumbler of ice and booze in his left hand.

"Yes," I said. "You are?"

"Theo Hornshoe. Sometimes malcontent, professional roustabout, and gambler extraordinaire." He stuck out a hand. "I'm one of the players who'll be joining you at the tables tomorrow."

"*Professional roustabout?*" said Shay as she shook his hand. "You're a circus laborer?"

"Not really," he said. "I just like that word. *Roustabout*. It sounds like someone who lays about, gets in tussles, and seduces fine women, don't you think?"

"Ah," I said as I shook his hand in turn. "Someone who likes to sail the spoken word into new and uncharted waters. A gnome after my own heart then. So tell me, Theo, how do you know who we are?"

"Well I am, after all, a gambler *extraordinaire*," he said. "And I wouldn't be so extraordinary if I wasn't so perceptive. I'd heard the rumors about our mystery competitors. A half-elf of unparalleled beauty, and her cavalier, a, ah... Well, that is to say, a..."

I waited. "A what?"

Theo smiled. "Why, a devilishly handsome chap such as yourself."

"Hah!" I said. "I like this guy. I'll be sure to treat you with kindness and respect as I slowly and methodically rob you of all your money over the next few days."

Theo snapped his fingers and took a sip of his drink. "Right back at you, big guy."

"So, Theo," said Steele. "Since you seem to have your finger on the pulse of the competition, why not give us a primer on our foes?"

"You want me to spill the beans on the rest of the players?" he said. "And what exactly am I to get out of this arrangement?"

"I don't think Sam was asking for any secrets you might've unearthed," I said, "although, knowing her, she wouldn't dissuade you if you wanted to volunteer them. Rather, we'd like to introduce ourselves, if possible, to the other players. Seeing as we only recently made it aboard the ship, we aren't sure who they all are."

"Other than Johann and Ghorza, I take it," said Theo.

I glanced at Steele.

"Yeah, that's right," he said. "I notice things. Store that in the part of your brain where you keep your cockiness. But seeing as I'm liquored up and feeling swell, sure, I'll give you the low down. Besides the old man and the orc matron and the three of us, there are four others. One of them is over there. Jimmy Frazier, though he goes by 'The Hammer.'"

Theo pointed him out, a hulking brute about the same size and shape as Quinto and with a similar complexion. He wore a felt ascot cap over his round melon, and his shoulders threatened to pop out of his suit.

"I don't know too much about him," said Theo, "other than I wouldn't want to be around him when he gets hungry. He likes to intimidate people with his size and a mean grin he pulls out every now and then. To be honest, it totally works. Then there's Orrin, a hard-nosed dwarf who doesn't say a whole lot. He hasn't arrived yet, but you'll notice him when he does. He's got a huge scar that runs down his face from eye to chin. There's also some woman named Wanda who as far as I can tell likes the color purple, unicorns, and moonlit walks on the beach in solitude."

I furrowed my eyebrows.

"That's a joke, by the way," said Theo. "Except for the last part. I haven't met her yet, but I don't think she cares for company. Then last but certainly not least there's Verona. She's around here somewhere. Let's see..."

Theo turned and cast his gaze into the room. After a moment he pointed. "There she is. Verona. Verona!"

An elf woman with heavily curled golden hair, wearing a grey-flecked white fur shawl and enough jewelry to sink a ship half the *Prodigious's* in size, paused in her walk toward the bar. She waved to Theo with a hand that held a long, thin jade cigarette holder, one currently occupied with a smoldering butt.

"Theo. Darling. How are you?" she asked as she approached.

"Verona. Let me introduce two of our newest gaming companions. The affable and overconfident Thomas Waters and his lovely, calculating bride, Samantha."

Verona took a drag from her cigarette holder, exhaled, and idly waved the smoke away with her hand. "Verona Quivven. Charmed."

From afar, Verona had come across as stunning, but up close, the wrinkles around her eyes and mouth were more evident, as was the hint of gray at the roots of her hair. In her heyday, she probably would've given Shay a run for her money—but only to those who didn't mind the smell of smoke. She reeked of a thousand cigarette butts. Being a full blooded elf, it was beyond me how the odor didn't bother her. I supposed she must not even notice it anymore.

"So, Verona," I asked, "how long have you been playing games of chance?"

"Is that a roundabout way of asking me my age?" she said.

"Ah...Theo put me up to," I said, pointing at the gnome. "Blame him."

"What?" said Theo. "I did no such thing. Though I like your deception, big guy. Pro tip: you're showing your hand early. Giving me ammunition to use against you tomorrow."

"Don't mind Theo," said Verona. "He seems to think every aspect of one's personality is a clue, and beyond that, a cudgel to be used against you. He's also rather loose with his lips."

"Loquacious is the word you're looking for," said Theo. "And what of it? Some gamblers hide behind a mask of silence and indifference while they play. I prefer bombarding my opponents with bullshit. I find it wears them down over the long run."

"I'm sure it does," said Verona. "Now if you'll excuse me, my lips are becoming parched." She gave Steele and me a nod. "Until next time."

She wandered off toward the bar. Theo shook his head as she left. "I can't quite get a bead on her, but I tell you what. I think she's a lot smarter than she lets on. I'm definitely keeping my eye on her."

Verona swayed as she walked, her dress tight. "You would."

"Pardon?" said Theo.

"Ah...nothing," I said. "So tell me, Theo, has this excrement barrage of yours already begun?"

"*Excrement barrage?*" Theo laughed. "You *do* like to play fast and loose with language. And perhaps other things as well." He gave me an exaggerated look out of the corner of his eyes.

"I'm not sure I follow," I said.

"I wouldn't expect you to, but it's all part of the game. Don't you love poker?" He lifted his glass only to find he'd reached the bottom. "Oh. My cup runneth dry, so I'm off to slither my way through the crowds at the bar. It was nice meeting you, and I wish you all the worst of luck in the days to come."

He smiled and toasted his empty glass in our direction as he left.

"He's a firebrand, isn't he?" said Steele.

"Yeah, but in a nice way, if that's possible."

Steele took a sip of her beverage. "So...should we meet the others?"

"Might as well," I said. "But only after a tour of the room's snack trays. I'm starving."

9

Following the whims of my stomach did not go without consequence. While I crammed eggs and delicate, slivered salmon down my gullet, Johann made his exit. Based purely on visual evidence—I was much too far away to hear the words he spoke—he excused himself to his entourage, spoke something to his thick-necked escorts, and headed for the door, but not before casting a long glance in the direction of Verona, who lounged by herself, smoking in the far corner.

With my belly momentarily sated, I headed to the bar to refresh Shay's and my drinks while my partner approached Ghorza, who she deemed to be the slightly less intimidating of our two remaining marks. I didn't envy her the task—between her obesity and facial warts, Ghorza was particularly unsightly, even for an orc—but after nearly twenty minutes waiting in line at the bar, I questioned if I'd made the right choice.

When I finally secured an apricot whiskey sour and a glass of merlot from the bartender, who apologized profusely for the delay, it was only to find Shay walking back toward me from Ghorza's direction.

"I take it I missed everything?" I handed Shay her glass and grabbed a miniature quiche from a passing tray.

"That you did." She nodded toward the crowd. "What took so long? There's only four or five people in each line."

"Yeah, well the bartender decided to grow the vegetables for one guy's Bloody Mary from scratch, and he made another drink from egg whites that involved seven or eight minutes of solid shaking. I'm surprised his arm didn't fall off."

"And you didn't switch lines?"

"Trust me, I thought about it. They kept filling in around me." I popped the quiche into my mouth. "So tell me about Ghorza."

"She's pleasant enough," said Steele as she sipped her wine. "Or I suspect she would be if she weren't drunk. She must've gotten an early start, because she's pretty far gone, to the point where she already seems hung over. She kept wincing and asking me to keep my voice down, and she seemed to have a hard time processing some of my questions."

"Did you get anything useful?"

"As far as the tournament is concerned?" Shay shrugged. "I wasn't able to progress the conversation past the trivial. Ghorza's manservant, Vlad, wasn't particularly interested in chatting, despite his sobriety. I think he suspected me of trying to take advantage of Ghorza's condition for my own benefit."

"Which, you know...you were."

I glanced at the mismatched pair, Ghorza sinking deeper into her overstuffed chair and Vlad cooling her with a paper fan. Shay was right. Ghorza looked on the verge of sickness. Vlad stuck out a hand, tested her forehead, and tucked a strand of hair behind Ghorza's ear.

"Is it just me," I said, "or is something going on between those two?"

"Something nefarious?" said Shay.

"Something romantic. Not that I'd understand it if it were. I mean, what kind of elf gets off on overweight orc chicks?"

"Don't be such a bigot," said Steele. "Interspecies love sprouts as easily as between like partners. I should know."

For once, I didn't take that as a thinly veiled expression of her love for me. She was talking about her parents, but our budding relationship was as good an example, as was the odd pairing between Quinto and the fae-blooded Cairny.

"As always, you're right," I said. "It's not my place to judge. Although it'll be difficult to abstain. I'm so good at it."

Shay gave me a small nod that showed she accepted the apology. "Don't mistake prosecution for judgment."

A bell rang near the exit. A white jacket-clad steward stood there with triangle and beater in hand. Once the sound permeated through the room, he spoke in a loud, clear voice. "Ladies and gentlemen. The ballroom is now open." He stepped to the side and swept his hand into the corridor.

Steele took a quick glance around the room as the masses began moving toward the exit. "Well, I think we've learned about as much as we're going to tonight. Shall we?"

I sipped my drink and leaned in. "Shall we what?"

"Proceed to the ballroom."

It took me a moment to process her meaning. "Are you...asking me to dance?"

"A lady asking a gentleman to dance? Of course not. That would be rather forward, wouldn't it?" Shay stood rooted in place and let the void of silence fill the space between us.

"I—" I stared into her bold blue eyes, wide and beautiful and expectant. "—would love to. But what about Jimmy?"

"I don't think he looks like the dancing type," said Shay.

"That's not what I meant."

Shay smiled. "I know."

"Fair enough. But I should warn you. It's been a while since I danced."

"As you might've guessed, my dress doesn't provide for the greatest ease of movement." Shay waved at her knees. "We'll wait until they play a waltz. I should be able to handle that, if you can."

"Believe it or not, I've danced it before."

I held out my arm. Steele took it, and I escorted her into the corridor. While I presented a mask of tranquility, a little person inside me ran around in circles screaming.

I hadn't lied. I *had* danced the waltz—something like four thousand years ago, when my ex-wife Nicole and I had just started dating and she'd dragged me along on all sorts of 'fun' outings I'd never truly appreciated.

The waltz, as I recalled, was one of the slowest of the ballroom dances, with a simple one-two-three, one-two-three pattern. The feet formed a box, moving forward and to the right and back and to the left over and over again. There was also supposed to be a corresponding rise and fall to the body where you elevated on your heels as you worked your way through the box, as well as numerous possible flourishes and twirls, though I could get by without performing any of those.

"Thomas?"

I glanced at Steele. "Yes?"

"You're bouncing up and down."

"Sorry. Muscle memory. For the waltz."

"You know, if you're not comfortable..."

I shook my head. "Nonsense. I'll have everything sorted by the time we start. Never you worry."

We followed the crowd into the ballroom, a broad two-story room that wouldn't fit inside most buildings let alone on most ships, but the *Prodigious* took delight in making otherwise enormous things seem insignificant by comparison. I led Steele past the stage, where a string quintet sat with instruments ready, to a section of armchairs at the perimeter that still hadn't been filled by guest posteriors.

The other gentlemen in the room had left the chairs for the ladies, so I did the same, waving my hand at a spot as the music began to play. "Care for a seat?"

"I would, but..." Shay tilted her head toward the dance floor.

I glanced at the quintet. "Is this a waltz?"

Shay smiled. "I don't have the best ear for music, but this sounds like three-quarter time to me. Which would mean it is."

Couples streamed onto the dance floor. "Just my luck. Might as well get to it, then."

"Again, if you're not feeling this..."

"No," I said. "And stop doubting me. Now, if you'd join me for a dance, my lady?"

Steele seemed taken aback at my tone, but not offended. Perhaps she hadn't expected me to take charge. Either way, she took my hand and allowed me to lead her to the dance floor.

The tiny agitator deep inside me screamed at the top of his lungs, yelling that I had no idea what I was doing and was about to make a fool of myself, but I ignored him. He kept yelling as I grasped Steele's right hand in my left and held my arm firmly out at my side. He kept yelling as I wrapped my right arm around her midsection, placed my hand against the middle of her back, and pushed her firmly against my right hip. Still he yelled as I met her gaze, and in a moment of clarity, I understood the protest.

I wasn't worried about making a fool of myself, or of proving myself a poor dancer, or even of providing my soon to be poker competitors with an inkling as to my true identity of a man not of means. I was afraid of disappointing Shay. Unnaturally afraid, given my rational knowledge of Shay's romantic interest in me, but afraid nonetheless.

Shay smiled at me, a genuine, heartfelt smile of affection like nothing I'd ever seen her give to anyone else, a radiant yet subtle, kind and caring smile that crinkled the corners of her lips and eyes alike. "Ready?"

The agitator rose inside my head. I downed him with a swift elbow to the face. "Absolutely."

I waited for the beat of the music to repeat and launched into the steps, leading Steele with a firm hand. Forward and right, close step, back and left, repeat, twirling a quarter turn with each movement. It took a fair mental effort to maintain, but only for three or four repetitions of the whole. At that point, the cycle became routine, and my mind and body alike relaxed. I forced my frame rigid as mandated by the dance, but I began to enjoy it, feel the bouncing rhythm of the waltz and the flow of the quintet's strings and so much more. My handhold with Shay became more than a point of contact, and with each full rotation, our bodies moved together in greater sync.

Steele kept her head titled slightly to the side, as was the style, but I noticed her glancing at me.

"Can't keep your eyes off me, can you?" I said. "Is it the tuxedo or the shave? Because I could ramp up my self-grooming regimen without too much pain. The clothes on the other hand..."

Shay turned her head and smiled. "You're a far better dancer than I expected."

"I can't tell if that's a compliment without knowing your expectations."

"It's a compliment."

Shay turned her head back, and I dared to be brave. I led her into a spin turn. Shay took it without missing a step, her dress whipping around and slapping me on the shins. Thanks to my success, I tried my hand at a double reverse spin, which proceeded with similar results.

Round and round we danced, Shay spinning and twirling and showing me an enticing stretch of bare back with each turn. Her arms lengthened and became more elegant. The music flowed through us, and our bodies grew closer with every rotation. Sweat beaded at my temples and at the small of my back. Shay's lilac perfume swirled around me, a musky, heady scent, and when I caught them, her eyes sparkled as brightly as her earrings.

The music stopped, and I brought us to a halt. Breath ran heavy through my nostrils, and I could tell Shay's did, too. Her mouth hung open by a sliver, and her bosom rose and fell rhythmically, a bosom that I had great difficulty keeping my eyes off of. Sweat kissed her skin like morning dew, and she looked at me with soulful eyes.

I wasn't sure what else she expected of me, but then I remembered my manners. I gave her a short bow. "Thank you for the dance, my lady."

"I, ah..." Shay swallowed. "My pleasure. Although...perhaps you'd accompany me to the deck? Suddenly I find myself quite warm, and some fresh air could do me good."

She wasn't the only one. My shirt stuck to my chest, and my heart beat like a drum, though not necessarily from physical exertion.

I nodded dumbly and held out my arm.

10

A cold breeze hit us the moment I cracked the door to the *Prodigious's* exterior, which was barren thanks to the wind's efforts.

Shay shivered. "Well, this isn't going to take as long as I thought."

I stripped my coat off and offered it. "Here."

Shay eyed it. "You sure?"

"I'm tough and thick-skinned."

"Liar. You hate winter."

"I'm also still warm from dancing. Maybe even more so than you."

Shay didn't respond to that. She presented me her back, and I helped her slip into the jacket. She crossed to the ship's railing, leaned over, and rested her elbows against the polished wood.

I took a place at her left. The moon shone high in the sky, probably three or four days shy of full, surrounded by a sea of stars that glimmered palely in the bright moonlight. In the distance, behind the ship's stern, New Welwic's lights burned like a second sky.

Waves slapped the ship's hull, playing out a steady beat. Behind the melody of the ocean, I detected a low murmur, deep and muffled and distant. The roar of the ship's engines, perhaps.

I tilted my head toward the city lights. "Hard to believe we're so far away already. I can't even tell we're moving, and my stomach is usually finely tuned to that sort of thing."

"You suffer from seasickness?" asked Shay.

"Depends on the size of the boat," I said. "This is more of a small island, though."

"Apparently, I don't either."

"*Apparently?*" I said.

Shay turned her head toward me and sighed. "Alright. Confession time. I'd never been on a ship until today."

"Really?" I said. "That can't be true. We were on that skiff together when we dove into New Welwic's underbelly."

"A skiff is not a ship," said Shay. "It's a boat."

"Correct you are, my nautically-informed dance partner," I said. "But small vessels are worse than big ones when it comes to sea sickness."

"We weren't at sea," said Shay. "We were in a cistern. My point is, I'd never set sail before today. Don't get me wrong. I've travelled, but it was always via land."

"Well then, you hit the jackpot," I said. "Because I *have* set foot on ships before, and this is by far the largest, nicest, most modern one I've ever seen. And it may be the first one in history with a ballroom in it."

"Jackpot..." said Shay. "Intended or unintended gambling metaphor?"

"Subliminal, perhaps?" I said. "It's hard to stop thinking about the poker tournament entirely, although...I did. During our dance."

Shay emitted something between a hum and a purr. "Likewise."

I felt myself drifting toward her, my elbows gliding across the railing and my shoulder closing on hers. Maybe the breeze pushed me.

Shay tucked her left hand under my right, and the clasped pair hung over the ship's lip. "So what is it about the tournament that preys on your mind?"

At the moment, nothing about the competition preyed on me. Shay did, though, with the breeze pressing the tail of her dress against her legs and pushing her hair over to the side, exposing the long, smooth lines of her neck. She sucked her lower lip in through her teeth and let it back out, succulent and wet.

I glanced over my shoulder to make sure we were alone. "Well, I suppose there are any number of things that concern me. Despite my braggadocio in Theo's presence, I'm not entirely sure how I'll place my bets with such a rich prize on the line, or if I'll be able to bluff properly. I'm concerned about our overall performance, and who'll come out on top. And I'm not sure if I'll be able to keep my wits about me if things go as I hope they do."

Shay did the thing with her lip again. "Are we still talking about card games?"

"I don't know what *you're* talking about. I'm trying to sell you a fine leather jacket."

Shay smiled and squeezed my hand. "You rouge."

The door behind us creaked, and we both turned. Out of it emerged a young man in one of the ship's navy and white sailor's uniforms. He took a look around and quickly locked onto Shay and me.

"Excuse me," he said. "Are you Mr. and Mrs....Waters?"

He hadn't come from the ball. His clothing made that obvious.

"Yes," I said. "What is it?"

He shifted his feet and glanced up and down the deck again, all while playing with his hands. "I'm, uh...sorry to interrupt. But Boatswain Olaugh instructed me to come get you. It's urgent. Could you follow me?"

"What's this about?" asked Steele.

He couldn't keep his hands still. "I really can't talk about it. But you're needed in one of the ship's luggage compartments. Please?"

I forced my annoyance down under my vestments. Shay wasn't going anywhere, after all. "Fine. Lead the way."

11

S hay and I trudged deep into the *Prodigious's* belly, following the sailor down several flights of stairs into darkened corridors. The smooth wood floors of the promenade deck were replaced by bare metal, and the paint on the walls transitioned from a gentle cream to a flat white. The air became musty, and instead of cigar smoke and hints of potpourri, it held traces of coal ash and salt. It left an iron tang on my tongue.

While revelers packed the halls of the first couple floors, well-dressed and cheerful and inebriated, they disappeared the further we went. We passed a few of the ships' crew, and then none at all for almost a minute. Given our escort's demeanor, I started to get a feeling of unease—why had I let Shay convince me to leave Daisy behind?—but then we turned a corner to find Boatswain Olaugh standing in front of a closed bulkhead door, just as the sailor had promised.

He didn't look happy, and I didn't drop my guard.

"So," I said as we walked up. "Can I ask what's going on now?"

"Almost. Steck's inside. He can explain better than I can." Olaugh cranked on the door handle and opened it.

Steele glanced at the crewman but stayed true to character. "Steck? Who's that?"

Olaugh nodded at the sailor. "He knows."

"He knows?" I said.

"I, uh...know," said the sailor. "Names. Occupations. Everything."

"How does he know?" I asked. "*Why* does he know?"

Olaugh clenched his teeth. "If you'd go through the door, I think you'd figure out why pretty darn quickly. Or you should if you're any good at what you do."

Any good at what we do? I stepped through the portal, and the sailor hadn't sold it short. It was a luggage compartment, though only moderately filled. There were a few stacks of suitcases and trunks and carpet bags, loosely tied down with rope to keep from shifting, but most of the space remained unused, which made sense. The *Prodigious* was large enough to undertake a lengthy journey, but her maiden voyage consisted of a quick jaunt around the Wel Sea. I couldn't imagine many of the ship's guests had packed heavy.

I spotted Steck's head past one of the stacks and called out to him. "Steck. What's going on? Why in the world—"

I cut myself off as fate gave me the answer to my own question. A broad-shouldered guy in a light gray suit jacket and matching slacks lay face down in a pile of suitcases and trunks that had come loose. An incision about an inch wide cut through the back of his jacket, just underneath his left shoulder blade, but that wasn't what drew my attention. The blood that soaked the entire back of his coat was.

"Gods, Steck," I said. "What the hell happened?"

"I...don't know," he said as he scratched his thin hair. "I...guess someone stabbed him, and he fell into these suitcases, knocking them over."

Steele joined me at my side, followed closely by Boatswain Olaugh and the crewman. She glanced at the dead body. "That's not what Daggers meant and you know it. You told us this was a vice and fraud case. That we were here to ferret out a card cheat or two. So what exactly did you fail to mention in the briefing this morning? What are we *actually* doing aboard this ship?"

"*What?* I don't know," said Steck. "I mean, I didn't keep anything from you in the briefing. This *was* supposed to be a vice case. Or a fraud case. However you want to label it. Nobody was supposed to die. I have no idea what happened, or why, or even *who* this is. I swear!"

Steck gestured as he talked, tucking his hands under his armpits, wiping them on his pants, tucking them into his pockets, but never letting them stay still for more than a second. He made the crewman seem calm.

"Alright," I said. "Let's settle down and tackle this like professionals. Steck, what happened? What do we know?"

He shook his head. "Ask James here. He found the body."

I turned to the sailor. "That's you?"

He nodded. "Yes, sir. James Willis."

"Tell me how you found this man."

James rubbed his hands together nervously. "I came down here in search of a bag for Mr. Tallsdale. He's one of the ship's passengers, up on the B deck. He meant to bring the bag with him, but it was put in storage by mistake. So I came down to retrieve it, and when I entered, I found this." He pointed at the dead body.

"And then what happened?" I asked.

"Nothing," said James. "I ran to the bridge to inform the Boatswain. He summoned Mr. Steck here, and he told me to get you and Mrs. Waters—er, I mean, Detective Steele. Whichever."

"No one else has been by in your absence?" I asked. "Nobody else knows?"

"Just the five of us, to my knowledge, sir."

"And did you touch anything?" I asked. "Has the scene changed in any way since you first arrived?"

"No, sir," he said. "Not to my knowledge."

I turned to Olaugh, who stood at attention with his hands behind his back. "Who has access to the luggage compartment?"

"Any of the crew, in theory," rumbled the half-orc. "All the *Prodigious's* interior doors that are capable of locking use the same key, apart from the staterooms, of course. Those have separate keys, for guest security."

"I assume the luggage compartment locks," I said.

"Yes," said Olaugh.

"And *was* it locked?" I asked James.

"Ah..." He scrunched his brow. "No, actually. I turned my key, but the latch didn't click. It was open already."

"How often is this area patrolled?" I asked Olaugh.

"Not often, during a regular trip," he said. "Even less so now."

"What do you mean?"

"The short answer is our staff is busy attending to the opening night festivities," Olaugh said. "The longer answer is we didn't think there would be a need. As you can see, the space is largely bare. We have storage to accommodate long trips, but this maiden voyage is quite short due to the poker tournament you'll be competing in. After we complete that, we'll dock and head on a longer voyage. Only a few of the guests are staying with us for that longer voyage. This is largely their luggage."

"So, basically, pretty much anyone on board could've gotten in here, and no one was likely to have seen who actually did." I sighed. "Wonderful."

I turned back to the body. Given the disorderly pile of luggage and Shay's restrictive dress, she couldn't kneel next to the body, so she'd settled for seating herself on a nearby trunk, her legs pressed together and folded off to the side. The pose helped bring the dress's mermaid inspiration to life, though I had a hard time imagining a mermaid in such a brilliant scarlet.

I waded into the suitcases beside her. "Well at least somebody picked the right color to wear tonight."

"As if you had any choice," said Shay. "But blood will stain this dress as easily as your shirt. They're completely different shades."

I took her word for it. "Find anything?"

Shay brushed back some of the stiff's hair. "Look familiar?"

"Sure does," I said. "Unless I'm suffering from premature Alzheimer's, that's Lumpy."

"*Lumpy?*"

"Yeah," I said. "One of Johann's three thugs. Humpty, Dumpty, and Lumpy."

"I'm not surprised you already named them," said Shay, "but I am surprised with your choice of monikers. Especially since there were three of them and only two names from that nursery rhyme to go around."

"Hence, Lumpy," I said.

"If anything, it should be Lumpty."

"*Lumpty?* That's not even a word."

"Neither are Humpty or Dumpty," said Shay.

"Fair enough." I pointed at the body. "So what else did you find?"

"Well, I can't tell a whole lot from this angle, but this incision appears to be the only one on his back, at least. As far as I can tell, it would be enough. See the angle of entry? It indicates a downward strike into his back, and given the placement of the wound, I think it could've pierced one of his lower ventricles, assuming the knife was long enough. It would explain all the blood, anyway."

I smiled. "Look at you. You're like a mini Cairny."

"I'm taller than she is, but I get your drift," said Shay. "Why don't you move him off the suitcases so we can look at him from the front and check his possessions?"

"And risk sullying my suit? Not on your life." I waved to Olaugh and James. "A little help?"

The pair came over, and under my supervision, moved Lumpty to the floor and onto his back. James almost dropped him prematurely due to his nerves, but Olaugh was a rock.

I knelt down and took a look at the guy. He had a bit of a scrape and a bruise on one cheek, but his face had been pressed against the brass-banded corner of a trunk. If he fell into it, it could've easily caused the contusion. Apart from that, I didn't spot any obvious scrapes, cuts, or bruises, and though his hands—empty, unfortunately—were callused, they didn't show signs of struggle.

"Stabbed in the back, plain and simple," said Steele, echoing my own thoughts.

I checked Lumpty's pockets and actually found things. Multiple things. His coin purse, filled with a fair amount of silver, a silk handkerchief, a pair of brass knuckles—not illegal, but not exactly encouraged either—and a key with a chain similar to the one on Shay's and my own room key. It read one thirty-five.

"That's a promenade deck key," said Olaugh. "It wouldn't get the man in here."

I knew that. I also had a pretty good idea whose key it was. I pulled one last item from Lumpty's jacket: a slim, black leather case long enough to hold pens. I cracked it open.

"Looks like Lumpty didn't need a key." I held up the lock picking set for everyone to see.

"Well, knowing one of our own isn't in on this makes me feel better," said Olaugh. "Though not much."

"We can't rule anything out at this point." I stood and turned to Steele. "What do you think?"

"I think a lot of things," she said. "I think this case just got a whole lot more complicated, *and* more dangerous. And I think Steck should be counting his lucky stars he brought us on board instead of a pair of detectives from another department."

Giving thanks seemed beyond Steck's ability at the moment. He still stood at the foot of the luggage pile, staring into the disorder.

I waved him over. "Steck. We need to have a pow-wow."

"What is it?" he asked. "Do you have some idea who did it?"

"Yeah, didn't you see the note the killer left tacked to the back of the stiff? Of course not, man. Get your head in the game. What we need to do is figure out a game plan."

"Why are you asking me, then?" said Steck. "You're the homicide detectives."

"Yes, but this isn't a normal case," I said. "We're undercover on a fraud investigation that hasn't even started yet, and already somebody tangentially related to said investigation has turned up dead. We're cut off from the rest of our support teams, and we're in international waters, which makes jurisdiction tricky. So the question is, how do we approach this?"

Steck sighed. "Guys, I'm not going to lie. Having this case slip through my fingers before it even starts is going to haunt me for the rest of my career, but we don't have a choice. A murder trumps a potential fraud any day of the week. The homicide investigation has to take precedent."

"Agreed," said Shay, "but that doesn't mean we should abandon our mission."

I thought I knew where she was going, but I made her say it nonetheless. "Go on."

"Given the rumors about something fishy going down during the poker tournament and the fact that

Lumpty here—Daggers' designation, not mine—was in the employ of one of our three prime suspects, I'd say there's about a ninety-nine percent chance his murder is related to the tourney and was perpetrated by one of the players. Because of our limited jurisdiction, we stand a better chance of figuring out who killed him by staying undercover than we do by blowing it."

I nodded. "I'm with Steele. This puts more pressure on our shoulders, but the mission is still the same. We're just going to have to unravel a murder while we sort out what we came here to do. And that means more work for you, too, Steck. We don't have additional detectives or a coroner or a CSU team, and because Steele and I have to remain undercover, you need to be our eyes and ears. You'll need to do the legwork."

"For what it's worth, we stand ready and willing to help," said Olaugh.

"And we appreciate it," I said. "You can start by giving us a full list of every passenger with luggage in this compartment. Maybe that way we can figure out what Lumpty was doing here. Steck—I'm going to need you to interview all the bartenders and waitstaff from the mixer. Steele and I know when Lumpty left the party, but we don't know precisely where the other potential suspects were and at what times. Hopefully some eye witness accounts can narrow down the suspect pool for us. And see if you can find any other crew that might've seen what happened down here."

Steck nodded.

"I'll make sure the staff comply," said Olaugh. "And I'll make sure they meet with Steck one on one. As far as they'll know, he's a compliance inspector, making sure people are doing their jobs."

"Good thinking," I said. "Olaugh. I'll need you and Steck to move the body to a safe, secure location out of sight from prying eyes. And someone's going to need to clean this place up. I'm guessing you, James, due to the muzzle we're keeping on the operation. Given what we know, that's about all we can do at this juncture, unless you know more about mortuary science than you appear to, Steck."

The vice cop adopted a horrified expression. "You're kidding, right?"

Shay nodded. "It's what he does."

"Just because somebody died doesn't mean we need to get sober," I said. "Although finding a dead body does have a way of taking the edge off a buzz. Regardless, we all need to keep a clear head from here on out. Stay in touch, stay vigilant, but keep your lips sealed. If word of this spreads, it could create a panic, never mind sending our killer into hiding."

"And it would create unnecessary negative publicity for the *Prodigious*," said Olaugh.

I wasn't particularly worried about that part, but I let Olaugh think I cared. As the ship's security officer, I'd need his help if I had any chance of solving the murder and Steck's fraud case, both.

12

After checking ourselves carefully to make sure neither of us sported any blood stains, and after returning my dinner jacket, Shay and I headed back up to the mixer, but by the time we arrived, things had largely died down. All our fellow competitors had exited the lounge, and the few we hadn't met didn't rush from the shadows to make our acquaintance.

Luckily, the waitstaff still lurked and were more than happy to unload their uneaten appetizers on me. I made up for my lack of a formal dinner with fifteen or twenty bite-sized morsels, all the while wishing I could round up everyone in the room and put their feet to the fire, but I'd simply have to wait and let Steck to the heavy lifting.

More drinks tempted me, but I followed Shay's advice and abstained. Apparently, the powers who ruled over the *Prodigious's* gaming enterprises determined eight o'clock sharp would be a good time to start a poker tournament despite teasing everyone with free beverages the night prior. With that in mind, Shay suggested we turn in early. I escorted her down to our suite, but as we walked, it wasn't thoughts of sleep that milled about my brain.

The murder of Johann's bodyguard had momentarily hijacked my thoughts. I kept revisiting the evidence in my mind's eye, but at the same time I hadn't forgotten my evening with Shay. The sultry, playful looks she'd given me at the mixer. The feeling of our bodies pressed against one another on the ballroom floor as music flowed through us and sweat slicked our skin. The coolness of the winter breeze and the warmth of Shay's touch as we stood shoulder to shoulder on the *Prodigious's* deck.

I doubted Shay's and my compatibility more often than I cared to admit. Not because of any serious *in*compatibility on our parts. Sure, there was an age difference between us, as well a difference in maturity, with Shay being the far more responsible and sensible of our pair. And we had different tastes in music and literature and art and even basic aesthetics, so it was only natural for me to wonder, even discounting the fact that I tended to overthink aspects of every relationship I'd ever been in—either that or underthink them, as my ex, Nicole, might argue. But we also shared moments that made it obvious whatever doubts I had about us were largely unfounded. Our locking of lips a few days prior was one. The smile Shay had given me on the dance floor this evening was another. Both of those had burned into my long term memory. I'd never forget them, and I'd never ignore what they implied about Shay's feelings for me.

With that knowledge firmly in mind, I still had no idea how to proceed as I turned the key to our room and opened the door.

Shay glided into the living room, trailing her hand against the wainscoting as she moved. Despite the vigorous dancing, the brisk sea breeze that had tousled her hair, and the trek into the ship's depths to discover a dead man, she looked as beautiful as ever. Her dress dipped low on her back, teasing me as it hugged her in all the right places. She paused at the door to her bedroom.

I followed her in and glanced at the clock. Ten-thirty, or close enough not to make a difference. "So...what time do you think we should rise in the morning?"

Shay shrugged. "Six-thirty or thereabouts, if we wish to eat and look presentable."

If. The eating I was fond of. The presentation less so.

I took a step toward the far wall and peered into my bedroom. I'd taken the quarters on the left and Shay those on the right. My bag sat on the bed where Steck had left it—one of them anyway. My garment bag still lay on the floor of the living room by the coffee table.

Perhaps in response to my motion, Steele spoke. "Daggers?"

I looked up. "Yes?"

Shay hadn't moved from the frame of her door. She'd averted her eyes to the floor and drawn her hair over her right shoulder, exposing the full of her neck. She did that thing with her lips again, where she sucked on her bottom one before letting it out.

"I..." She lifted her head, drawing her gaze slowly across the floor, past the coffee table and the garment bag. She paused and blinked.

My heart thumped heavy in my chest. "Yes?"

"I...think someone's been in our room."

It wasn't what I'd hoped to hear, but I knew better than to doubt her observational prowess. "How do you know?"

"Your garment bag. It's been moved."

Instinct took over. I reached for Daisy, despite her absence, before darting into my bedroom to check for intruders. With that completed, I rushed to Shay's room to do the same. Once I'd satisfied myself in regards to our safety, I returned to the living room.

"Check your things," I told Shay. "See if anything's missing."

I opened my garment bag. I'd placed my suit back into it following my change. The jacket, slacks, shoes, leather belt, and thin tie were all there, even the cuff-links, though I couldn't tell if anything had been moved—mostly because I hadn't paid attention as I stuffed it in. I was, however, glad I'd left my badge back at the precinct on Steck's insistence. If someone *had* gone through my things, my identity would've been revealed.

"I don't suppose it was Steck who dropped by," called Shay as I moved back to my bedroom.

"Don't you think he would've mentioned it if he had?" I said. "Besides, he doesn't have a key to our room."

I went through the second bag on my bed, and while I couldn't remember every last piece of peacockery

Steck had made me bring along, neither could I spot anything blatantly missing or out of place.

When done with my search, I zipped the bag up and crossed over to the suite's exit. I snapped the deadbolt into place, put the additional safety bar in, and headed back to the living room.

Shay stood there having finished her own inspection, hands clasped before her. "I didn't find anything missing. You?"

I shook my head.

"Thoughts?" said Shay.

"I don't know," I said. "I'd be comfortable wagering it was one of our fellow poker competitors or their underlings who broke in, but beyond that? I suppose it could've been Lumpty, but the timing might've been difficult. What do you think?"

"What I think is we're not the only ones expecting hijinks," said Steele. "I'd bet several of our competitors heard the same rumors Steck did. They're looking for evidence that'll reveal who's going to pull the con, and I'd wager Lumpty found it. Either that, or he got a little too close for comfort."

"Yeah," I said. "But what did he find?"

Shay shrugged. "Think we'll be safe here tonight?"

"I locked the door and put the latch bar in, but I'll tuck a chair under the doorknob just in case."

Shay nodded and glanced at the clock. "We should probably hit the hay. We'll have an early morning."

"Yeah. We should. There'll be plenty of time to mull over this tomorrow."

Shay turned toward her room, but she paused at the edge. "Daggers?"

"Yes?"

She glanced at me and shot me a shy smile. "I had a nice time tonight."

I smiled back. "So did I. Although I could've done without the murder and the breaking and entering."

"Likewise. Goodnight."

"Goodnight."

Shay stepped into her room and closed the door, and I retreated to my own quarters. I stripped my shoes and coat off and lay on my bed face up. The mattress welcomed me with arms of purest down, far more comfortable than my own slab of concrete at home. Nonetheless, I suspected I'd have a hard time sleeping. I had far too much on my mind.

Very little of it had anything to do with police work.

13

I stifled a yawn as Shay and I stood at the entrance to the restaurant on the promenade deck, waiting for the host to return.

"You going to make it there, princess?" Shay, wearing a svelte burgundy cocktail dress that ended at her knees, smirked at me.

"Waking up this early should be criminal," I said. "At the very least, I suspect it's unhealthy."

"That goes against conventional wisdom."

"Yeah, well conventional wisdom also says bloodletting prevents disease and that regular applications of mercury ointments cures syphilis."

"Point taken," said Shay. "But it's not as if we had much choice."

"No kidding. This outfit took forever to get into." I gestured at my getup, a deep navy suit with a faint tartan design. It hadn't actually been that time consuming to don, but combined with a shower and a shave, the process had necessitated an early start.

"Now you know my pain," said Shay.

"What are you talking about?" I said. "As if you wear evening gowns and put your hair in an updo on a regular basis."

"I put a fair bit more effort into my appearance than you do."

"Something I thought you enjoyed," I said.

"To an extent," said Shay. "What I don't like is the expectation that I *always* be so presentable."

I stroked my chin. "Have I given you that idea? Honestly, if you want to get a little slovenly every now and then, it won't bother me in the least."

"I didn't mean you personally," said Shay. "It's more a cultural thing. Don't worry about it. It's one of the many societal injustices I hope to one day overturn."

The host returned, a clean-cut gentleman of early middle age. "Apologies, sir. Madam. A table for two?"

"Something in a corner if you can," I said. "My lady and I have private matters to discuss."

The host nodded and waved for us to follow. As he led us through a dining room full of the clatter of knives and forks, spirited chatter, and the clacking of teeth, I noticed a few familiar faces. Verona sat at the bar by herself, enjoying what appeared to be a liquid breakfast and ignoring the ill effects it might have on her later. Ghorza lounged in a chair at a centrally-located table looking decidedly worse for wear. She moved sluggishly and wore a feathered hat and shaded glasses to guard against the early morning glare. Of Jimmy, I saw not a trace. Neither did I spot Johann and his men. I wondered if he'd figured out what had happened to Lumpty, and if so, how he'd react.

I did spot Theo, however, in the far corner. He shared a table with a surly looking dwarf wearing a smooth brown vest over a crisp orange dress shirt with the sleeves pushed up to his elbows. A golden chain, the tail of a pocket watch, hung from his breast pocket to his belt. A large scar trailed from his eye to his chin, obvious even underneath the thick shock of his beard.

I elbowed Shay softly. "Orrin?"

"Can't imagine there are too many other scarred dwarves in first class," said Steele. "Especially those who would suffer Theo's company."

Suffer was right. Orrin didn't seem to be enjoying the gnome's chatty nature, as I'm sure Theo was well aware. Apparently he hadn't lied when he said he liked to bombard his opponents with verbal horse droppings.

"Sir. Madam. Your table." The host pulled out a chair for Shay.

We thanked him and seated ourselves. Within seconds, a pert waitress arrived to take drink orders. I gave her instructions to bring coffee and tea, as well as an assortment of eggs, cured meats, fruit, and biscuits. I knew better than to think her prompt arrival would be a harbinger of her ongoing attentiveness, and we had time constraints to keep abreast of.

I eyed our competitors casually, but none seemed to have their eyes trained in our direction. I turned to Shay. "I don't suppose you can overhear any of their conversations."

"In this din?" she said. "Not a chance."

"Good," I said. "Your hearing's better than mine, and I figured if you couldn't hear any of them, it was probably safe to talk."

"What about?"

"The possibility of us sharing a dining room with a killer."

Shay smiled. "Oh, so just your regular light breakfast conversation, then."

"For us, anyway."

"And you don't think we should wait for Steck to bring us his additional input?" said Shay. "Like the testimony of the bartenders, waiters, and waitresses from last night's mixer?"

"You know I'm not a thumb twiddler," I said. "I theorize regardless of how little evidence I have. But given our and everyone else's presence at the mixer last night, I think we can narrow the field a bit even without their eyewitness accounts."

"Disagreed."

"Oh really?" I said. "And how do you figure that?"

"We left our room for the mixer at seven, which means we arrived about ten after. We spent maybe an hour there, but Johann and his men left roughly twenty minutes before we did, putting their departure at a quarter to eight. We then moved to the ballroom and danced. Total time elapsed, half an hour. Then we moved to the ship's exterior and spent approximately another twenty minutes there before James found us. That gives us an hour and ten minutes from Lumpty's departure to the point at which we found him dead. We were isolated from everyone else for the latter fifty minutes of that—plenty of time for anyone, including those we left at the mixer, to follow Lumpty to the luggage compartment and murder him."

I lifted an eyebrow. "Where were you hiding a watch last night? That dress didn't leave a lot to the imagination."

Shay blushed, but only slightly. "I have a good internal clock."

"Okay. I trust you," I said. "Sounds about right to my own estimations, anyway. But if you're right, that means we can't narrow our pool of suspects at all."

"We can't. Steck can. Give him time. He'll come through."

"I hate it when you bat my arguments down with sound logic," I said. "But if we can't do anything until Steck interviews the staff, what am I supposed to do to occupy my overactive thinking cap?"

"How about putting it to use on the task at hand?" said Shay. "Namely studying your opponents. In addition to a murder to solve, we still have a poker tournament to win and a con-man to catch."

"Right. Gambling." I glanced at the opposition again. "Still think we have a chance to win?"

"Are you kidding?" said Shay. "Somebody was stupid enough to kill a man. They might've had the upper hand coming in, but these folks are playing on our home court now."

I smiled. I appreciated Shay's attitude even if I lacked her confidence—if it was that. Could be she was already practicing her bluffs.

The waitress returned with our meals. I began to scarf down eggs, sliced sausage, and fruit salad with little regard for decorum, but I hadn't put my jaw to the grindstone for more than a minute when I noticed

Ghorza stand and head for the exit. Theo and Orrin noticed her and followed.

I gave Shay a nod and spoke between bites. "Something's afoot."

"Yeah," she said. "The tournament's about to start. We need to hurry."

I looked around the room, but I couldn't spot a clock anywhere. Apparently, Shay hadn't lied about her internal timekeeper. Hopefully, she'd use it to keep us from being late.

14

An escort led us through the casino proper, past craps tables and roulette wheels already busy with patrons, to the high stakes poker room that would become our immediate home. It had all the usual trappings of a casino—beige on cream paisley rugs, lots of artificial light, and velvet drapes hung over solid walls, because windows would only give patrons an excuse to stand up and leave—but it had been outfitted in ways the common rooms hadn't. Round tables with three high-backed stools apiece dotted the corners of the room, and on the side, a bartender with a black vest and bowtie staffed a bar with at least a hundred bottles of expensive liquors set into the wall behind him. A delicate crystal chandelier hung from the center of the space, and underneath it was a green felt-topped poker table that had never felt the touch of an elbow upon its unblemished edge.

Of course, to call it a *private* room was definitely a misnomer. Above us, a second floor gallery allowed spectators to peer upon the gladiators below. The space was mostly barren at the moment, but I had no doubt that as the action on the table thickened, so would the crowds. Our poker tournament was intended as a draw, after all, and the casino's operators would be remiss in their duties if they didn't take the opportunity to sell drinks to onlookers and take side bets on our performances.

A quick glance around the room revealed we weren't the last of the players to arrive, though we were close. Orrin, Theo, and Jimmy were there, as was Ghorza with Vlad and Johann with Humpty and Dumpty. The textile mill owner didn't look pleased, but then again, he hadn't before one of his men had gone missing. He must've suspected Lumpty's death. Why else wouldn't the man have reported back to him following whatever task Johann had set upon him?

In addition to the known commodities, I noticed a lone woman in the corner at one of the round tables. She was slight and of middling height, with raven dark hair cut in a pageboy, the bangs of which reached to just over her eyes—not that you could see them. Like Ghorza, she wore darkened spectacles, but with wide lenses rimmed in white. Rather than a dress, she wore a black turtleneck sweater and matching pleated slacks. She nursed a glass of clear liquid between her hands, probably water unless she preferred her vodka straight.

She had to be Wanda. Seeing as she was alone and the game had yet to begin, she seemed a fitting target for investigation, but Orrin had isolated himself on the opposite side of the room.

Shay noticed my gaze. "Divide and conquer?"

"It's the best strategy, if one has the resources," I said.

"I'll make the acquaintance of the lady in black, then," said Shay. "Best of luck in the tournament, my sweet."

We'd both firmed up our personas on the walk over. "I make my own luck. But you already knew that, didn't you, dear?"

Shay shot me an elevated eyebrow as she pivoted and glided toward the presumed Wanda. I could watch her walk away for hours on end, and the heels she wore made the sight even more pleasant, but I had work to do.

I approached the scarred dwarf in the corner and extended a hand. "Orrin, is it? Thomas Waters."

Orrin's hands were stuffed in his pockets. He eyed my hand and kept his in place. "Yes?"

"I'm introducing myself."

Orrin didn't flinch.

I pulled my hand back. "The customary response is to reply in kind, but it's alright. Perhaps you have an infectious disease you're trying to keep me clear of, or you suffer from erratic seizures that prohibit you the full use of your arm. Those are the most flattering explanations I can come up with, anyway."

"I'm not here to make friends," growled Orrin.

"I think we're all here for the same reasons," I said, "but neither am I here to make *enemies*. I think it's a mutually compatible goal with making money."

"Not the way I play," said Orrin. "Or the way you do, for that matter."

I lifted an eyebrow. "You've watched me play before?"

"Don't act stupid, Waters. The first hand hasn't even been dealt and already you've more than doubled your odds of winning. I'm not sure who you bribed to make sure your wife would get a spot at the table alongside you, but I assure you, that kind of underhanded move hasn't gone unnoticed."

"Samantha?" I said. "Well, I could try to convince you we're playing independently and that she'd secretly love to win it all to get out from under my oppressive boot heel, but I don't think you'd believe that. Still, we each put up our own entry fee. Should we lose, we lose twice as much as any of you."

"You're right," said Orrin with a scowl. "I *don't* believe any of that. But believe you me. Whatever signs you've established to share information with each other through the game? I'll figure them out. And I'll use them against you. So you'd better hope you can take me out early, because otherwise I'll run you into the ground late."

Orrin stormed off toward the bar, leaving me to wallow in solitude. If Orrin really thought Shay and I'd be working in tandem to win the tournament, he'd be sorely disappointed. There was too much risk involved in such a strategy, and with less than a day to prepare, we simply hadn't had the time to put such a system in place. Still, I was glad Orrin had voiced his concerns. Better to know you have a target painted upon your back to give you some chance of avoiding the arrow when it comes.

"Lovely guy, isn't he?"

I looked down. Theo had snuck up on me again. "Not particularly, no. I'd ask him what I did to anger him, but he told me right to my face, unprompted."

"I wouldn't take it personally," said Theo. "He didn't like me either. Said I was too chatty. *Me.* Too chatty. Can you believe that? And all I did was come up and try to be nice to him at breakfast. The poor guy was sitting all by his lonesome. Figured he could use some company, as could I. Might as well break our fast together, right? But I tell you what. I had to carry that conversation. He didn't pull his weight *at all.* By the end of it, he all but told me to shove off."

"Orrin did that?" I said. "And after you went out of your way to brighten his morning, with no ulterior motive or possible gain on your part. How dare he?"

Theo smiled. "I know, right? Some people..."

I nodded toward Shay and the woman in black. "You get a chance to meet Wanda?"

"Oh, yeah," said Theo. "She's a real chatterbox. Look at her go. I think she's uttered three whole words to your piece of arm candy over there. Oh, wait. Scratch that. Four."

"What was it you said last night? About some people hiding behind a mask of silence?"

"In her case, maybe it's not a mask," said Theo. "Maybe she's naturally quiet. Or maybe it is a mask but the kind that hides a painful secret, some yawning chasm of darkness within her that's screaming and clawing as it tries to get out."

I lifted an eyebrow. "That's a little dark."

Theo laughed. "Oh, come on, man. I'm kidding. *Or am I?*"

Verona entered the room, a drink clasped in one hand and her jade smoking stick held in the other. Her eyes were glazed, but she walked without any missteps despite wearing three-inch high stilettos. My guess was she'd had a lot of practice—both at drinking and walking in heels while inebriated.

A woman with dark blonde hair wearing black slacks and a blouse with white suspenders over it followed her. She paused in front of the poker table and cleared her throat. "Excuse me. Ladies and gentlemen. May I have your attention, please?"

Theo rubbed his hands together. "Oh, yeah. Here we go, baby. Let's do this."

Once the chatter died, the new woman continued. "I hope you're enjoying your time aboard the *Prodigious* so far. Let me be the first to officially welcome you to the ship's inaugural high stakes, no-limit hold'em poker tournament. My name is Patty Hiller, and I'll be your dealer for the course of this event. I've received word from our head manager that you've all deposited your initial buy ins, and with the arrival of Madam Quivven, we are complete. So, without further ado, place your drink orders with our bartender if you so desire, please have a seat, and let's begin."

I eyed Steele across the room. She gave me a curt nod. I took a deep breath and approached the table.

15

"Aw, come on, man," said Theo. "Are you serious? You can't be serious with these cards right now. It's like the gods have a vendetta against me or something."

"Don't you ever shut up?" said Jimmy. The big bruiser sat wide with his elbows out to his sides. Even accounting for the size of the table, he would've been tight on space if not for that fact that he'd been seated between Theo and Wanda.

"Not really," said Theo. "Besides, I haven't said if I'm going to check, raise, or fold yet."

"After all that, you're *not* going to fold?" said Jimmy.

"What?" said Theo. "Nah, I'm kidding. I'm folding." He pushed his cards toward the dealer.

Jimmy drained the last of his whiskey and soda—his third so far—and tapped his fingers on the table to indicate he checked, sending the bet to Wanda.

Clockwise from the dealer, we sat: Johann, Shay, Theo, Jimmy, Wanda, me, Orrin, Ghorza, and Verona. We'd played for several hours already if my rumbling belly was any indication, but in that time no major changes had taken place. I'd grown my pile of chips slightly and Shay's had dwindled by a similarly small amount. Wanda had done the best for herself so far, building her fortune by about twenty percent, and Johann had fared the worst, but even he was only down about five thousand crowns.

Only five thousand crowns... How quickly my estimation of the value of money had declined.

Wanda folded, and I did the same. Orrin scowled and grumbled and pulled on his beard, but eventually he folded, too, sending the bet to Ghorza.

The orc woman had remained quiet and reserved so far, hiding under her hat and shades, but I'd yet to figure out if it was her intended strategy or merely a result of her hangover. She finally removed her glasses and set them on the table. She puffed out a breath of air, took off her hat, and fanned herself with it.

"Oh, my," she said, breaking her silence. "I feel warm. Am I the only one? No? No one else? Goodness. Vlad? Be a dear. Get me more chilled water?"

The elf servant stood at the back of the room. He sprang into action on request, heading to the bar.

"Hey, Ghorza," said Theo. "Nice to see you've joined us. Finally fighting off that brown bottle flu?"

"I don't know what you're insinuating," she said. "I've simply been feeling under the weather."

"Hmm." Theo elbowed Jimmy and gave him a wink. "Sure she doesn't. Am I right, big guy?"

"Don't make me eat you," said Jimmy. "Flossing afterwards would be a nightmare."

Theo held up his hands in mock horror.

Vlad brought the water. Ghorza took a sip, waited a moment, and raised. Verona folded. Jimmy matched, and Patty put the three flop cards down. Jimmy and Ghorza went back and forth a bit before Ghorza eventually took the hand on the river.

Patty collected the cards, shuffled them, and dealt everyone a new pair. "Next hand. Madam Quivven to start."

Verona took a peek at her cards before pressing them back against the table. She took a drag from her cigarette holder and pushed forward her required bet due to her starting position, known as the small blind.

Johann played with his chips, intertwining and separating them one-handed with fingers far more deft than age would indicate. His face was cool and composed, and to my observation, he hadn't shown any signs of disquiet following the disappearance of his man. Humpty and Dumpty, who sat at one of the round tables in the corner nursing their drinks, seemed far more on edge by comparison.

By virtue of his secondary position, Johann was required to double Verona's initial bet, but he pushed forward a much larger pile of chips than he needed. About two thousand crowns worth. "Let's raise the stakes."

"Aw, come on, man," said Theo. "And I finally had a good hand."

"Then play it," said Johann.

"And waste a good hand on you? No way." He pushed his cards forward. "I'm saving my good hands for Jimmy, and I can already tell he's not going to play. You going to play, big guy?"

Jimmy scowled and folded. Wanda and I did the same, minus the scowling, but Orrin matched. Vlad had taken over fanning duties for Ghorza, but the big orc woman took her time sipping her chilled water before eventually folding as well.

Verona wore a similar outfit to the one she had the night before, a ruched golden dress, a heavy fox fur shawl, and twenty pounds of jewelry. She trailed a hand down the fur to her martini—like Jimmy, her third—lifted it, and took a sip. In a drinking contest, I'd have to go with Jimmy thanks to his bulk, but Verona had that glazed, even keel look of a functional alcoholic, never fully alert but never truly drunk either. Her liver was probably so porous by now the alcohol passed right on through.

She set down her drink, took another long drag from her cigarette holder, and blew the smoke roughly in Johann's direction. "Very well, Johann. Let's see where this goes."

She pushed her chips forward to match the bet.

Patty flipped three cards down onto the table, the flop: the queen of hearts, seven of diamonds, and five of hearts.

Johann stroked his chin. "So, you'd like to dance, Verona? I have to admit it's been a while. Though my feet have slowed in my old age, I think you'll find my mind is as deft as ever." He pushed forward another three thousand crowns worth of chips.

Orrin grunted and cracked his neck. He stared at his chips, but after a moment of contemplation, he flicked his cards back to the dealer.

"If nothing else, I'm glad to see you haven't lost your nerve." Verona matched Johann's bet. "But let's be honest, dear. It's not enough to keep one's mind from dulling. If anything it needs to sharpen over time."

Dear? It wasn't necessarily a term of endearment—many women referred to men in such a fashion, especially those who'd been groomed in high society—but I couldn't recall Verona greeting *me* that way last night.

Patty turned over the fourth card, the turn. A seven of hearts.

Johann tapped his fingers on the table to indicate a check.

"You see what I mean?" said Verona. "You need to stay sharp. To be able to anticipate the cards." She pushed forward another two thousand crowns worth of chips.

"The cards can't be anticipated," said Johann. "Only the opponent. I'm all in."

The stately old man pushed the rest of his chips forward into the middle of the table, soliciting a murmur from the crowd that had started to gather in the gallery. He sat back and leveled his gaze at Verona.

She took a long drag from her cigarette holder and let it out slowly. "Of that, you are undoubtedly correct. It's too bad you could never anticipate *me.*" Verona waved at her chips. "I match."

Patty set down the fifth and final card, a two of diamonds. Johann flipped his cards, a pair of queens.

"Full house, queens over sevens," said Patty.

"What's the matter, Verona? You're looking a little *flushed,*" said Johann.

Verona waved her cigarette dismissively. "Not as much as you will be."

She turned her cards. Rather than a pair of hearts, as Johann clearly expected, she revealed a pair of sevens.

"Oh, snap!" said Theo.

"Four of a kind," said Patty. "Game to Madam Quivven."

Johann's cheeks reddened as the crowd above gave him a smattering of applause, but to his credit, he took his loss with poise. He stood, straightened his jacket, and nodded to the remaining players. "Ladies. Gentlemen. Best of luck in the rest of the tournament."

He motioned to his men, turned, and exited through the door at his back.

Patty collected the cards. "On that note, I suggest we break for lunch. We'll resume the tournament in an hour and a half's time."

Everyone rose, other than Verona who busily stacked her chips. Orrin and Jimmy headed toward the bar while Theo headed for Ghorza, apparently thinking some jawing could help banish the remnants of her hangover. Wanda, however, made a beeline for the exit.

Shay joined me. "Well, that was interesting. I was starting to think the table would never see any real action."

"Can we talk it over in a minute? There's something I'd like to follow up on." I nodded at the door. "Save me a spot at lunch?"

Shay caught my drift if not necessarily my intention. "Sure. See you in the dining room."

I nodded and hastened for the door, hoping my pace wasn't too obvious.

16

I stepped back into the heart of the casino proper and blinked. Though I'd thought it bustling before, I'd been wrong. At least twice as many people packed its halls now, drinking and laughing and huddling around card tables. Cigar smoke choked the air, that of fine tobacco but overpowering nonetheless. A ball clacked and clattered against the hardwood sides of a roulette wheel before it was drowned in a cheer from the surrounding crowd.

I scanned the room. The men wore suits of rich fabrics in dark colors, blacks and navy blues and browns, but the women had by and large dressed to stand out. Gowns of bright yellow and purple and red dotted the landscape, like flowers bursting from the ground after the last winter thaw.

To me, they were a distraction. I kept my eyes on the black coats and shirts, scanning them for anyone too small and diminutive to be of the male persuasion. A flash of natural light caught my eye, and suddenly I saw her. Wanda, sliding through one of the exits into the *Prodigious's* interior.

I'd had my eyes on her throughout the morning, or at least a single eye, given her position at my right elbow. Theo hadn't lied about her. She made Orrin, the table's resident brooder, seem downright chatty. She hadn't uttered a single word during the morning's session—not one—instead choosing to communicate with the dealer entirely through table taps, finger gestures, and flicks of her cards. In addition to that, she'd barely moved. She played every hand as if it were the same, giving no indication as to her cards or her psychology or even if she needed to use the bathroom. Not that she would. She hadn't drunk anything either.

It wasn't her table demeanor that interested me, however. It was her public presence. She hadn't attended the mixer the night before, nor the ball, and I hadn't spotted her at breakfast in the morning, either. It could be she simply wasn't social—in fact, I'd bet money on it—but while her antisocial nature might preclude her from fraternizing with her opponents over drinks or a meal, it didn't say anything about her ability or desire to meet with them one on one in private in their rooms or, say, a baggage compartment.

Her hasty exit from the high stakes room certainly didn't do anything to quell my suspicions. I hurried after her, mouthing apologies as I bumped into the backs of people in the space between tables. When I made it through the same exit she'd taken, I glanced up and down the hallway, but I didn't spot her. To the right beckoned the exit to the ship's deck, while to the left lay access to the rest of the ship's bridge deck and the staterooms on the promenade deck.

I'd never considered myself the world's best tail, mostly due to my lack of fleet feet and my larger than average size, but I did know a bit of the science behind the art. Half the battle was thinking quickly and predicting the most likely course of action of the subject. Despite her turtleneck, Wanda wasn't dressed to spend time outdoors, and given all our presences in the high stakes room, our staterooms were unoccupied, meaning there was a better than average chance she'd headed toward the bridge deck.

I went left. I chose correctly. I spotted a glimpse of black slacks as I turned the corner, disappearing into a stairwell.

I trailed at a distance, following her up the stairs, down the main portside corridor on the promenade deck, and around a corner. I'd expected she might stop at one of the staterooms, either hers or someone else's, but she surprised me, hooking a right away from the guest quarters and toward a part of the ship I hadn't yet visited. After two dozen paces, she pushed her way through a pair of swinging double doors. I caught a flash of natural light and a healthy dose of green, but little else.

I didn't think she'd noticed me, but I needed to proceed with caution. I wasn't sure what I was heading into, and if Wanda did make me, I'd lose the only advantage I had. I counted to twenty seconds in my head and followed her in.

The brightness caught me off guard. The room that opened up before me had high ceilings of solid glass, and sunlight from an abnormally cloud-free day poured in. Thousands of plants, from ankle high creepers to ten foot tall trees, soaked in the rays, some in wide communal troughs, others in terracotta pots, and still others in hanging baskets, but the room wasn't solely a greenhouse. Rather it was some sort of conservatory, with white wicker chairs and tables strategically distributed throughout the greenery. It was a beautiful space for whiling away the daylight hours—or for escaping detection.

I made my rounds, walking up and down the aisles separated by thick rows of vegetation, but I already knew I'd been beat. Other than an elderly woman reading underneath a wide-fronded tropical tree and a snoring gentleman who looked like he'd enjoyed the overnight festivities a little too much, I found nothing—except for another staircase at the far side of the room, that is.

I followed it and made my way back to the dining room, where I found Shay seated by herself at a corner table.

"There you are," she said. "I took the liberty of ordering, seeing as we'll be short on time. I hope you're in the mood for a bouillabaisse. The waiter said it's scrumptious. Has fresh caught rockfish, not to mention mussels and sea urchin."

"Seriously?" I said as I took a seat. "You ordered me a *fish stew?*"

"Well, yes. I..." Shay's face fell.

I felt as if she'd kicked me in the chest. I could be such a heel sometimes. "Look, I didn't mean it that way. I'm sure it'll be delicious, and you know I—"

A smile crept across Shay's face.

"You didn't really order me the stew, did you?"

Shay snickered. "I'm sorry. I had to. You're so easy sometimes. And be honest, if you were in my shoes, you totally would've told me you'd ordered me a baloney sandwich or something equally insipid. But never fear. The bouillabaisse is mine. You have a steak and mashed potatoes on the way."

I breathed a sigh of relief. "You know, I'm confident in my bluffing skills, but forcing my way through that would've put them to the test."

Shay glanced into the dining room, but it was as joyous and loud as before. "So...who'd you follow? Johann or Wanda?"

"The latter," I said. "But she must've made me. I lost her upstairs. But it wasn't a complete loss. I found a space up there I think you'll love."

Shay lifted an eyebrow.

"A greenhouse," I said. "Lots of gorgeous plants, and seats to sit and relax."

"As if we have time to do any of that."

"You never know," I said. "We might get this wrapped up by the afternoon. Then it's all paid vacation from here on out."

"Your optimism is unsettling, especially given your recent failure with Wanda."

"I know, but it's better than the crushing pessimism I usually carry around and hand out for free, wouldn't you say?"

Shay smiled. "Either way, thanks for thinking of me. I'd love to go up there after the afternoon's round of poker."

I nodded, but Shay didn't have to thank me. Thinking of her had become one of my favorite pastimes of late.

17

I took a slow sip of my apricot whiskey sour, which I'd been nursing since sitting down at the poker table hours ago. As much as I enjoyed the beverage, I had no intention of letting the drink's demons inhabit me, as they had a way of making themselves at home and refusing to leave one they did.

Jimmy didn't seem to suffer the same misgivings. He'd been drinking like a fish ever since we'd returned from lunch, and even with his impressive mass, the spirits were taking their toll. His eyes drooped, the stench of alcohol sweat rolled off him, and correspondingly, he'd hit a rough stretch. Now he'd turned noticeably snappier, and his joking threats had taken on a sharper tenor.

Jimmy snarled at Theo. "You gonna bet, shrimp, or what?"

"Hey, no need to get personal," said the gnome as he tapped his fingers on the table. "You don't see me calling you derogatory animal-based names because of your size, and trust me I could. There's lots to choose from.

Rhino. Elephant. Whale, though I'm not really sure if that's a good one. You're big, but thick. I don't know how well you'd float. You practice your strokes?"

Jimmy repeated himself, but slower this time and angrier if possible. "You gonna bet, or not?"

"I'm thinking," said Theo. "You know, using the old gray matter? This is game of intellect. If you don't think through everything, you'll never win. Seriously, you might want to write that down. I don't give that sort of advice out free of charge most of the time, but I'm feeling generous due to your...eh, *chip situation*. I mean, seriously? Come on, man." He waved at Jimmy's pile, which had dwindled to about half its initial size.

Jimmy growled at the rest of the table. "Would someone please make this midget bet before I tear his fingers off and use them to plug my ears?"

"Whoa there," said Theo. "No need to threaten violence. Thought it does make my choice on this hand easier. I fold." He tossed his cards toward the dealer.

"Finally." Jimmy pushed half his chips in, about five thousand crowns worth. "I raise."

Wanda folded, silently as always. After skipping lunch in the dining room, she'd appeared back at the high stakes poker room right at the top of the hour. She hadn't changed her strategy one iota. If she had in fact spotted me, she didn't plan on letting me know, nor had she made any move that made me think my presence at her elbow made her uncomfortable. She was cold as ice. Maybe she *had* spent time on the *Prodigious's* breezy deck, after all.

I had a queen and a jack, off suit. Not a bad hand, but nothing to wager five thousand crowns over. I shook my head and folded. "Too rich for my blood."

Orrin folded too, sending the bet to Ghorza, who'd started the hand. Her initial bet was on the line, but it paled in comparison to Jimmy's recently pushed forth pile.

Ghorza stroked her chin between thumb and index finger and took another sip of water. She'd drunk nothing else all day, but the most basic of beverages seemed to have worked its magic. The woman's complexion had finally improved, and she'd abandoned her hat and glasses about an hour ago. She'd also begun to put more effort into the game, at least to my eyes. I'd noticed her stroking her chin on more than one occasion, but every time she'd done so she'd ultimately folded, so I hadn't been able to put my knowledge to use.

Ghorza set her glass down and pushed her cards forward. "Go ahead and take my small blind, Jimmy. I don't want it that badly."

I suppressed a smile. I'd been right about Ghorza. Now if only she'd stroke her chin like that on a bet, I might be able to take advantage of her.

Verona puffed on her cigarette holder and eyed Jimmy. She'd put forth the hand's big blind, but it had barely made a dent in her chip pile, swelled by her defeat of Johann and a few other successful hands. An empty highball glass sat in front of her, red half moons on the top from where her lipstick had rubbed off. Amazingly, it had sat there for nearly two hours without her having waved at the bartender for a refill. Perhaps even she had her limits.

"So, Jimmy," said Verona. "It appears no one is willing to challenge you. But I suppose you're used to subservience, aren't you?"

"I'm used to getting what I want," he said. "And I crush anyone who gets in my way. That's why they call me The Hammer."

"Well, you're blunt if nothing else," said Verona. "But I think it would behoove all of us to know if your newfound bluster is warranted or is in fact just that. So I'll call your bet." She pushed forth enough chips to match. She blew smoke across the table through puckered lips and flicked her fingers at the dealer for more cards.

Patty obliged, putting three down on the table. The jack of spades, ten of hearts, and two of clubs.

Jimmy chuckled and flashed an evil smile. "Wrong move, Verona. Get ready to feel the weight of my hardened steel face." He stuck his hand out and let it hover over his remaining chips.

Theo snorted. "Dude, I've got to say, that hammer metaphor is getting pretty tired. But if we're using metal-based analogies, I'll throw another one at you. If you're going to make threats like that, at least have the brass leg slappers to go through with it. Come on, man. Take a stand."

"Shut it, you little weasel. I make my own choices." Jimmy's fingers danced over his chip pile for another few seconds before he pushed the entire thing toward the middle of the table. "I'm all in."

All eyes shifted to Verona. She considered the cards that had been turned as she smoked. After a moment, she shrugged, rolled her eyes, and tossed her cards face up on the table. "Fine. I call."

She revealed the king and queen of hearts, putting her an ace or a nine shy of a straight but with nothing but a high card for the time being.

Jimmy flipped his cards face up, too. The jack of diamonds and ten of clubs. That gave him two pair right off the bat—not a bad hand given what Verona had revealed, but not particularly good either, and worse than my own starting hand. The off suit jack ten certainly wasn't anything I would've wagered five thousand crowns on right off the bat, but maybe Jimmy was a looser player than I thought. I'd have to remember that if he won the hand.

Patty set the fourth card on the table. The five of hearts. Verona was now a heart, a nine, or an ace away from eliminating the game's second player.

The elderly elf woman tapped her cigarette's ashes into a tray. "Still feeling confident, Jimmy?"

"You've got nothing," he said. "And hammers don't sweat."

But sweat he did. Moisture dotted his brow, and veins stuck out on his forehead, probably from the force with which he clenched his jaw.

Patty flipped the final card. The nine of diamonds.

Jimmy stood and slammed his fists into the table, knocking over several of our stacks of chips. "NO! DAMNIT!"

"King nine straight over two pair, jacks and tens," said Patty. "Game to Madam Quivven."

"This is bullshit. BULLSHIT!" Jimmy turned and punted his chair, sending it crashing into the wall. The crowd above gasped. "This game is rigged! A nine? Give me a freakin' break. And you!" He jabbed a thick finger at Theo. "You egged me into it, you little slime!"

"What? *Me?*" Theo pushed himself as far back into his chair as he could and shrunk down, trying to hide among the padding. "I didn't tell you to go all in. That was all you!"

I stood up and put my hands out in an appeasing manner, all while a pair of the ship's security officers came in through the door in response to the noise.

"Settle down, Jimmy," I said. "You knew the risks when you signed up for this, same as we did. It's a game of chance as much as it is skill."

Jimmy glared at me with burning, whiskey-fueled eyes as the two guards converged on him, taking positions at his sides. One of them gestured toward the door. "Sir?"

"Don't touch me," said Jimmy. "I can see myself out. And I hope all of you rot in hell."

Jimmy snapped his jacket over his shoulders and stormed out the exit. Boos rained down on him as he left.

To her credit, Patty didn't miss a beat. She gathered the cards and helped move the pile of chips to Verona's spot. After shuffling the cards, she set them aside. "I apologize for that unpleasantness," she said, as if she'd had anything to do with the matter, "but on that note, I think it's time we break for the evening. We'll resume the tournament tomorrow morning at eight o'clock sharp."

I crossed to Steele's chair to help her from her seat. "Doing alright?"

"Of course," she said. "Why wouldn't I be?"

I shrugged. "Jimmy's outburst." Theo had crossed to the bar, but he still looked shaken. A brazen front could only get you so far when you were a gnome going up against a troll-hybrid.

"As if I haven't dealt with worse."

"It's just that it was very...violent," I said. "And sudden."

I think Steele figured out I was thinking about more than what happened at the poker table. "Would you care to head to our quarters to discuss it in more detail?"

I held out my arm for Steele to take. "Let's."

18

I unlocked the door to our stateroom, held it open for Shay, and locked it behind us. Shay took a seat in one of the opulent chairs in our living room, and I joined her, seating myself across from her.

"So," said Shay. "I take it you have theories about Jimmy you wanted to run by me?"

"Theories might be too strong a word," I said. "These are loose collections of thoughts I haven't sifted through yet."

"Hunches, then? Inklings? Misgivings?"

"Even suspicions and funny feelings."

"Well why don't you fetch me a glass of water and a thesaurus while you figure out which."

I stood and crossed to our bar, where I lifted a pitcher and pulled a glass off a rack. "The point is, I'm concerned by Jimmy's behavior. It should be obvious why. The guy's established himself as hotheaded and violent, and those are traits to be aware of when searching for a guy who just stabbed someone else in the back. And let's not ignore the fact that he's big, tall, and strong. For him, it would've been easy to—"

"Daggers?"

"Yes?" I set the glass of water on the coffee table in front of Steele.

"The couch cushions are misaligned. Someone's been in our cabin again."

I swore. "You've got to be kidding me. Okay, standard protocols. Check for stowaways, see if any of our personal belongings are missing, and keep an eye out for evidence that might've been left behind."

I checked Shay's room first, in the wash closet and under the bed, to make sure she'd be safe before retiring to my own quarters. There I sifted through my bags of clothes and shoes again, which I still hadn't unpacked. Everything seemed to be there, although I had no idea if it was precisely where I'd left it or not. My sense of placement with regards to minutiae wasn't nearly as acute as Shay's.

From there, I moved to my chair, over which I'd draped the tuxedo I'd worn the night prior. As I checked the pockets, Shay joined me.

"Don't tell me you forgot to hang this up," she said.

"I didn't forget," I said. "I chose to leave it here."

"But there's a crease in the jacket, now," she said. "It'll need to be pressed before tonight's opera."

"Opera?"

"*The Pirates of St. Gustifere,* by Smotrycz and Gullivan. What did you think we were doing tonight?"

"I hadn't given it any thought," I said. "But more important than the jacket at the moment is whether or not you found anything missing in your room. Or anything added, if that makes any sense."

Shay shook her head. "All my belongings are where I left them, more or less. I could tell someone had been through them, though. As for clues? No obvious ones. Whoever went through it was careful."

"You know, I'm really starting to miss our CSU team," I said. "Remind me to buy them a round of drinks when we get back."

"Do you think it was the same person who broke in last night?"

I finished with the jacket pockets. Nothing missing. "Not unless the person who broke in last night was Wanda, because I know for a *fact* it was her who busted in here."

Shay lifted an eyebrow. "You do?"

"When I say fact, I mean it's another hunch. Why else would she have ditched me through the greenhouse? Nobody else was missing during the lunch hour."

"Just because she caught onto your tail and managed to lose you doesn't mean she came here afterwards," said Shay. "She might've been up to something nefarious elsewhere, or she might've not been up to anything at all but rather suspected *you* of misdeeds. And you're wrong. She wasn't the only one missing during lunch. Johann and his men had already left, and Verona hopped out of the dining room early."

"All true," I said, "but you're not supposed to point it out. You're supposed to buttress my hunches with facts that prove my point."

Shay tilted her head and lifted her brows. "Daggers..."

I heard a knock at the door. I shared a glance with Shay before moving to the front and opening it. It was Steck.

I nodded him in and closed the door behind him. "About time you showed up. I don't suppose you've noticed anyone other than us coming in and out of our room, have you?"

Steck narrowed his eyes. "Pardon?"

Steele joined us in the living room. "We've had two break-ins. One while we were out last night and another at some point today during the poker tournament."

"You're sure?" asked Steck.

"This is kind of what Steele does," I said. "Trust me, she's sure."

Steck sighed and threw up his hands. "Look, I don't know. I've barely been around. But I can ask. Some of the crew might've seen something. I'll...add it to my to-do list."

"Long day?" asked Steele.

Steck nodded. "You could say that. It's been challenging isolating all of the staff from last night's events, but I've met with all of them now and taken their statements. And I've had a chance to go through said statements and try to find common ground between what they claimed."

"And?" I said.

Steck pointed at the water glass, still untouched on the coffee table. "May I? I'm parched."

Steele gave him the go ahead.

Steck took a long draught. "Ah. Better. Okay. First, the bad news. No one saw anyone entering or exiting the luggage compartment. I talked to several of the crew that work on the lower levels and gave them descriptions of the people in the poker tournament, but they couldn't even confirm if they'd seen any of them at all, much less near the hold. I can't blame them. With last night being the first aboard the *Prodigious,* everyone's face is fresh. Hard to distinguish one partier from the next."

"But there's good news?" said Steele.

"To an extent," said Steck. "The bartenders, waiters, and waitresses from last night's mixer all agree. Verona Quivven, Jimmy Frazier, and Theo Hornshoe were in the bar area throughout the evening. None of them left for more than a few minutes at a time, probably to use the facilities. If Detective Steele is right that Johann's man died roughly thirty minutes before our crewman, James, found him, then that eliminates them as suspects. If we also assume Johann or one of his other guards didn't kill the man, that narrows the suspect pool even further."

"Don't ever assume anything in this business," I said. "But you're sure about Jimmy?"

"I'm only sure of the waitstaff's testimony," said Steck. "But they all agreed. Remember, I interviewed them individually. Why? Do you have reason to suspect him?"

"Verona eliminated Jimmy from the competition prior to breaking for the day," said Shay. "He didn't take it well. He blew up, making threats and throwing furniture. But we don't have any specific reason to suspect him of the murder—unless there's something you failed to mention to me, Daggers. We did get sidetracked with me discovering evidence of another intrusion."

I pursed my lips. "Nothing specific. I mean, there are various elements of Lumpty's murder that would seem to eliminate certain parties. The angle of the wound would indicate a downward trajectory of the blade into Lumpty's back, making it difficult for someone short like Theo or Orrin to have dealt the blow. Similarly, the blade pierced pretty deep. Someone weak like Wanda might've had difficulty mustering up the strength for that. But short people can jump or dive off stacks of luggage, and even weak people are capable of surprising feats of strength when faced with stressful situations. Rather, I was more concerned with Jimmy's overall behavior during the afternoon poker session."

"You mean his drinking?" said Shay.

"Well that's part of it," I said. "Jimmy's playing behavior changed from the morning to the afternoon. He started to get looser with his bets, and from the hands he played, I'd say he made some mistakes. His drinking would explain that. It could've made him cocky and reckless, but why was he drinking to that extent in the first place? Theo was being a prick when he said it, but he was right. Poker's a thinking man's game. If you drink that much, you're going to lose."

"Unless you're Verona," said Steele.

"Even she slowed down in the afternoon," I said. "And she got lucky with the river in the hand that eliminated Jimmy. But my point is Jimmy seems like a guy who's played a hand or two. And he'd know better than to get that sloppy, or to bet the way he did."

"What are you getting at?" asked Shay.

"He bet five thousand crowns with an off suit jack ten starting hand," I said. "Then he went all in with two pair. It turned out Verona didn't have him beat right off the bat, but he couldn't have known that. All I'm saying is that if I wanted to make my exit, that's how I'd do it, and I'd be sure to throw a fit at the end like he did."

"You think Jimmy threw the hand?" asked Shay. "Why would he do that?"

"I don't know," I said. "But there's supposed to be some sort of fraud going on here. If Jimmy did throw the hand, there must be a logical reason for it."

Steck snapped his fingers. "See? *This*. This is exactly why I brought the two of you on. The Captain said if there was even a whiff of corruption, you two would sniff it out. It's possible someone paid Jimmy to lose, or someone's blackmailing him—and maybe others— toward financial gain. So what else have you noticed?"

"That's not enough?" I asked.

"I...well..." Steck sighed. "Sorry. It's been a long day, and stuff that's actually related to vice excites me. Trust me, I'd rather be playing card games than talking to waiters and waitresses."

"You know what I don't get?" said Shay. "Johann. He's one of our prime suspects, one of his men dies the night before the tournament starts, and yet he's the first one out."

"It doesn't mean he's not involved," I said. "As I said. Assume nothing."

"I suppose so." Shay chewed her lip, and we all contemplated our thoughts for a moment. Then Shay clapped her hands. "Either way, we need to get moving.

The opera is set to begin in a couple hours, which sounds like a lot of time, but considering we haven't eaten and still need to get into our evening wear, I'd say it's pretty tight."

"We need to change *again*?" I asked.

"You remember when I asked about your tuxedo jacket?" said Steele. "There was a reason for that."

"Right," I said. "Steck, I don't suppose you've gotten that list of passengers with luggage in the compartment where Lumpty was murdered, do you?"

Steck slapped his forehead. "Dang it. I knew I was forgetting something. My fault. I'll get it tonight. Anything else you need?"

"Well, actually..." I glanced toward my quarters. "Do you know how to press a tuxedo?"

Steck took his time answering. "I'm going to regret asking that question, aren't I?"

"I think you already do. But seriously, leave it hanging in my closet for when Steele and I get back from dinner. And if you could tidy up a little while you're at it..."

Shay frowned. "Daggers..."

"*Kidding*," I said. "Your toil is appreciated. I'll owe you one."

19

I tapped my fingers on the armrest of my chair. I glanced at the grandfather clock in the corner of the sitting room and contemplated the nature of time. I continued to tap.

"Are you about ready?" I called out.

Steele's voice drifted over from her room, slightly muffled by the closed door. "Almost. Give me another five minutes."

"Five minutes..." I tapped my fingers some more. When Steele mentioned we had a little over two hours until the start of the opera, I'd figured we'd have plenty of time, especially considering the speed with which the waitstaff in the restaurant had served us breakfast and lunch. This time around, the waitresses and cooks hadn't disappointed, but I hadn't accounted for the glacial pace of female preparation.

"You know," I said in a voice loud enough to be heard, "it surprises me the disparity in time it takes for men and women to get dressed, specifically in regards to formal attire. Women clothe themselves in a dress,

shoes, a few pieces of jewelry, and undergarments, unless they're feeling frisky, whereas men end up donning
at least three times as many items. I'm wearing under-
wear, slacks, a shirt, a vest, a coat, socks, shoes, and a
tie, not to mention cuff links and shirt studs. So tell me,
given all that, why does it take women three times as
long as men to prepare? That's a ninefold disparity in
the ratio of clothes put on per unit of time."

Steele's voice drifted over again. "Did you style your
hair?"

"I combed it."

"And did you put on makeup?"

"What do you think?"

"Do you think perhaps you've answered your own
question?"

I drummed my fingers on the armrest and neglected
to further the conversation, mostly because in doing so
I'd make myself look more foolish than I already had.

"We're going to be late, you know," I called out. "And
I'm not warning you for my own benefit. I find the mer-
its of a show sung in a language and tenor that's completely unintelligible to be dubious at best."

"Very well," said Steele. "I'm all done with my
makeup. If you help me zip into my dress we could
probably be out of here in a minute or two."

"Zip into...? How tight is this thing?"

"Quite, in the places where it needs to be," said
Shay. "Now come in here and give me a hand."

I stood and crossed to her door. I rested my hand on
the doorknob, wondering if I should ask whether or not
she was decent, but she *had* told me to come in. No
need to be overly reticent.

I pushed my way in and found Shay standing in front of her mirror, wearing an ankle length strapless black evening gown with a sweetheart neckline and a fair amount of lace in the bodice. She had her back to me, and though the dress came to just under her shoulder blades, the majority of said back was currently exposed. A single clasp held the dress together under her armpit, but the zipper on the side was completely undone, showing off a length of creamy skin that reached from her ribs down to the curve of her derrière.

"Well don't just stand there," said Shay, looking at me through the mirror. "Come help me."

I crossed to her side and took hold of the zipper's pull tab. Shay collected her hair and drew it over her opposite shoulder. She'd curled it slightly and treated it with a different perfume than normal, a jasmine scented one if I wasn't mistaken.

"Be careful not to catch my skin. As I said, the dress fits snugly."

"I'll be careful." I pulled the dress's fabric tightly toward me and worked the tab north, moving it in hitching increments until catching a groove and sliding it all the way home.

"Perfect." Shay turned and smoothed the front of her dress. "So...what do you think?"

Her hair tumbled across the side of her face, cupping her cheek before cascading over her shoulder in a jumble of curls. A touch of rouge brightened her cheeks while a hint of dark liner made her azure eyes pop like pools of the clearest ocean shoal. Her lips had been enhanced with a natural-colored balm that somehow made her seem fresher and more beautiful than she already was. I wanted to dive in and kiss her.

"You're gorgeous," I said.

Natural forces conspired to enhance the effects of the rouge. "Thanks. Now let's go, otherwise we really *will* miss the show. We'll need a little luck as is."

I ushered her to the front, but I paused with the door a few inches shy of closed. "Oh, one thing," I said. "Before we leave, could you pluck one of my hairs? One of the gray ones, if you can find one. I won't miss those."

Shay's eyebrows furrowed, and she opened her mouth. "You know what? I'm not even going to ask. Hold still."

Shay's fingers dug into my scalp. I felt a tug followed by a sharp pluck. I winced but didn't yelp.

"Thanks," I said.

Shay eyed the hair. "And what am I supposed to do with this?"

"Put it in the doorframe as I close up."

"Ah. Got it."

With the rudimentary alarm in place, we set off down the hall and into the stairwell. Our feet clattered off the steps and echoed off the ship's steel walls.

"Daggers, can I ask you something?"

"Shoot," I said.

"Are you self conscious about your gray hairs?"

"Well, that depends," I said. "If you mean am I aware of them, then yes. If you mean do they bother me, then still yes."

"You shouldn't be, you know," said Shay. "They don't impede your charm in the least."

I snorted. "That's nice of you to say, but I suppose it's one of the perks of going prematurely gray. People are taught to be kind to the elderly."

"I'm serious. I don't mind them."

I opened my mouth, ready to launch into a joking, thinly-veiled tirade of self-loathing wherein I tore myself down, assuring anyone nearby I was unattractive and thoroughly unlovable, but I stopped myself in the formative stages. For one thing, I didn't really believe that anymore. I'd seen the effects of my diet and exercise regimen, and those physical changes had helped spark a psychological renaissance. I wasn't anywhere near as repellant as I'd once convinced myself I was, and if Shay liked the way I looked...well, who was I to dissuade her?

I nodded and smiled.

Apparently, we weren't the only ones running late. A crowd swelled against the face of the ship's theater, crashing into the overwhelmed ushers out front in waves. We joined the sea, shuffling back and forth and back and forth before eventually working our way to the front of the mass. There, I flashed one of the ushers our room key, and he herded us in through a set of thick, velvet drapes.

If not for the slightly lower than normal ceilings, the theater would've been indistinguishable from one on land. Over a dozen rows with thirty seats apiece stretched back from a full-sized stage, one currently closed off by heavy red curtains. A single layer balcony provided additional seating at the sides, though exactly how much I couldn't tell. The lights had already been dimmed, and my eyes were in the process of adjusting.

The usher showed us to our row. We excused ourselves to the other patrons as we shuffled past them into our seats—not particularly close to the stage, but at least centrally located in the row.

"Apparently, money can't buy quite everything," I said as we seated ourselves.

"What are you complaining about?" asked Shay. "As if any seat in this house is a bad one."

I would've replied, but our tardiness didn't provide me with an opportunity. The orchestra sprang to life, the crowd's communal voice dwindled to a murmur, and the red curtains drew apart.

20

The lights from behind the curtain cut through the dark, revealing a backdrop of pristine blue, dark for the water below and bright for the sky above. Wide-leafed palms thick with coconuts hung over the sides of the stage, and in the back, up high, white clouds shifted back and forth. The orchestra quieted, but the void of the music was filled with heavy thumping.

A man raced forth from stage right, dressed in a billowing white shirt, torn brown trousers, and with a bandana wrapped around his head. He looked about wildly before exiting stage left. Moments later, a band of pirates followed him from the right, racing across the stage without pause, bellowing all the while. The first man reappeared after their exit and hid behind one of the palms, only to have the pirates reappear and race back across the stage in the opposite direction. He paused after they'd left, looking to his left and right before eventually leaving the safety of the tree and moving to the center of the stage. He placed his hands on his hips and shook his head. The music started back up, and the man erupted in song.

I couldn't understand a word of it.

Maybe ten percent, if I was being honest. As it turned out, *The Pirates of St. Gustifere* wasn't performed in a foreign tongue, but that didn't make it any more intelligible. I caught snippets here and there, something about the man's past as a carpenter turned sailor and the appearance of a press gang. I had to admit his booming voice and rich baritone made for a final product that was pleasing to the ears if hard on the gray matter.

The gang of pirates returned, as did a woman who I gathered was the love interest. The pirates threatened the man. The woman pleaded for his life, and they all joined together in song. The orchestra intensified, further muddling the already jumbled vocals, and I began to lose interest.

As I did so, my eyes wandered. They'd finally adjusted to the light, letting me see into the furthest reaches of the balcony, which wasn't that far away, all things considered. Each balcony contained a modest three rows, four seats wide apiece. The accommodations seemed a little finer than those in the central portions of the theater, and I wondered just where our tax dollars had gone if not to provide Shay and me with the finest luxuries possible.

As I scanned my eyes across the balcony, I spotted a pair of familiar faces in the back of the one furthest from the stage. Jimmy and Ghorza, with their elbows in a heated war over the shared armrest between them. How they'd come to be seated next to one another in such a spacious theater I had no idea, but despite the cramped quarters, they didn't appear particularly displeased. In fact, it seemed as if they were talking. Was Vlad back there, too? I couldn't spot him, even accounting for my dark-adjusted eyes.

I glanced at Steele who had her eyes trained on the stage. The corners of her lips turned upward, and her eyes sparkled in the dim light.

I dipped my head low next to hers and spoke in a hushed tone. "Jimmy and Ghorza. Balcony, left side. Sitting together."

"Hmm?" She glanced in their direction before immersing herself back in the action. "Oh, yes. Good find."

Good find? Did she even care? Why *were* we at the opera, anyway? With the mixer, our presence had purpose: to meet our fellow poker competitors and learn their strengths and weaknesses, or at least a little of their backgrounds. But with the opera? Shay had mentioned nothing of the sort. She'd simply insisted we attend. And how would we perform reconnaissance, anyway, with us restricted to our seats and limited by social norms? All of which meant she'd seen the event as nothing more than an opportunity for us to spend a nice evening together.

Why wouldn't she, though? I enjoyed the luxuries offered to us by the cruise: the food, the drink, the time with Shay. It was only fair she do the same.

I let her bask in the show while I scanned my eyes over the rest of the crowd. After a bit of effort, I located Orrin, a few rows in front of us near the aisle. I didn't envision the gruff dwarf as a fan of opera, but his intense focus on the stage said otherwise. I did, however, expect to find Verona and perhaps even Johann at the show, but try as I might I couldn't spot them among the crowd. Neither could I spot Wanda, but that didn't surprise me. She'd already proven herself a recluse. Theo was another matter. He seemed just the sort to enjoy a boisterous show, but just because I couldn't see him didn't mean he wasn't there. With his stature, I'd be surprised if I *had* laid eyes on him. I wondered if perhaps they reserved the front row for gnomes and other breeds of similar stature. Within our capitalist society, probably not.

I glanced back at Ghorza and found the situation in the gallery had deteriorated. She and Jimmy no longer amiably shared space, instead appearing to be involved in a heated if hushed argument. Jimmy jabbed an angry finger in Ghorza's direction, and his mouth moved quickly. The opera attendees in front of them looked back at them with stern eyes and pursed lips.

I nudged Shay and nodded in their direction. "Check it out. Squabble at eight o'clock."

Shay looked again. As she did so, Jimmy stood and stormed off through the back of the balcony. Ghorza threw up her hands before crossing them over her stomach, shaking her head all the while.

"Think I should go over there?" I whispered.

"To do what?" asked Steele.

"Spy on them. Talk to Ghorza. Follow Jimmy. I don't know."

"Don't you think they'd find all that a mite suspicious?" whispered Steele. "Remember, we're here to enjoy a few days of luxury on the high seas. You can't poke your head into other people's matters willy-nilly.

And unless you can fly, you'd have a hard time tailing Jimmy."

Shay had a point. By the time I shuffled past the other guests in our row and hiked up to the back of the balcony, Jimmy would be long gone.

I shook my head nonetheless. "I don't like it. What are Jimmy and Ghorza talking about? Jimmy's already out of the tournament. Do you think he and Ghorza have a deal? That he threw his hand for her?"

Despite our hushed tones, our neighbors had started to give us less than pleasant glares as well.

"Perhaps these are things you could investigate *after* the opera," said Shay, "when we all retire to the bar."

"There's a post-play mixer?"

Shay nodded.

Now I understood. Even if Shay had intended our operatic outing as a pleasurable one, she'd hadn't meant it purely as such.

"Why don't you focus on the performance?" said Shay. "Try to enjoy yourself for once."

I sighed, pushing down my suspicions as I turned to face the stage. Given the nature of the beast, enjoying myself might be a stretch, but for Shay, I'd certainly try.

21

Shay and I filed out of the theater, following the other patrons as we snaked our way into the adjoining hallway.

"Oh, that was lovely, don't you think?" said Shay, her hand resting over my proffered arm. "Despite the publicity associated with the *Prodigious's* maiden voyage, I didn't think they'd get top shelf talent for their onboard entertainment, but I'm glad to have been wrong. Stanislaw Thatcher was superb as Captain John James Ringleford the third, and Betty...what was her last name? Well, she was a revelation as Elizabeth Beets. So strong and feisty and clever. I loved her."

"I wonder why," I said.

"Oh, come off it," she said. "I'm nothing like Elizabeth."

"I seem to recall you asking for a thesaurus earlier," I said. "Maybe I'll include a dictionary when I gift it to you, because your definition of 'nothing' isn't the commonly agreed upon variant."

"Well, perhaps in attitude we're similar," said Shay. "But in terms of dress and mannerisms and our situation in life, we're polar opposites. Besides, I'm far more elegant than she. And I don't care for sand between my toes."

"I can't comment on that last part, but I do agree with you on the elegance."

"Good. Because if you didn't, there'd be something wrong with you." Shay nodded toward the stairwell. "Should we head to the lounge?"

"If we can make it there."

We waded through the sea of humanity and up the steps to the promenade deck, then back over to the bar where we'd wet our lips with champagne the night prior. Crowds hadn't yet packed the space, but I had no doubt they'd be close behind, as I hoped would our poker compatriots. As it stood, only a single member of the crew had arrived, but at least it was the right one: Jimmy, who sat in a corner with nothing but a drink to keep him company.

Shay noticed him, too. "If you want to talk to him, go ahead, but I'd take a cautious approach. Don't pepper him with questions, otherwise he's liable to clam up. Or leave. Or punch you."

"You don't plan on joining me?" I asked.

She shook her head. "In the little time I've spent with him, he hasn't warmed to me. Not that he has to you, either, but at least your personality type matches his better than mine. Besides, if the two of us go over there, he might feel overwhelmed."

"Fair enough," I said. "So what's your plan?"

"Head to the bar. Get a drink. See if anyone else comes in and play it by ear."

"Don't overexert yourself."

"I'll try." Shay leaned in and gave me a peck on the cheek. "I'll send a waiter over with a drink."

"Make it two," I said. "Keeping Jimmy well lubricated is part of my plan."

Shay headed to the bar, and I worked my way toward the corner, where Jimmy sat hunched over in a booth, resting his forehead on intertwined hands. He didn't look up as I approached.

"So, I take it you're not a fan of the opera," I said. "Or pirates. Or both."

"What do you want?" Jimmy's voice rumbled forth, sloppy and slurred. How much of the tipsy had he already imbibed, I wondered?

I helped myself to a seat. "Between your bad luck on the draw of the cards and that spat with Ghorza in the theater, I figured you might need a friendly shoulder to lean on. But try not to lean too hard. As stout as I am, I'm not sure I could support you if your angle gets too acute."

"If my *what* gets too cute?"

"Never mind," I said. "That was a geometry joke and not a very good one. My point is, how are you holding up?"

Jimmy lifted his head. His eyes were bloodshot. Had he been crying, or was it just a side effect of all the booze he'd slammed down his gullet?

"Why do you care?" he asked. "I'm out of the tournament. I'm not a threat to you anymore. Isn't that enough?"

"That's precisely why I *do* care," I said. "Look, I'm here to make money, not enemies. Ask Theo, or Orrin. I told them the same thing. And now that you're out, I can risk extending a helping hand without fear of you ripping it off. So tell me. What's the problem? Is it girl trouble?"

"Girl trouble? What are you talking about?"

"You know. The spat. With Ghorza."

Jimmy blinked and shook his head, through the action seemed to pain him. *"You think I like Ghorza?"*

"Hey, I don't know," I said. "Some guys are into that sort of thing...I suppose."

Jimmy snorted and retreated back into his hands. "It's not a...*relationship* problem."

He didn't elaborate, so I tried to figure out a way to further the conversation without seeming like I was prying.

"Mr. Waters?"

I looked up. A waiter had arrived, carrying a tray of drinks. "From your wife at the bar."

"Thanks." I accepted the drinks. I kept the apricot whiskey sour for myself and extended the other to Jimmy. "Whiskey and soda?"

Jimmy looked up again. "You remember what I drink?"

"We're all poker players. Keeping track of minor details is kind of our trademark, isn't it?" I lifted my beverage. "Cheers."

I paused for a moment to see if Jimmy would meet my glass with his, but when it became apparent he wouldn't, I went ahead and took a sip. Despite choosing not to partake in the toast, the big man did bring the glass to his lips. He hummed in approval and set the glass back down.

"Hmm. Good whiskey."

"Some of the best," I said. "Do you take yours malted?"

Jimmy nodded.

"Good man."

We sat there for a moment letting the liquor seep into our veins, or out through our pores in Jimmy's case. As the silence stretched, I took another stab at the conversation.

"I hope I'm not being presumptuous," I said, "but I never pegged you as a loose player. Clearly your bluff worked on me."

Jimmy blinked. "My bluff?"

The alcohol must've been dulling his mental faculties as it had during the poker game. "You know. The off suit jack ten. I mean, it's not a terrible starting hand, but betting five thousand crowns on it is a bluff in my book. And it would've worked if not for Verona."

"It would've worked if not for that *damn nine* that came up on the river. But...argh, I don't know." Jimmy sighed and wiped a meaty hand across his face. "I keep playing that hand over and over again in my head. Jack ten. Two pair. Maybe I shouldn't have gone all in. What the hell do I know? I just...made some mistakes. Not only on that game, but leading up to it. Played some hands I shouldn't have. Not my fault though. I wasn't feeling like myself. It's like I couldn't... Couldn't..."

"Think straight?" I offered.

Jimmy lifted his glass. "Yeah."

"Maybe it was the all the whiskey and sodas."

Jimmy drained his beverage and slammed the empty tumbler back down. "It wasn't the drink."

"All I'm saying is when I have a few too many—"

"It wasn't the drink." He glared at me and blinked a few times. It might've been my imagination, but in doing so, some of the redness in his eyes faded. "What the hell are you doing here anyway? Get lost."

"Just sharing a drink with—"

"Get...lost."

I knew when a retreat was in order. I grabbed my glass, gave Jimmy a truncated wave, and headed back to the bar. There I found Steele, seated at a stool with a cosmopolitan in hand and with her legs crossed such that the slit in her dress displayed the creamy skin of her calf.

She wasn't alone. A pair of young men, one human and one elf, both handsome and well-dressed, fawned over her, standing tall, laughing when she laughed, and flashing their pearly whites.

"Well, this looks like a fun conversation," I said. "Mind if I join?"

"Ah, Thomas," said Shay. "Meet Bertrand and Fanduil. A pair of fellow opera enthusiasts."

"Enthusiasts is too light a word, I think," said Fanduil, unless he was Bertrand, in which case the other young man's decidedly human parents had played a cruel joke upon him at birth. *"The Pirates of St. Gustifere* has always been one of my favorites, and who would've expected such a marvelous performance of it aboard a ship, of all things—although it's rather appropriate considering the subject matter. Let's hope we all avoid contact with any Ringlefords, however."

"What about you, Mr. Waters?" said Bertrand. "What's your favorite Smotrycz and Gullivan?"

"I'm more of a Frank and Gregg man myself," I said. "Though I can honestly say it was the most spirited performance of *Pirates* I've ever experienced."

The looks of confusion on the pair's faces told me my mystery writer joke had gone over their heads, but both were too polite to put a voice to their questions.

"I hate to cut our conversation short," said Shay, "but do you mind if I have a moment alone with Jake?"

"Of course," said Bertrand. "Mr. and Mrs. Waters. A pleasure."

He nodded his head, as did Fanduil, and the pair moved off. They laughed and joked and Fanduil clapped Bertrand on the shoulder in a brotherly manner.

"You know, as I first walked up, I was sure they were here to gain favor with you," I said. "But now I'm not so sure they'd be interested."

"Either way, you dealt with it well," said Shay, taking a sip of her bright red drink.

"Why wouldn't I?"

"You've had jealousy issues in the past."

"And I plan to keep them there," I said. "Besides, neither Bertrand nor Fanduil has quite the same *seasoning* I do. I'm the far tastier treat."

"Are you saying you're old?"

"Salt and pepper are the most fundamental of the spices. I hear you're into both."

Shay smiled. "Find anything useful?"

I took a deep breath and let it out slowly. "Not especially. But there's definitely something going on between Jimmy and Ghorza. I'd bet money on it. Speaking of which, you didn't seek her out?"

"She hasn't come in yet," said Shay. "Orrin arrived, but he's such a drag. You can't blame me for choosing to spend time with a pair of charismatic young opera lovers over a bitter, ill-mannered dwarf."

"Who also happens to be an opera lover," I said. "Seriously, I saw him. He was fully absorbed by the performance."

"Excuse me? Mr. and Mrs. Waters?"

I turned at the familiar voice and found our intrepid baggage compartment worker and fellow confidant standing behind me. "James? What brings you here?"

The crewman bobbed his head. "I bring news, from, ah...Mr. Steck. If you could come with me?"

James had resorted to twisting his hands and shuffling his feet again. I didn't take that as a good sign.

"Very well," I said. "Lead the way."

22

"Could you at least tell us where we're going?" We exited the stairwell onto the bottom level of the *Prodigious* and headed up the hallway.

"I'm sorry, Mr., um...Waters," said James. "We'll be there in a moment."

James had been less than talkative as he led us into the ship's underbelly. I'd wracked my brain trying to think of what piece of news would be important enough for Steck to have called us to him—the list of people with luggage in the hold, perhaps—but if the implications from said news were so dire, why not come to us himself? And why bring us to...well, *wherever* it was we were headed? It certainly wasn't back to the hold.

We reached another bulkhead door, this time with a burly crewman standing guard at the front. James gave him a nod, and he nodded back.

James gestured to the door. "After you, sir. Madam."

"And this is...?" I asked.

"The pool, sir," said James.

The *pool*? Did Steck have a late night dip planned? I cranked on the handle and let myself in.

Dim light glimmered off the water within, water that shifted back and forth gently in tune to the rhythm of the ship's swaying—swaying I couldn't even feel, but my mass was a tiny fraction of that which filled the twenty-five by sixty foot pool. Warm moisture wicked through my jacket and into my shirt's armpits, and the smell of pool chemicals drifted through the air into my nostrils. Bubbles burbled to the surface at either end of the pool, warming the body of water with waste heat from the ship's engines. In the center, ripples trailed out from the end of a long pole. Boatswain Olaugh held the other end from the edge of the pool deck.

He was fishing out a body.

Steck stood next to him. He noticed Shay and me walk in and gave us a halfhearted wave.

I paused to rub my forehead. "Not this again."

"Just when you think you're going to have a nice, quiet night, am I right?" said Steele.

"Hey, at least the killer waited until after the opera ended," I said.

"Did they?"

"Good point. Let's find out."

I approached Steck and, correspondingly, the body, which Olaugh had nearly pushed to the lip of the pool. It was that of a woman. She was missing her fur shawl, but her jewelry, flaxen hair, and slightly too short dress instantly gave her away.

"Son of a bitch," I said. "It's Verona."

Steck nodded.

"What happened?" asked Steele.

"How should I know?" he said. "Why do you think I called the two of you here?"

"Don't give me that again," said Steele. "You know what I mean."

Steck sighed. "Fine. A couple, those two over there—" He pointed them out, a young man and woman, seated on a bench in a corner. The woman had a towel over her shoulders, and the man rested his arm over it, comforting her. "—came down here for a dip, not fifteen minutes ago. That's when they found Verona. They screamed, and Wilton came running. He's the guy guarding the door. He sent for Olaugh, Olaugh sent for me and for James. I sent him for you, and here we are."

"No one else was down here when the lovebirds arrived?"

"I don't think so," said Steck. "Go ask them to make sure."

"We will," I said. "But first let's get Verona out of the water."

I stripped off my jacket, took off my cufflinks, and rolled up my shirtsleeves. Olaugh pushed Verona against the pool deck and set down the pole. We both knelt.

"Ready?" I said.

He nodded.

We each grabbed an arm and pulled the body out, dragging her to a bed of towels someone had laid out prior to our arrival. There we set her on her back. I placed her arms down at her sides.

"She's still warm," I said to Steele.

"No kidding," she said. "It's a heated pool."

"Derp. Sorry. Still, she had to have died recently. What do you think? Within the hour?"

"I'm no Cairny, Daggers," said Steele. "But based on her complexion...maybe? I can't imagine she could go for longer than that without being found."

I turned to Olaugh. "Same question as last night. How often is this place frequented?"

"More often than the luggage compartment, that's for sure," said the burly boatswain. "But I'm afraid I can't give you a much better answer than that. This is only the second day of our maiden voyage. I don't yet have a good idea of where the guests congregate at what hours. But at this time of night, with the opera and everything else going on in the upper decks? I can't imagine many people would come down here. Just would be lovers like the pair in the corner."

"We'll have to talk to that guy in the front," I said. "Winston, or whatever his name is. See what he knows. In the meantime, we should check Verona for signs of struggle. See if we can figure out what killed her."

"You don't think she drowned?" said Steck.

"If so, I think someone probably helped her along that path."

I knelt down next to Verona's body and swiped a lock of wet hair out of her face. With her makeup largely washed off and without the cloud of cigarette smoke, perfume, and better-than-thouness surrounding her, she seemed markedly older—the wrinkles around her mouth and at the corners of her eyes more pronounced and her hair more like wet straw than spun gold. Heavy earrings pulled her lobes down, and the massive, jewel laden necklace around her neck hung askew, giving her an air of sloppiness she'd never had in life. But as for the rest of her...

"Can someone get me a lantern?" I said. "I can't see if her skin is bruised in this light."

"On it," said Olaugh.

He stepped away, and Steele knelt down on Verona's opposite side.

"Daggers. Check this out."

Shay pointed to a brooch pinned to the top of Verona's dress over her left breast. It was a rather simple thing: a single emerald surrounded by smaller ones, set in a forest of silver filigrees.

I chewed on my lips. "Was she wearing that at the poker game?"

Shay shook her head. "She never changed out of her dress, but that's new." She extended a hand, unpinned it, and turned it over in her hand. "Looks old."

"Check it for prints," I said.

Shay lifted her eyebrows.

"Come on. It's a joke."

Olaugh returned with the light, and I gave Verona a once over. The pool was too dark to tell if she'd bled into it, but my perusal of her extremities didn't reveal any incisions or puncture marks. She didn't seem to sport any bruises, either.

"I don't mean to rush you," said Olaugh. "But if we're trying to keep this under wraps, and I assume we are, then we need to move this investigation somewhere more private. Wilton is guarding the door, but the longer he stays posted there, the greater the opportunity for suspicion to grow."

Rushing went against my police training, especially when it meant abandoning a murder scene, but I had to remember I wasn't dressed in my ratty leather jacket with Daisy in my pocket and a team of detectives and crime scene investigators at my back. Shay and I were operating undercover, without a CSU team to canvass the scene. The pros of further digging had to be weighed against the cons.

"Olaugh's right," I said as I stood. "We need to move out of here. Steck, get a cart to help us transport Verona's body somewhere secluded. Olaugh, I need you to figure out where we're going, what to do with the witnesses, and I'll need you and James both to check the surrounding area. Look for dropped personal items, clothing, scuff marks even. It's a pool deck, but we might get lucky. Shay and I will talk to the witnesses. We need to be ready to move when we're done."

The team sprang into action, and Shay and I headed to the far corner to speak to the young couple. They looked up as we approached, fear in their eyes.

"Excuse me," I said. "We understand you're the pair who found the victim in the pool?"

"That's right," said the young man. "And you are?"

"I'm Shay Steele, and this is Jake Daggers," said Shay. "We're with the NWPD's homicide division."

"You're...cops?" said the man. "How did you get here so fast? And why are you dressed like that?"

"We're here on an undercover mission," said Shay. "First and foremost, the two of you need to understand you're not in any danger. The case we're investigating involves a small, select group of individuals, none of which have any reason to harm anyone but each other.

But I do need to stress that Detective Daggers and I, as well as Detective Steck who was poolside, need to remain undercover. Boatswain Olaugh will make sure you're protected and compensated. Is that understood?"

"Of course," said the young man. "Just...do whatever you need to do. We'll help however we can."

"Tell us what you found," I said.

The young man gave us his spiel, pretty much word for word what Steck had already related. He tried to involve his female companion in the tale, but every time he prompted her, she muttered something barely audible and shook her head.

"So when exactly did you arrive at the pool?" I asked.

"I'm not sure. Maybe twenty minutes ago," he said.

"And no one else was here?"

He shook his head.

"What about on the way here? Did you notice anyone suspicious? Anyone leaving? Anyone in pool attire?"

"I'm sorry. No one. But I wasn't particularly paying attention."

Of course he wasn't. I glanced at the young woman. I knew what he'd had on his mind. Unfortunately for him, his intents were now a lost cause.

"It's alright. We appreciate your help." I looked to Steele. "Should we talk to the goon at the door?"

"Might as well, though you might not want to call Wilton a goon to his face."

"Wilton. See, I wanted to say Wilfred. I knew it started with a 'w,' though."

We crossed to the front and exited to the corridor. Wilton and his muscles were still there, but so was

Steck, approaching with a luggage trolley. Talking would have to wait.

23

Steck wasn't a dope. He'd gathered the trolley from the nearby laundry room, but instead of emptying it before carting it our way, he'd left it full of the soiled bundles of sheets with which he'd found it. Those proved useful in two ways. First, they gave us something to wrap Verona's body in, and second, they gave us something to hide Verona's body *under*. As someone who'd moved corpses before, I could attest to the fact that a body with a sheet draped over it fooled absolutely no one.

Because of the size of the cart, we had to fold Verona a little to make her fit. Her body hadn't yet cooled, which made the process easier, if no less creepy. Then it was a simple matter of filling in the spaces with bundles of sheets and off we went.

Wilton took the cart while Steck went to rouse the ship's medic. Given the lack of obvious external evidence for Verona's death, Steele insisted we perform an autopsy as it might give us more clues toward the identity of her killer or even her time of death. Lacking

Cairny, the ship's medic seemed like the next best option. Of course, it meant adding one more soul to our ever growing list of those aware of our undercover mission, but at this point, it couldn't be avoided.

Wilton wheeled the cart into an oversized dumbwaiter, secured the pulleys, and began to haul on the rope. Steele and I headed up the stairs to the floor above and extracted the cart once it arrived. From there, we pushed it toward the hold. Apparently, Olaugh had stored Lumpty's corpse in one of the empty sections, and it was as good a location as any for me and Shay to poke and prod Verona's leftovers.

As we wheeled the cart past the stairwell, I heard footsteps, followed by a familiar voice.

"Mr. and Mrs. Waters. Well, this is a surprise."

Johann descended the steps, dressed in another of his sharp, tailored three piece suits but without his usual entourage. He seemed taller than before, and his feet danced over the steps with a greater dexterity than I remembered. Perhaps he'd been drinking, although that usually had the opposite effect. It was still a more logical explanation than him discovering the fountain of youth somewhere in the *Prodigious's* steel depths.

"Mr. Preiss," I said. "This *is* a surprise. What brings you down here?"

"Just meeting an old friend. Someone I didn't realize was aboard this ship before we departed but who I'm nonetheless glad to have found." He glanced at the cart full of soiled sheets. "And you?"

"Well, there was an...*incident.*"

"Incident?" Johann adopted a more serious look. "What sort of incident?"

A red blotch on the top set of sheets inspired me. "A...wine incident. Samantha enjoys her merlots, you see. She was drinking in our quarters—which isn't particularly ladylike, and trust me, I've told her not too, but she did it anyway. Needed to relax after the stresses of the day, she said. Well, you know how the drink affects one's motor skills, and wouldn't you know it, I hear a crash and she's tumbled into her bed, spilling wine all over the sheets. So here we are."

Johann nodded slowly, taking it all in. "I...see. But why are you here *with* the sheets? Why not have the ship's cleaning services replace them for you?"

Shay's cheeks had reddened, indicating she didn't particularly approve of my fib. It looked as if she were blushing from embarrassment, however, so it still worked to our advantage.

"I'm quite particular about my sheets, Mr. Preiss," she said. "I wouldn't deign to sleep in the ones provided to us by the ship, and so I packed my own. Hand-picked Argolian cotton, with a thread count of eight hundred. It's like sleeping on a cloud. So you can imagine I wouldn't trust the ship's cleaning crew to launder them properly, or not to misplace them. My night's sleep is on the line."

"Yes, of course. Quite a thorny situation, that. I'll, ah...leave you to it then. Best of luck." Johann nodded and headed back into the stairwell, eager to be free of us and our crazy linen preferences.

As his footsteps receded, Steele turned to me. "A *wine incident?*"

"It got him to leave, didn't it?" I said. "The more important question is, what's he doing down here?"

"You don't buy his answer of meeting with an old friend?"

"Down here are third class and ship's crews quarters," I said. "If so, Johann has friends in low places. I'd be much more likely to believe he was on his way to either the ship's luggage compartment or the pool, if you catch my drift. But his men aren't with him, and he's not dressed for a swim."

"We can sort out his motives later," said Steele. "Right now we need to move before anyone else magically arrives."

I nodded, and together, we pushed the cart down the hall, into the hold, and to the secluded room Olaugh had pointed us toward. I unlocked it with the key he'd provided me and entered.

The interior was empty except for Lumpty's body, lying face up on a plain white sheet. I spread out one of the sheets from the cart next to his body and started discarding soiled blankets into the corner. When I reached Verona's body, I unwrapped the sheet from over her and waved to Steele.

"You want to give me a hand with this? I'll get her under the arms and you can grab her feet."

Shay sighed. "Just a moment. I'm not dressed for moving corpses."

"And I am?"

"You can move and bend and lift easily. It's close enough."

Shay toed off her heels, leaving them kicked in a corner, and hitched up her dress before joining me at the cart. I slid my arms under Verona's armpits. "Ready?"

Shay grabbed her ankles. "Ready."

We lifted on three, shuffling her over before dumping her on the sheet next to Lumpty.

"Well, that wasn't so bad," I said, dusting my hands on my pants. "Apparently you don't pack on many pounds when all you consume is booze."

Shay nodded toward the corpse. "Did you see that?"

"See what?"

"When you put her down. Verona's head sort of...*flopped* to the side."

"She's dead now," I said. "That's what bodies do. They flop."

"Don't be a lummox. Let me take a closer look."

Shay waved me back and knelt down above Verona's still damp hair. She placed her hands on either side of the elf woman's head. She turned it to the side, held it there for a moment and turned it the other way. On the back twist, the neck responded with a crunchy rasp.

"Hear that?" said Shay.

"How could I not," I said. "That sound is going to haunt my dreams tonight."

"I think her neck's broken."

"I think you're right. The question is, how did it happen? Was it deliberate? Or an accident, as she fell into the pool, perhaps?"

"You don't honestly think it could've been an accident, do you?"

"I don't think she was hanging out poolside by herself before slipping and falling in a puddle, no," I said. "But she could've been pushed by someone who didn't intend to kill her."

A knock at the door drew both of our attentions. I instinctively reached for Daisy, but she was nowhere to be found. Not that I'd need her. An intruder who meant us harm wouldn't have knocked.

"Who is it?" I said.

"Zander Lowhall," came a muffled voice. "Ship's medic."

I opened the door, and in walked a dwarf dressed in a crisp navy and white uniform with his beard tightly woven in two long braids. A red medic's bag hung from a single strap over his shoulder.

He took one look at the bodies and grimaced. "Good gods. I didn't want to believe it, but there you go. Two people. Dead."

I shut the door behind him. "I'm Detective Daggers, and that's Detective Steele. We're with the NWPD, homicide. Don't mind the get-ups. It's a long story. Have you been brought up to speed?"

Zander nodded. "More or less. That Steck fellow described the situation to me, but...well, it's worse when you actually see them, isn't it?"

Shay eyed the man's medic bag. "I see you've brought equipment. That's good. Before you arrived, we'd come to the conclusion this woman, Verona Quivven, had her neck broken. As I'm sure you've been informed, she was found afloat in the pool downstairs. So the question is, how did she break her neck? From a fall? Or did someone inflict the damage to her directly? And was she still alive when she fell in the pool, or was she long dead?"

Zander stepped to Verona's side. "Um...alright. And how would you suggest I determine those things, exactly?"

"Well," said Shay, "if Verona fell and broke her neck on impact, I'd expect to see a single impact fracture in one or more of her neck vertebrae, as well as a fracture of some sort on her skull. If someone grabbed her and forcibly broke her neck, I'd expect more of a spiral fracture in the vertebrae. And as for determining whether she was alive or dead when she hit the pool, that's simple. We need to check if there's water in her lungs."

Zander held up his hands. "Whoa, hold up. Are you suggesting I *cut this woman's body open?*"

"What's the big deal?" said Shay. "I know you're not a coroner, but you have to dissect cadavers in medical school, don't you?"

Zander cleared his throat. "Ah. Yes. About that..."

"*You're not a doctor?*" I said.

"I never claimed to be," said Zander. "I'm the ship's medic. Technically, I'm a registered nurse."

I ran a hand through my hair. "Oh, wonderful."

"Please tell me you at least have a scalpel and some tweezers on hand," said Shay.

"Well, of course I do," said Zander, hefting his bag. "I have a whole host of medial supplies and equipment."

"You just don't know how to use any of it," I said.

Zander glared at me. "Hey, now. That's uncalled for. Slicing up bodies wasn't part of the job requirement."

"He's right, Daggers. No need to get snippy. Now Zander, the scalpel and tweezers, if you please. Daggers, give me a hand."

Now it was my turn for surprise. "Are you suggesting *we* perform the autopsy?"

"When I hang out with Cairny, we don't just giggle and talk about shoes," said Shay. "I've learned a lot from her, and while I may not possess her level of expertise, I know what I'm looking for. We can do this. It's not like we have any better options."

I glanced at Verona. Lumpty's death was one thing, but her? The memory of her sitting at the table, laughing idly, teasing people and blowing smoke in their faces was fresh in my mind. Now I found myself in the position of having to drive a sharpened steel blade into her not yet cool flesh.

As for Shay? I shook my head. "You know, it feels like yesterday that you wandered into the Captain's office and he sent us to investigate that dark elf with the hole burned through his chest. I razzed you mercilessly, calling you green and trying to make you queasy. Now look at you."

"It doesn't feel like yesterday to me," said Shay. "It feels more like a lifetime ago. I've grown a lot since then. And I dare say you have, too."

Wasn't that the truth. So many things had changed, and so many of them for the better. But those changes still didn't make me excited for what we had to do.

I sighed and held out a hand. "Zander? Scalpel me. Shay and I have work to do."

24

With Shay at my side, I trudged back toward our stateroom, exhausted, emotionally spent, and even a little hungry despite the grisly nature of the work we'd completed. While I'd anticipated how challenging the dissection of Verona's body would be on a psychological level, I hadn't guessed how *physically* taxing it would be. My fingers and forearms ached, and I couldn't wait to get them some rest—but not before washing them. I had enough dried blood, skin, and bits of assorted gore under my fingernails to create my very own Verona voodoo doll.

I stopped in front of our door and dug in my pocket for the keys.

Shay put a hand on my arm. "Wait." She nodded at the frame.

"Huh?"

It took me second to figure out what had drawn her eye, but then it dawned on me. My hair was gone.

I growled under my breath. "Will this day never end? Alright, stay behind me. Keep your eyes peeled. No guarantee they'll be gone or won't have left any nasty surprises for us just because that was the case the last two times."

I turned the key in the lock and pushed on through.

I was right. The intruder *hadn't* left. They'd chosen to hang out in our living room in plain sight. And take a nap, apparently.

Luckily for Shay and me, the intruder was Steck. He startled awake as I slammed shut the door.

"Good gods, Steck," I said. "You would've given me a heart attack if I hadn't already known you were in here."

He stood quickly and shook his head. He blinked several times. "Oh, I, uh...sorry. I must've fallen asleep. It's been a long day, and—wait, you knew I was here? Who told you?"

"No one," said Shay. "We have our ways. But what are you doing here? How did you get in?"

"Ah, well..." Steck reached into his pocket and produced a thin, notched piece of metal. "Skeleton key. Olaugh lent it to me. You see, after I roused the ship's medic, I met back up with the Boatswain and James in the former's quarters. I had some matters I wanted to discuss, and I also needed to pick up that list of guests with items in the luggage hold which Olaugh had promised me was ready. With that in hand, I thought I'd deliver it to you, but to be perfectly honest, I didn't want to come by and watch you perform an autopsy. I, uh...get queasy."

I lifted an eyebrow. "Really?"

"Hey, I'm a vice cop for a reason," he said. "I figured I'd wait for you here, but waiting outside your quarters in the hall would look suspicious if anyone were watching. So Olaugh lent me the skeleton key. I guess I fell asleep. That couch is more comfortable than it looks, and that's saying something."

"So...the list?" I said.

"Oh. Right." Steck patted himself down before eventually finding what he was after in his interior vest pocket. He produced a sheaf of papers and held them forth.

I stilled him with a hand. "Just give us the highlights."

"Oh. Sure. Well, let's see. Four of your competitors actually have bags in the hold. Theo, Johann, Ghorza, and Jimmy."

"And what does each of them have down there?" I asked.

"I don't know. Bags," said Steck. "I mean, I can tell you their approximate sizes and colors, but I have no idea what's in them. We can't crack them open without probable cause, and as far as we can tell, none of the bags owned by the stated parties were forced open by Johann's man."

"So Johann has a bag in the hold?" said Shay. "That means Lumpty might've been down there accessing Johann's own possessions. I wonder if his death stemmed from a robbery. That might explain why none of the bags were forced."

"I suppose, but that's pure speculation." I rubbed my chin and started to pace around the living room. "Okay, look. I know it's late. We're all tired, and we need sleep. But we're also all here, and we've had two murders in the past two nights. Clearly something major is afoot, so let's go over what we know. Shay and I just completed a rudimentary autopsy on Verona. Her lungs had a bit of water in them, and we found a rotational fracture in two of her vertebrae, meaning someone broke her neck and tossed her in the pool as she was sucking her last gasps. Verona's skinny, but she's no pixie. Someone strong must've killed her. Jimmy, Ghorza, Orrin, or one of Johann's thugs, maybe. Possibly Johann himself, depending on how much muscle still lingers under those suits of his."

"But given the timing of her death, we have to eliminate Ghorza and Orrin," said Shay. "We saw both of them at the opera, and they stayed throughout."

"Which leaves Jimmy and Johann," I said. "But neither of those feels quite right to me. When we bumped into Johann, he seemed downright chipper. And I talked with Jimmy at the bar following the end of the opera. While he was surly and drunken, he was more concerned about the results of the day's card game than anything else."

"A card game he lost to Verona," said Shay.

"True," I said. "But what's his motive for murder? He can't steal Verona's poker earnings. The house still holds those. So what then? Revenge? For losing a hand he admitted he probably shouldn't have gone all in on in the first place? I didn't get that vibe from him."

Steck tapped his chin. "You know, if you narrow your suspect pool to Jimmy and Johann, only one of those wasn't accounted for at last night's mixer. Johann."

"But you're assuming the same individual committed both murders," I said. "And we've already gone over this. Why would Johann murder one of his own men?"

"One of our problems," said Shay, "is that while we have a plausible motive for the murder of Verona—that being revenge or anger due to the results of the poker tournament—we have nothing of the sort with regards to Lumpty's death. We need to figure out *why* someone would want to kill him. If I'm right about my robbery theory, it could've been anyone."

"Which means we need a better idea of who had the opportunity to off him. Or the means." I snapped my fingers. "Steck. That skeleton key. It can get you into any of the staterooms?"

"I don't think I like where you're going with this," he said.

"We need to find the knife that was used to murder Lumpty," I said. "If we find that, we find our killer."

Steck wiped a hand across his face. "Look, Daggers, you know as well as I do I can't go around breaking into people's rooms. Never mind all of our covers would be blown if anyone chanced across me, but even if I did find a knife, we couldn't do anything about it. It would be inadmissible evidence."

"But would it really be breaking in?" I said. "You have a skeleton key, and the approval of the boatswain—not to mention we're in international waters. And you're not really looking for the knife. You're looking for the knowledge of who has knives in their possession. The knowledge is all we're after at this juncture."

Shay crossed her arms. "Daggers, you're toeing a thin line with that reasoning, and it's a line were not supposed to be anywhere near."

"Alright, fine," I said. "We'll save that as a last resort. But we need to keep it on the table. Lives are on the line."

Steck nodded, as did Shay, reluctantly. After a moment of silence, Steck spoke up.

"Look, guys, you know I'm willing and able to help with this investigation in any way possible, but as you already said, Daggers, it's late, and I'm tired. I've already crashed once."

"I hear you," I said. "We all need sleep. Our minds will function better in the morning."

"Thanks." Steck took a step toward the door.

"One last thing, though," I said.

He paused, his face sagging. "Yes?"

"Can you keep an eye on Wanda for me? I don't trust her. She's always missing at crucial points in our timelines, and I'm ninety-nine percent sure it was her who broke into our apartment this afternoon. I want to know what she's up to."

Steck nodded. "I'll do my best."

He left, and I locked the door tight behind him. Steele lingered in the living room.

"Well," she said as I returned. "I think I'm going to take a quick bath before turning in. I feel like I have corpse stink all over me. With any luck, it won't linger on the dress. *That* would be a tragedy."

"Likewise," I said. "Hopefully I won't have to wear this tux again tomorrow night. Then again, maybe the smell will fade if I hang it up. Or maybe it's all in our minds and the smell will fade along with the memory."

"Perhaps." Shay smiled. "You know, despite it all, I had a nice time tonight. Again."

"Me, too," I said. "Two nights in a row. That must be some sort of record."

Shay pshawed. "For you, perhaps."

"I meant for us."

Shay's smile widened. "Good night, Daggers."

I bobbed my head, and she closed her bedroom door. Again, it wasn't the end to the night I'd hoped for, but considering the circumstances, it could've been far worse.

I glanced at my fingernails, grimaced, and headed to my bathroom.

25

escorted Shay back into the high stakes poker room at the back of the ship's casino, my belly full of sausage and eggs and my eyes surprisingly wide open thanks to the restorative efforts of three cups of coffee. Even Shay had forced down a cup, more out of necessity than desire—or so she claimed. I'd make a convert of her eventually.

Despite our late night, we'd beaten some of the others to the room. The gallery was oddly empty, but Theo sat on a stool in a corner, dangling his toes in the air. I spotted Orrin at the bar, and surprisingly enough, Johann had arrived as well. The latter sat at one of the corner tables with a deep scowl embedded into a granite visage. His two toughs, Humpty and Dumpty, stood at his chair's back, their arms crossed and their chests puffed. They practically dared anyone to come within swinging range.

"Well, he doesn't look anywhere near as chipper as he did last night," I said under my breath.

"And so the mystery deepens," replied Shay in kind.

She turned to stand in front of me, straightened the lapels of my jacket—today a warm chocolate brown with cinnamon pinstripes—and adjusted the knot of my cream-colored tie. "So...should we mingle?"

I took a second to admire my partner's own attire—a light grey and black cocktail dress that hugged her torso before poofing out at the waist. She looked spectacular as usual, which was both a blessing and a curse: a blessing for obvious reasons, a curse because it would make focusing on the cards that much more difficult. I could only hope it would distract the others equally.

"We could try," I said. "But it doesn't look as if Johann is in much of a mood to chat."

"Oh, trust me, he's not." Theo approached, having descended from his throne. "I already tried. His goons almost tore me in half, and Mr. Preiss himself said not a word."

"Good to see you again, Theo," said Shay. "So...any idea why he's here, then? I can't imagine he'd want to watch the rest of the game without having a stake in the result."

I wasn't sure if that last line was meant to be so lucid, but if Theo picked up on it, he didn't reveal it.

"Your guess is as good as mine, my lady," he said. "He's been here the whole morning, as far as I can tell. At least he beat me here, and I was the next earliest to arrive, which made for conversational awkwardness, as you might imagine. It didn't get any better when Orrin arrived. I get the feeling most of our fellow competitors are getting annoyed by my talkative nature."

"And who says we're not?" I smiled.

Theo smiled back. "Touché, Mr. Waters. But if I do annoy you, at least you're kind enough not to show it. Or smart enough not to. One of the two. I have my thoughts as to which."

I heard a swish of fabric, and Ghorza entered through the door, wearing a voluminous purple dress. Her manservant, Vlad, followed her closely. She gave our trio a nod before heading toward the bar.

"And now the wait is down to two," said Theo. "Tell me, who do you think will be the last to arrive? The elusive, secretive Wanda, or the lush, Verona? Unless Jimmy shows up, of course, in which case I'd have some questions about what the heck is going on."

It was such a simple question, and yet not one I'd prepared for. It did beg another, though. With Verona's death, how would the tournament proceed? Would it, even?

The gods decided I'd suffered enough over the last few days and granted me a small boon. Wanda walked in through the front door, black turtleneck hugging her chin and with her large, circular tinted glasses shadowing her face.

"Well, that answers that," said Shay. She delivered the line calmly, without a hint of emotion. She *had* come a long way.

"And so two becomes one," said Theo. "Can't say I'm surprised, really. With as much as Verona had to drink yesterday? If I were in her shoes, I'd probably sleep for a week and not shake off the buzz."

"You would've keeled over by the third martini," I said.

"I am small, I admit," said Theo. "But when it comes to distilled beverages, I punch heavier than my weight, trust me. And despite my size, I've never disappointed a woman in bed. So, you know...keep that in mind, Mrs. Waters."

Shay snorted and lifted an eyebrow. "Are you coming on to me, Mr. Hornshoe? And in front of my husband, no less?"

"Hey, there's always a chance you'll get tired of old tall and handsome over here," he said. "I strike out more often than not, but my strategy has always been volume."

Patty entered through the front and took a seat at the table. She opened a brand new deck of cards and began shuffling, but she didn't make any announcements.

Theo eyed the table, then us to see if we had any insight. A number of the other players behaved in a similar fashion.

Once again, I heard the swish of fabric from the drape that hung over the front door, announcing yet another arrival. Boatswain Olaugh, this time.

"Well, that's not Verona," said Theo. "Not as pretty as Verona, either. And before you ask, no I didn't hit on her, too."

"Seems an odd thing to mention, unprovoked," I said.

"Ok, fine. I did. Like I said, volume."

Olaugh cleared his throat. "Excuse me. Ladies and gentlemen? I'm Boatswain Olaugh, and I require your attention. As you've all noticed, Madam Quivven has yet to arrive. I regret to inform you she will *not* be joining you. There's no easy way to say this, so I will simply say it. Madam Quivven suffered a fall last night while in the ship's pool area. She slipped into the water, and...well, she's no longer with us."

I heard several gasps and murmurs, but they were drowned by Johann's powerful voice. "LIAR!"

The older man had stood, his face beet red and his jaw quivering. He pointed an accusatory finger at Olaugh. "Liar, I say! You expect us to believe she simply *slipped* and *fell*? Through no malicious action? Bollocks! If that were the case, why would you hide this from us?"

"Sir," said Olaugh. "The event occurred late last night. This is the earliest you were all gathered, and of course, we had to enact our own investigation into the matter—"

"Lies! If any of that were true, you would've also revealed that my man Ignatius has been missing since the night before last." Johann swept his accusatory finger around the room. "That's right! One of my men has been missing for thirty-six hours, and I don't for a *second* think he's gone rouge. He's dead! I know it. Someone killed him, and someone killed Verona! There's a *murderer* among us!"

"Sir, I must ask you to keep these baseless accusations to yourself," said Olaugh. "Not only are these rumors slanderous, but they risk creating a panic where none is needed. Now, seeing as you've already been eliminated from the tournament, I must ask that you leave. Peacefully."

"Oh, a panic is needed, all right," said Johann. "But you won't have to lay hands on me. I can see where your loyalties lie. But the rest of you need be aware of what's going on. Watch yourselves, or you might find your head on the block next!"

Johann stomped out the door, his thugs hot on his heels. After he'd left, Olaugh nodded to the room. "My apologies. Know that as the ship's boatswain, security aboard the *Prodigious* is my number one concern. I offer you my sincerest assurances that none of you are in danger. Now please. Proceed with your tournament."

On cue, Patty gave the cards one more shuffle and held her hands out to the chairs. "Ladies and gentlemen? If you could take your seats."

I helped Steele into her chair and headed toward my own, all the while wondering about Johann's outburst. He'd been downright furious, not only at the murder of his own man but at that of Verona. Why had he let everyone know? If he were behind either of the murders, wouldn't it behoove him to keep their knowledge secret? Or did he have some reason to incite a panic in the remaining players as Olaugh had suggested?

Either way, the cat had torn its way free from the bag, and it was time to play.

26

"Three of a kind, queens, ace high over three of a kind, queens, ten high. Game to Miss Skeez." Patty gathered the cards and redistributed the chips. "And on that note, why don't we pause for a quick mid-afternoon break. We'll begin again promptly in ten minutes."

I stood and stretched. The morning session had flown past, followed by a quick lunch in the dining hall and more poker, but now halfway through the afternoon session, I felt the game wearing on me—despite having done fairly well for myself. I'd grown my fortune to about twenty-eight thousand crowns. Ghorza has similarly fared well, but some of the others hadn't, namely Orrin and Shay, unfortunately. She was down to under ten thousand crowns, and if our fellow competitors were wolves, they'd be licking their chops.

I made a quick trip to the facilities. When I returned, I found Shay standing at one of the corner tables. She waved me over.

"Hello there, beautiful," I said. "How are you holding up?"

"What do you think?" Her face said it all.

"Come on," I said. "The situation isn't that dire. You can recover."

"Really?" she said. "I lose leverage with every chip of mine that drifts into someone else's pile. I'm on the ropes. It won't be long before someone comes after me, either with a good hand or a strong bluff, and I'm not sure I can fend off either."

"Well then, you'll just have to keep fighting and hope the right cards come your way. What other choice do you have?"

Shay lifted an eyebrow and lowered her voice. "It's sweet of you to believe in me, but let's be honest. You're better at this game than I am. There's no sense denying it. And because of your wins you're in a much stronger position than I am."

"I'm listening."

"You know as well as I do someone is going to take me out sooner or later. For our mutual benefit, it would be best if that person were you."

"Well, Orrin will be happy about this if he finds out," I said. "It's exactly what he accused me of the first time we talked."

"It may be dishonest, but the ship's management let us play together," said Shay. "It's not strictly against the rules. And in poker, strategy stretches beyond the edge of the table."

"So how do you propose we do this?"

"We establish a cue," said Shay. "Some way for you to notify me you have a good hand, one you know you'll win with. I'll have my own cue to signify I have a decent hand, too. Not great, but good enough to make it look respectable. After there are enough cards down for you to know it's a go, I go all in, you take the hand, end of story."

"And what sort of cue do you have in mind?"

"Something simple," said Shay. "Maybe something you already do every now and then so people won't suspect anything's amiss. Like rubbing your thumb and forefinger together."

"I do that?" I said.

Shay nodded. "It means you're thinking, so it's not really a tell in the traditional sense. I'll respond with a chew of my lip, just the edge, on the left side. Does that work?"

Patty piped up from the table. "Ladies and gentlemen? If you could once again take your seats."

"Works for me," I said. "Let's do this."

We returned to our seats. The crowd in the gallery above similarly gathered, having been let back into the space following Olaugh's announcement about Verona. I wondered what sorts of rumors swirled up there regarding her disappearance. Surely some suspected a nefarious exit, but if Olaugh was smart, he'd already spread competing rumors of an illness or excessive drinking being the cause of her absence.

Patty dealt the cards. My first two hands were terrible, and I folded straight away. The third was better, but not by much—certainly nothing to try and take Shay out with. Unfortunately, it was a portent of things to come, as it set off a string of mediocre hands that left me betting little or nothing at all. After almost an hour,

Patty finally dealt me something worthwhile, the king and jack of spades, but when I rubbed my thumb and forefinger together, Shay failed to chew on her lip. She had nothing.

It wasn't a total loss, though. I won a fair number of chips from Wanda with the hand.

More time passed, and a well-dressed waiter came by with a tray full of appetizers: fried shrimp covered in a sweet and savory sauce, peppers stuffed with goat cheese, lobster balls, and something by the name of crudités—which sounded exotic and appetizing but turned out to be nothing more than thinly sliced raw vegetables. I helped myself to a small plateful and sent the man away with my drink order, with which he promptly returned. An old fashioned, similar enough to my go-to whiskey sour to be palatable but strong enough to keep me from guzzling it.

I took a sip and ate a few shrimp and sat out another hand. Patty dealt me two more cards. A three and a seven. Another early fold. Lobster balls. More shrimp. Two more sips of my drink.

My stomach gurgled, and I felt a twinge in my abdomen. Perhaps my belly's way of reminding me of my diet? I fed it a carrot to appease it and took another drink.

The carrot didn't help. I felt another twinge, but this time it was accompanied by a feeling of warmth, spreading through me not from the belly up but from the heart out. Moisture beaded at my temples, which I dabbed away with a handkerchief I'd tucked into my front jacket pocket.

What was going on? Was it the lobster balls? I didn't have a shellfish allergy. Maybe the shrimp had been undercooked, but I'd only just eaten them. From prior experience, I knew stomach bugs took a few hours to wreck havoc on my colon.

Patty dealt me more cards. A jack, ten, off suit. Not a particularly good hand, but I'd gotten it before. When Jimmy went out, I thought.

Theo started the bet, putting forth the required small blind. Wanda put in the big blind and sent it to me. I tried to run the numbers in my head based off Steck's simple mathematical system, but I was having a hard time remembering how it went. There were the points for the high card—a jack was five—and then you had to add points for straight potential. So I had, what...four there? How many points was that?

"You gonna bet there, champ?" said Theo. "You know my strategy. If you're on the fence, just go for it. I mean, come on, man. What's the worst that could happen? You lose it all? To me? Doesn't sound too bad, does it?"

I felt Wanda's eyes boring into me even through her glasses. Screw it. Why not? I tossed forward enough chips to match.

I lifted my drink as Orrin folded, hoping a bit of booze might settle my stomach, but I paused before it reached my lips. Could it be the bitters? No, that made no sense. Bitters were alcoholic concoctions of herbs and spices and bark, among other things. I'd never had an allergic reaction to them before, so why would I now? And the only other ingredients in the drink were whiskey, sugar, and water. Unless...

I recalled Jimmy, sitting at his chair the day before, sweating and swaying and looking green around the gills. I'd assumed he'd drank too much, but what if he hadn't? What if something *in* his drink had rattled his senses?

I set my glass down, untouched, but the damage had already been done. A cloud descended over my mind, and it took all I had to sit up straight, keep my lunch in place, and not drown in my own sweat.

The hand came back to Theo, and he raised on the flop. I folded, as I did on both of the next two hands, despite one of them being decent—I think. I couldn't for the life of me remember the point values Steck had instilled in me. I felt as if I'd aged seventy years over a period of two minutes. I might not remember my own cat's name if anyone had asked me. Not that I owned one, but I barely remembered that either. My head pounded, blood rushed through my ears, and the sweat continued to flow. I dabbed my head with my kerchief again, but I could tell it was soaking through. Surely the others had noticed. They'd be blind not to have.

Patty dealt another hand. Shay started, putting in her blind, and Theo doubled the bet as was required. I realized I hadn't even looked at my cards. While Wanda folded, I took a glance. Pocket kings. Even in my addled state, I knew those were among the best possible starting hands.

I picked out some chips and threw forth enough to match Theo's bet. Orrin sucked on his teeth, considering his options, but I felt as if I were forgetting something. Something important. Related to the poker game, undoubtedly, but what? Oh! The signal to Shay. But what was it? Chewing my lip? No, that was her move.

Orrin matched, sending the bet to Ghorza. Oh, goodness, what was I supposed to do? Blasted drink! It was something simple, something tactile.

I sat there, rubbing my fingers together as I desperately tried to think of what I was supposed to do when I noticed Shay chewing her lip. She knew? How'd she know?

I glanced at my fingers. Oh. Right.

Ghorza folded, and Shay matched Theo's bet. Patty turned over the next three cards. The eight of diamonds, the eight of clubs, and the five of clubs.

Shay eyed the cards. "Well, well. Interesting."

"Does this mean you're finally going to play a hand?" said Theo. "Because for the last hour, you've been playing tighter than a, uh..." He glanced at the ladies present. "Well, let's just say you've been playing tight."

"As a matter of fact, I will." Shay pushed forward five thousand crowns worth of chips.

Theo rolled his eyes. "Oh, come on. Really? I guess this is what I get for egging you on. Fine. Have it." He tossed down his cards.

Between my two kings and the pair of eights, I had a decent hand going. Besides, I knew my role to play with Shay. I pushed some chips forward—hopefully the right amount. "Yeah. I call."

"And I raise." Orrin pushed forth a huge pile of chips, maybe ten thousand crowns worth.

Crap. Shay and I hadn't planned on someone else hijacking our hand—had we? I couldn't even remember, but it seemed a stupid thing to bank on.

Shay glanced at the pile and chewed her lip. Was that part of her sign, or was she concerned?

"Well, I suppose I'm all in, then." Shay pushed the rest of her chips forth.

My forehead felt as if it were on fire. My eyes wanted to pop out of my skull. I stared at Orrin's chips. He only had about three thousand crowns worth left.

"So, *Waters*," said the dwarf. "What's it going to be? You in on this one?"

I swallowed hard. "Let's make this interesting. I raise. By however much you have left."

A murmur ran through the crowd.

"Fine. Let's ride this one out." Orrin flipped his cards, the queen of clubs and the queen of hearts.

Shay flipped hers, the jack and ten of clubs. I tossed my two kings down, and Orrin growled. Patty flipped another card. The three of clubs.

"Oh, ho, ho," said Theo. "And the script flips."

With the fifth club, Shay now had a flush, beating both of my and Orrin's two pairs. I blinked. That hadn't been the plan, right?

Shay smiled, though it seemed forced.

"Don't get cocky," said Orrin. "One more queen and those chips are mine."

I kept my mouth shut. Patty flipped the final card. The eight of hearts.

Theo whistled. Orrin grunted and swore under his breath. The crowd oohed. Shay seemed relieved. I wasn't sure what had just happened.

"Full house, eights over kings," said Patty. "Game to Mr. Waters."

I blinked. I'd won—apparently.

Patty reorganized the chips and collected the cards. "Given the hour and the departures of Mrs. Waters and Mr. Wyvernjaw, I'd suggest we end the betting for today. For those still in the game, we'll meet tomorrow morning at the same time."

Orrin pushed free of his chair and headed for the bar. I nodded to Patty, loosened my necktie, and bolted for the exit.

27

"Thomas! Thomas, wait up!"

I barreled through the ship's hallway, Shay's voice distant and muffled in my ears. I couldn't slow. Our room beckoned. The bed, specifically.

I'd almost made it to our door when Shay caught up with me. She grasped me by the arm and twisted me to face her.

"Daggers, what's going on?" she said in a hushed voice. "Are you okay? Is something wrong?"

"Drugged," I said. "Somebody...spiked my drink. Must've. I feel...dizzy. And lightheaded. Can't think straight, and there's a...cloud of some sort hanging over my brain."

I dug in my pocket for the keys, stumbling as I brought them out.

Shay helped steady me. "Here. Let me."

She unlocked the door and took my arm, herding me into my room. She led me to my bed, fluffing a pillow for me before easing me onto my back.

"Let me get you some water," she said.

I nodded, regretting it as the pounding in my head worsened, but Shay had already left. She returned a moment later with a tall glass from the bar. She held my head as I gulped the contents down greedily, then removed my shoes and tie and undid the top few buttons of my shirt.

"Stay right there," she said. "I'll be right back."

"Where would I go...?" I said, but Shay had already disappeared again. She returned with a cool, damp cloth that she lay over my forehead, as well as another glass of water. She made me drink it all, which I did though more slowly this time.

"Feeling any better?"

I rested my head on the pillow, the coolness of the towel seeping into my skull. "Yes, actually. Thank you."

"What are your symptoms?" she asked. "Take your time, with breaks if you need to, but I need to know them all."

"Let's see," I said. "Dizziness. Sweating. Hot flashes. Stomach pain. Confusion. And, uh...there was something else. Oh, right. Memory loss."

"Was that a joke?"

"Was *what* a joke?"

"Never mind." Shay sat next to me on the bed. She extended two fingers and held them against my throat.

I gave her a few seconds. "How am I—"

She shushed me and held up a finger from the opposite hand. I went quiet again. After fifteen seconds, she pulled her hand back. "About a hundred and ten beats per minute. Elevated, but not to the point of serious concern, especially if you're starting to feel better. You *are* feeling better, right?"

I gave her a thumbs up. "Honestly. Truly. I am." And I wasn't kidding. Since becoming horizontal and guzzling the water, the fuzzy cloud over me had started to break, and the rushing torrent of blood through my ears had dwindled to a mere flood.

"I should get you something to calm your stomach," said Shay. "Food to absorb whatever chemicals were given to you. Bread or crackers, probably. And I should get the medic. Zander may not have been much use dissecting a corpse, but this seems more in his wheelhouse."

"There's no need, Shay," I said. "Really. Some rest, more water, I'll be fine. Physically, anyway. I'll still want to strangle whoever spiked my drink."

Shay shook her head. "No. I'm finding Zander. He may know some tricks I don't. You stay right here, okay?"

"You got it."

"Great. Be back soon." Shay exited the room. I heard the pitter-patter of her feet, the slam of the door, and then nothing.

I took a few deep breaths, closed my eyes, and enjoyed the silence—until someone ruined it with a knock.

"What is it?" I called out. "You forget something? Or just change your mind?"

A voice came back, muffled and distant, but from the closed door, not the drug-induced cotton jammed into my head. "Mr. Waters? Sir? Can I have a moment?"

It sounded like Steck.

"Come on in," I said. "The door's open. I think..."

Again I heard the creak and close of the door, followed by footsteps. I didn't lift my head from the pillow, but I shifted my eyes toward the entrance to my quarters.

Steck appeared, pausing at the foot of my bed when he saw me. He was breathing heavily. "Daggers? Are you feeling alright?"

"Splendid," I said. "This is how I relax after an invigorating poker game."

Steck's eyes narrowed and his brows furrowed.

"Sorry," I said. "Force of habit. Truth be told, I've been better. Somebody spiked my drink."

"You're kidding," said Steck. "With what?"

I sighed. "You know, if you're trying to avoid the wrath of my snark, you should stop asking me stupid questions whose answers are either plainly obvious or totally inscrutable."

"Fair enough," said Steck. "I don't suppose you saw who dosed you?"

I thought about shaking my head but instead chose a more headache friendly option. "No. Must've been the waiter or the bartender. I'd guess someone paid them off."

"And Steele?"

"Went to get the ship's medic," I said. "Should be back soon."

Steck snorted and planted his hands on his hips. "Of course she did."

"You need her for something?"

"Not her necessarily," said Steck. "But someone. And given your condition..."

I sat up to a forty-five degree angle. Miraculously, my head didn't complain. Much. "What's going on?"

"Remember how you asked me to trail Wanda?"

I nodded and winced. My head was far from perfect, apparently.

"I followed her after the end of the poker game," said Steck. "She headed into the engine room."

"The engine room?" I said. "What would she be doing—no, scratch that. I need to take my own advice about stupid questions. You're sure she went in there?"

"Absolutely," said Steck. "I followed her down five flights of stairs and saw her enter with my own two eyes."

"And then what?" I asked.

"What do you mean, then what? I ran back up here as fast as I could to tell you."

I wanted to slap my forehead, but I was smart enough not to. "Let me guess, Steck. You don't have a whole lot of experience tailing people."

"You...think I should've followed her in?"

"Don't get me wrong," I said. "I'm glad to know she was headed somewhere suspicious, but next time I tell you to follow someone, please do so until they *actually* commit a crime or meet with another party."

I sat up the rest of the way and ripped the cloth from my head. "You said you ran up here?"

Steck nodded. His breath had slowed, but it still gave credence to his claims.

I stood, wincing. "Good. If we hurry, we might be able to find out what she's doing down there."

"But...what about the drugs in your system?" said Steck. "And Steele?"

"I've taken down a herd of doped-up dwarves while mildly concussed. I think I can handle a dose of roofies. And as for Steele? Well, hopefully she won't be too angry with me, but that's my battle to fight, not yours. Still...got a pencil?"

The vice cop turned porter patted his pockets. "I'm not sure. What for?"

"Really, Steck? Again with the stupid questions?"

His cheeks reddened, but it wasn't my fault he kept asking things with obvious answers.

"Never mind," I said. "I think there's a fountain pen and pad in the living room. Let's hoof it."

28

Though a single bulkhead door separated the *Prodigious's* second most lower level from her engine room, it felt like much more than that. The portal transported me from a clean, well lit hallway into a dark cave reminiscent of a preacher's promise for the eternal damnation of sinners. A crashing wave of damp heat rolled into me, bringing with it scents of sulfur and soot and engine grease. A din enveloped me—the pounding of iron on steel, the push and clank and screech of pistons and crankshafts, and the distant shouts of burly men, all set over the constant roar of flames.

I blinked in the shadowy expanse, amazed at how a space filled with the blaze of coal briquettes could be so dim, even though I already knew the answer. The fires need be contained, funneled toward the boilers to create the heat and pressure needed to drive the ship's engines. As my eyes adjusted, I made out the huge drums that held the bitumen, dotted with hundreds of rivets already blackened by coal dust.

Sweat beaded over my face, and I longed for the cool cloth Shay had laid over my forehead, but if I knew anything about humidity, the cloth wouldn't work the same way in the boiler room's swampy embrace. My head pounded, made worse by the cacophony of enormous, moving engine parts and rageful death cries of the ship's fuel, but at least I could walk straight and remember things for longer than a goldfish could.

I turned to Steck, shouting over the noise. "You say you saw Wanda come in through here. Any idea where she might've gone?"

He shook his head. "I never followed her in. As soon as she disappeared through the door, I made my way to your chamber."

My eyes continued to adjust, bringing to life more of the details in the engine room: huge carts of pitch black coal, thick spools of braided wire and heavy chains, and hazy clouds of steam seeping through connecting pipes from boiler units large enough to live in. I also spotted a pair of stokers, one as bald as an egg and the other with a pompadour, seemingly held in place by nothing more than engine grease. Both wore plain white undershirts over canvas pants, though the shirts had been turned a murky shade of gray by the environs.

They spotted Steck and I before we did they.

The bald one shouted at us and mounted the bare metal stairs leading toward us from the engine room floor. "Oi! What'cha be doin' here? This ain't no place for dandies such'as yerself. And what ya be doin' bringing 'im here? Don'tcha know better?" He shot a thick, coal-darkened finger at Steck as he said that last part.

I didn't have time to play games. "You seen a woman come in here? Dark hair, dark clothes, dark glasses?"

The greaser joined his pal Baldy on the stairs and elbowed him in the ribs. "See? Told you I wasn't crazy."

"You saw her?" I asked.

The greaser nodded. "Maybe five, ten minutes ago. Harry here thought she was a shadow. I said she wasn't. We had ourselves a spat about that."

I suppressed a chuckle. Of course the egghead's name was Harry.

"You's a loon, you is," said Baldy. "Maybe's y'all are. T'aint no woman prowlin' 'bout the boilers. T'aint nobody else, neither, no matter how many times ya stamp and spit during the spat."

"Somebody else?" I said.

"More shadows," said Baldy. "T'aint nothin' but that. And don't let 'im fool ya into thinkin' otherwise."

"I'm telling you I saw someone else," said the greaser. "At least...I think I did."

I glanced at Steck. "Sounds like Wanda's meeting someone down here." Then, to the stokers: "Any chance you saw where this woman, or that shadow that most definitely wasn't a person, were heading?"

"Well, what sorta stupid question is 'at, now, mate? Askin' done we seen where a shadow done run off ta?"

"To be fair, we're both in a bit of a stupid question funk," I said.

Baldy narrowed an eye, the coal dust caked against his face cracking from the effort. "Who'd ya say the pair of ya was? And what'cha want with a pair of humble stokers here in the ship's taint, by the by?"

"I could tell you," I said, "but it would take too long to fetch Boatswain Olaugh to prove it to you. Suffice it to say we need to find those two shadows. Steck, let's split up. Head to the right. You can take Bald—er, Harry with you. I'll head left. You, with the pompadour. Stay here and keep an eye on that door. If the woman or the shadow come back, I'll want to know."

Steck eyed me dubiously. "You sure about this?"

About not having to endure Baldy's charming, low country dialect and having to explain to Wanda what I was doing in the man's company when and if I found her? Of course I was. "Trust me, I'll be fine. I can handle myself. Now go. We don't have much time. Probably."

I didn't wait for Baldy to tell me why I couldn't delve into the engine room, heading off into the depths all while hoping Steck could handle the mess I left in my wake. I wove back and forth between huge pieces of machinery and boilers that radiated heat into my face, trying to formulate a plan of action for finding Wanda and coming up with nothing.

To some extent, it made sense she'd descend into the *Prodigious's* bottommost pit for a clandestine meeting, assuming she wanted one. The constant break-ins of Shay's and my room gave credence to the idea that everyone in the poker tournament was spying on everyone else—although I was fairly sure at least *one* of the intrusions into my room had been by Wanda herself. Either way, the darkness and noise of the engine room made eavesdropping nearly impossible.

Unfortunately, it did the same for tailing, or for finding subjects who'd been lost due to a vice cop's misinterpretation of orders. The most I could do was head into the engine room's deepest shadows and hope for the best.

Sweat poured down my face as I popped between patches of orangey-yellow coal-fired glow to darkness and back. My shirt stuck to my chest like glue, and I considered ditching my coat on an unattended coal bin. After another minute and a pint of perspiration lost, I did more than consider it. After all, the coal dust had likely ruined it, and weren't the clothes mine to do with as I pleased?

As I peeled the garment from my damp sleeves, I spotted a hint of motion behind a steam expansion cylinder twice my height. Something dark. Probably not another stoker. Those blokes were smart enough to wear short sleeves, and in white to make themselves more visible.

I tossed my jacket to the side and followed the movement, not sure if it had been Wanda but figuring there couldn't be too many other interlopers in the dark, cavernous space. Of course, it could've been a piston or a flywheel or any number of other inanimate components, but given the size of the ship those all moved glacially, and the movement I'd seen had been sharp.

I turned the corner and blinked. It was dark as night behind the piston chamber—darker even, given the absence of stars—but a bit quieter than near any of the open furnaces or next to a giant rotating crankshaft.

"Hello?" My voice came across clear in my ears, though muffled by the ever present background roar. I squinted, searching the darkness for any evidence of milky skin not covered by a black turtleneck and shades.

Could that be why she wore the glasses? To prepare herself for a predetermined spelunking expedition into the ship's underbelly? It seemed a rather elaborate ruse just to give her an edge for whatever meeting she must've planned here.

I heard a whistle, like that of a blade cutting through air, and dropped instinctively. Something clanged into the cylinder behind me, followed by a grunt. Not a feminine one.

I kicked out a leg and made contact with something meaty. Another grunt followed, as well as a whoosh of air. A shadow blotted out what little light reflected off the edge of the engine compartments before crashing into me, knocking the breath from my lungs.

A powerful smell of liquor rolled off my assailant, mixed with a stale sweat stench and a hint of something sour. Hands grappled at my face and arms, hands I couldn't clearly see but that felt large and strong and rough. One tried to hold me in place while the other pulled back.

I mustered my strength and rolled to the side, hoping to avoid the blow I expected if not saw. The figure above me grunted again, and I felt their weight release from my ribs. A clang sounded, maybe that of a head or an elbow ricocheting off the nearby metal cylinder.

I sucked in air to appease the burning in my lungs and called out for help. "Steck! Steck!"

Another thump from near the cylinder. I rolled in the opposite direction, then cast my hand about the floor for a weapon. Anything hard that could cause damage to a skull. Nothing.

Footsteps towards me. Could my assailant see better than me? I crouched low and braced myself.

Knees smacked into me, rattling my skull and sending shooting pains lancing into my brain, but I held on, pushing and twisting at the same time. My assailant tipped and fell, crashing to the floor. Their cry was accompanied by a resounding metal clatter, the banging and bouncing of at least a dozen reverberating poles. Rebar, perhaps.

A glimmer caught my eye, and my hand found it. The cool metal fit easily into my hand just as Daisy's would've if I'd been smart enough to bring her along, but the bar's balance was off. It was too heavy, and it torqued on my hands, probably due to its length.

Somewhere in the distance I heard a shout, and I called back. "Steck! Here!"

Another clang sounded to my left. I turned and swung, missing everything. I twirled like a top.

The shadow in front of me drifted to the right, and I heard another footstep. I swung again.

This time my aim sailed true. The bar impacted at chest level with a meaty whump, sending a vibrating jostle through my hands. My mystery attacker yelped— a pierced cry of pain that could've stemmed from any number of voice boxes.

More cries. Nearby now. I could make out the words. "Waters? Waters!"

The yelp trailed off into a whimper, and I heard a rapid patter of heavy feet.

"Hey! Wait!" I called, but my voice rasped and didn't carry. Coal dust choked my lungs, which burned fiercely, to say nothing of the rhythmic, lingering thumping that coursed through the blood vessels in my head.

Steck's voice drifted over clearly now. "Waters? Where are you?"

I stumbled toward his voice and the light—meager though it was, it seemed bright against the pitch black of the corner tucked away behind the piston chamber walls.

Steck materialized through the edge of the darkness, the side of his face lit in dim oranges and yellows. Baldy and another stoker, wide-necked and swarthy, stuck to his back like glue.

"Good gods, man," said Steck as he laid eyes on me. "What in the world happened?"

I felt the weight of the iron bar in my hand, its patterned edge biting into my skin. I dropped it with a clatter. "That bad, is it?"

"You're covered in sweat and coal dust, your shirt is torn, and...is that a welt on the side of your face?"

"Probably from the flying knee," I said.

Steck's eyebrows furrowed.

"I was attacked," I said. "As if that wasn't obvious from my screaming."

"Who?" asked Steck. "Wanda?"

I started to shake my head, then stopped as needles poked through my eyeballs. I winced and leaned over, resting my elbows on my knees. "No. Someone big. Strong. Soaked in booze. Didn't say a word, and I didn't get a good look at them. It's dark back there. They knew that. I thought *I* was following *them*. Guess I was wrong."

Steck stepped over to my side and lay a hand on my shoulder. He lowered his voice so only I could hear it. "Daggers...are you doing alright?"

"My head feels like it's going to burst," I said through clenched teeth. "Turns out working yourself into a lather and taking a knee to the noggin isn't much fun when you're still half doped up on goofy pills."

"We need to get you back to the room," said Steck. "Harry. Give me a hand, will you?"

Baldy took a step forward, and I lifted my hand, ready to argue that what we really needed was to go after the mystery assailant, but did we? *Really?* Whoever it was had melted into the shadows and run off. The engine room was cavernous, not to mention dark as a mineshaft and ten times as loud. My attacker had done their homework. Chances were they'd scouted the rest of the engine room as well, and without being spotted by the stokers all the while. What chance did I have of finding them, all while nursing a drug hangover and a probable mild concussion?

Baldy extended a hand, and I took it, pulling myself upright. "You're right. Let's get to the room, before anything else happens to my poor brain."

29

Steck helped me back to my quarters, lingering in the living area as I headed into my bathroom. It wasn't until I'd guzzled another two glasses of water, washed my face, combed my hair, and gotten halfway through changing my shirt that it hit me.

Shay hadn't returned.

I popped the last couple buttons into place, tucked the shirt tails into my slacks, and headed back into the living room. There, I found the note I'd penned for Shay exactly where I'd left it. I glanced at the grandfather clock.

"Steck," I said. "Where's the ship medic's office?"

"What?" He blinked. "Why? Have you taken a turn for the worse?"

"Think, Steck. Shay went there. Where is it?"

"Oh. I, uh...let's see. On the B deck. Toward the front, near the bridge."

I did some mental math. Given how long it should've taken Shay to get there and back and my own time spent in the engine room, Shay should've returned a good ten or fifteen minutes ago, at least.

I turned toward the front door. "Let's go."

"You can't be serious, Daggers. You need rest. If Steele were here..."

Steck trailed off as he noticed the look on my face.

"Right," he said. "I'll lead the way."

We took the most direct route from my stateroom, passing through the bulk of the promenade deck, past the mixer lounge, and down a flight of stairs. There, toward the ship's prow, we found an open bulkhead door with the word 'MEDIC' printed above the molding in bright red.

I stepped inside to a small room with walls of pristine white. A pair of examination tables with white padded cushions and chromed legs populated the space, as did a couple more traditional hospital beds, each dressed in white linens and with the privacy screens drawn back. They were all empty, but the desk at the front of the room wasn't. Zander sat there, facing the wall. He tapped a pencil against a sheaf of papers—a stack of reports by their appearance—but he turned at the sound of us.

Zander leaned back and tugged on one of his beard braids. "Oh. It's you, again. I sincerely hope you didn't come to have me revisit the events of last night. Once was enough, thank you very much."

"Where's Samantha?" I asked.

"Pardon?"

"You know. My partner. Steele. She was here not ten or fifteen minutes ago. Where is she?"

"Oh. Her." Zander pointed his pencil at the doorway lazily. "Well, the last person through that door was a woman by the name of—well, for patient confidentiality purposes I can't say, but she was suffering severe indigestion for eating too many shrimp at the ship's buffet. That was well over an hour ago."

I glanced at Steck.

"Why do you ask?" said Zander. "Is there...a problem?"

"You've just been enlisted," I told the dwarf. "I'll need you to work down the port side of the ship. Steck, you can take the starboard side. I'll go back through the middle."

"Daggers, I can understand your concern," said Steck, "but are you sure a full blown manhunt is necessary?"

"You didn't see her when she left," I said. "She was adamant I stay right there in the room and wait for her to return, which she'd do with Zander in tow. She was determined, Steck. And in her mind, I was in despair. I needed help. She wouldn't lollygag about knowing that, go frolic in the ship's gardens or stop at the bar for a few drinks."

Steck regarded my face again and nodded. "Very well. Given what just went down in the engine room...well, better safe than sorry."

"She's wearing a light grey and black cocktail dress, Zander," I said. "I can count on you, right?"

The dwarf seemed to have mostly followed along despite the gaps in knowledge. "I'll help look for her. Protect and serve, that's what I do."

"Good. Let's go."

I headed back into the ship's interior, walking up the stairs to the promenade deck and working my way toward the aft portions. I stopped a porter and a crewman, asking them about Shay with no luck, before pausing outside the double doors to the mixer lounge. Despite my claims about Shay not stopping for a drink, I went in anyway. A number of people milled about inside, from bartenders to waiters to patrons. Someone might've seen something.

I approached the bar, where a young man in a white shirt and black vest rattled a cocktail shaker above his shoulder.

"Excuse me. Barkeep? I don't suppose you saw a young elven lady pass this way. Tall, beautiful, chocolate brown hair. Wearing a black and grey dress?"

The bartender cracked the shaker and poured the contents into a martini glass. "Ah, yes. Madam Samantha."

"*Samantha?* You know her? And you're on a first name basis?"

The bartender smiled as he washed out the shaker. "She gave me her last name but insisted I call her by her first. You must be her husband, Mr. Waters."

A mixture of annoyance, relief, and curiosity coursed through me. I forced it all down to the same place I'd shoved my lingering headache. "Perhaps you could start at the beginning. What was she doing here, and where is she now?"

"I'm not sure I can answer all those questions," said the bartender as he scooped ice into his shaker. "I first noticed Madam Samantha about twenty, twenty-five minutes ago. She's hard to miss, as I'm sure you're aware, sir. She loitered for a few minutes before heading here to the bar and taking a seat at the end." He pointed out the stool. "I served her a drink. Sangria with a touch of limoncello. We made light conversation, but she wasn't terribly focused on it. Kept looking over her shoulder, as if she were expecting someone."

Or trying to spot someone, I thought. "And then?"

"She left, perhaps ten minutes ago. Out the front doors."

"Alone?" I asked.

The barkeep nodded.

"She head left or right?"

The barkeep pursed his lips, his brow furrowed.

"Don't act as if you don't know," I said. "I've watched her walk away. It's hard to peel your eyes from her backside, even when she's not wearing a dress. So I'll ask again. *Left or right?*"

"Ah...right, sir."

"Thanks."

I headed out and turned right, back in the direction I'd already scoured. Clearly Shay hadn't been standing around in the main promenade deck hallway, otherwise I'd already found her, which meant...

I headed into a side corridor and down the stairs, popping open the door to the *Prodigious*'s exterior. A chill wind cut through my dress shirt, bringing with it a salty spray that cleared the remaining flecks of coal dust from my nostrils. The sun had disappeared from the sky, though the last vestiges of its light trickled over the horizon and painted the sky in deep purples and blues.

I headed down the deck, looking for Shay, but apparently the cold had forced everyone inside. Far off in the distance, a pair of men in navy and white uniforms coiled rope. I headed toward them, hoping they might've seen something to aid my search.

The wind gusted, and I put my head down against it, all the while thinking about what the bartender had said. Shay had come to the lounge, loitered, and paused at the bar. But why? She'd thought me in distress, so it would've taken something serious to make her deviate from her plans. Perhaps she'd been followed and hoped to discover the identity of her tail? It would explain her lingering at the bar, glancing over her shoulder, but spotting a tail in a crowd at a cocktail lounge would be a hard task. Much easier would be to isolate the tail. Like, say, on a largely deserted ship deck...

I paused, my head still tilted down against the wind and my eyes trained on the polished wood underfoot. A deep scrape marred the otherwise glossy wood, cutting across the boards from the halfway point of the deck all the way to the railing. It ended roughly halfway between a pair of lifeboats that hung over the side, but there was something else there, too. In the joint between two of the railing poles, a scrap of cloth fluttered in the wind—a lacey light grey fragment with a hint of black stitching.

I gripped the railing and cast my eyes over the side. The fading light made the surface of the ocean appear as one churning dark mass, with only the tips of the waves glimmering in the glancing rays. I squinted, doing my best to counteract the night's oncoming wishes.

And then I saw it. A shimmer. It could've been sea foam, or algae.

Or it could've been a grey dress.

I turned to the seamen and shouted at the top of my lungs. "HO! MAN OVERBOARD!"

With my hands trembling, I planted my foot against the top of the railing, heaved, and launched myself into the abyss.

30

Frigid darkness exploded around me, stabbing me with icy needles and nearly knocking the breath from my already battered lungs. I kicked out and pushed my arms through the water, once, twice, thrice until I broke the surface. I gasped and flicked my head to shake the salty water from my eyes, casting about for direction. The *Prodigious,* like a floating mountain, was impossible not to see, but where was Shay?

Think, Daggers, think. I'd spotted the glimmer to my right, toward the ship's aft. With the ship at my back, I shifted my gaze, but it wasn't until I rode the height of a swell that I saw it. A goodly ways away, floating upon the roiling ocean surface. A length of dark fabric.

Above me I heard shouts and cries for help. They registered in some far off corner of my mind as I lashed out toward the floating form, forcing my muscles to work. The cold had already worked its way deep into my tissue, setting my teeth to chattering, and it was only a matter of time before it reached my bones.

Despite its omnipresence around me, sucking me of my warmth, the icy water meant nothing. The shouts and cries meant nothing. My headache, the blow to my ribs, the coal dust in my lungs, all of it meant nothing.

Action meant everything.

I churned my arms and kicked my legs, fighting the ebb and flow of the waves along with the cold and my own emotions. Arm out. Twist. Pull. Breathe. Kick. Repeat. Salt water forced its way between my lips only to be spat back out. My heart pounded and my muscles burned.

I reached another crest and saw her in the trough. Shay, on her back with her arms out, the dress floating lifelessly to her sides and her skin pale.

I reached her in a couple wild strokes. "Shay! SHAY!"

She didn't respond. I pulled her to me as best I could with trembling hands. Her skin felt cold to the touch, but surely that didn't mean anything. My own fingers were little more than meat popsicles.

"Shay!" I shook her, but still she didn't respond. Somewhere in the background I heard a whir and a slap of the waves and more cries.

I glanced at Shay's face, ghostly in the dim light. Her eyes had closed, and her lips had faded from a warm pink to more of a champagne.

I tore my eyes away. She was on her back. She could breath. She'd be fine. She had to be. She had to.

Another cry sounded, closer this time. I turned my gaze toward the ship, where one of the lifeboats had been lowered into the water. The two sailors from the end of the ship manned it, one at the oars and the other perched at the prow.

I waved and shouted, then hooked an elbow under Shay's armpit and cast out in their direction. My muscles burned despite the glacial water, a fiery frigid mixture possible only in the deepest depths of hell.

Splash. Splash. Splash. Over and over I plunged my free arm into the water, kicking with every ounce of my might as I tried to make headway against the tide. The darkness deepened, but it must've been in my eyes only, as I couldn't have been swimming for so long, could I?

An oar materialized in front of me, and then a hand.

The water slapped off the side of the boat and back into my face. "Shay!" I shouted as I spat it back out. "Take Shay!"

The hands grasped her and pulled her up, then came back for me. The boat dipped and tilted, and I flopped into her belly with all the grace of a dying fish.

Somehow, being pulled from the water only made the chill worse. The breeze blew and I began to shiver uncontrollably, unable even to move to Shay's side to help her. Luckily, the sailors were more than capable. One had already begun chest compressions.

Pump. Pump. Pump. He leaned over and blew into her mouth.

Nothing happened.

Pump. Pump. Pump. He leaned over and blew again. I shivered.

Nothing happened.

Pump. Pump. Pump. Breathe. Pump. Pump. Pump. Breathe.

My heart slowed. I held my breath.

Shay coughed and sputtered. Her eyelids fluttered, and a spasm wracked her body. She turned her head and vomited seawater into the bottom of the boat.

I took up religion.

31

"**S**he's alive!" cried the sailor.

The other had already taken up position at the oars and begun to row us back toward the ship. I could barely lift my head due to the shivering, but in my peripheral vision, I spotted lights and warm bodies and motion on the deck of the *Prodigious*. People shouted. Ropes and life preservers splashed and plunked as they met the water's surface.

I ignored it all. I couldn't tear my eyes from Shay a second time.

She tilted her head, blinking slowly. Her skin might've paled, but her azure eyes remained as fierce as ever.

"Jake?" Her voice was raspy and soft, but it didn't shake like my own. That was a good thing, right?

"I'm here, Shay," I said through chattering teeth. "You're going to be okay."

The next few minutes passed by in a blur. The *Prodigious's* sheer cliff face loomed large. The sailors' hands moved quickly, attaching ropes to pulleys and yanking on them with superhuman strength. Bright lights burst into life as our boat cleared the ship's lip, like a sunrise breaking free of the horizon. Hands grasped me and pulled me free, then helped me back up when my own legs wouldn't hold me. Warm blankets draped my shoulders. People milled about, most of them dressed in the navy and white of the deckhands but others in the uniforms of stewards and officers as well. Steck was there, as was Zander, shouting orders in a voice loud, strong, and firm.

I searched for Shay and found her nearby, draped in warm blankets like myself and held vertical by a pair of sailors. Zander shouted more orders. The helping hands around me sprang into motion, herding me into the ship's interior and up the stairs. I stumbled. Sailors picked me up. Shay was carried.

I tried to formulate thoughts, but my brain moved sluggishly. My only concern was for Shay. Was she too cold to walk? How long had she been in the water?

Suddenly we'd arrived at our quarters. Sailors whisked me into my room and began stripping the clothes from my body. My sense of modesty protested weakly, but I was too cold to give it a proper voice. Shirt, pants, and undergarments were all discarded, and a new blanket, deliciously warm to the touch, was draped around me in recompense. I heard more shouts and footfalls from the living room, as well as a loud hiss and pop. The sailors dragged me into the common room, depositing me onto the thick fur rug in front of the fireplace. A blaze crackled there merrily, one I swear hadn't been alive moments ago, but then again, perhaps it hadn't. One of the stewards jabbed it with a poker, puffing on it and feeding logs into the flames.

A sailor produced a teapot and situated it over the fire. I heard a voice. Zander's. Someone slammed the front door. Then Shay appeared. A heavy blanket hugged her body like a sausage casing, and a second, smaller blanket had been wrapped around her hair as if it were a turban. Zander stood at one of her shoulders, and at the other stood a woman in a waitress outfit. They led Shay to the fire—she walked slowly, in a hitching manner and on the verge of falling, but walk she did—and helped her down onto the rug next to me.

Zander knelt at the side of the fireplace, making sure not to get between us and the flames. "Steck! Get more warm blankets. You. Waitress. Get me some mugs. And some honey if you can find it. Miss Steele? Can you talk? How are you feeling?"

Shay's teeth now chattered fiercely. "I... What...?"

"It's alright," said Zander. "You're suffering from moderate to severe hypothermia. One of the symptoms is confusion. It'll pass as you heat up, but we need to get warm fluids in you as soon as possible. You're lucky Mr. Daggers saw you. Based on the probable water temperature and your condition, I don't think you would've lasted another five minutes."

The waitress returned with mugs and a small jar as the teapot began to whistle. Zander fished it out with a pair of tongs and filled the mugs. He held one out to me.

"No tea bag?" I asked.

"Shut up and drink it," said Zander. "You can hold onto the mug yourself, correct?"

I snaked an arm out from under the blanket and found that my hand no longer shook. "Yeah."

"Miss Steele. Let me help you." Zander held the mug up to Shay's lips, forcing her to take sip after sip.

I took a drink of my own, and though the mug held nothing but water, the warmth flowed through my esophagus and into my belly as if it were a stiff shot of alcohol. I took another gulp and another, feeling my body temperature return to some semblance of normal.

Steck returned with more blankets. Zander accepted them, then waved him, the waitress, and the remaining sailor off. They exited, and I heard the corridor door shut.

Zander brought the mug back down, now empty. "Better, Miss Steele?"

Shay's teeth still chattered, but not so fiercely. "Yes. Thank you."

"Good," said Zander. "Another then."

He refilled the mug, this time adding a dollop of honey from the jar, and again helped Shay drink it. It could've been a trick played on my eyes by the flickering light of the fire, but by the end of the second cup, it seemed as if her lips had brightened and a touch of color had returned to her cheeks.

Zander began to refill the mug with honey and water. Shay wiggled an arm out from under her blanket and pressed her hand against Zander's forearm. "It's alright. I think I can manage it from here."

Zander eyed her hand and pressed his palm against her forehead. "Well, your shivering has largely subsided. That's good. Body temperature seems to be on the upswing. How are you feeling overall? Memory clearing up? How many fingers am I holding up?"

"Four," said Shay. "And yes. I'm feeling better. Much more so."

"Good. Let me get that towel off your head. We need your hair to dry."

Zander stood and removed the towel in question, spreading Shay's wet locks across the back of her blanket.

Shay peered at him out of the corner of her eyes. "Um...thank you, Zander. I appreciate your help. Honestly. Daggers and I both do. But I think we can manage it from here."

"Please." Zander rolled his eyes.

"I'm serious," said Shay. "I won't lie, I'm still cold, but I can think straight. I can tense and release my muscles. All I need now is time."

Zander straightened and eyed the both of us, concern still etched in his face. "Hmm...well, normally I'd keep someone in your condition under observation for a couple hours, but given what I know about you, you're both fairly capable. I can understand the desire for privacy, but you're not out of the woods yet. I suggest you keep drinking warm, sweetened beverages for the next hour. Try to get a little food in your system if you're up to it, but keep it simple. I'd suggest bread or toast. Maybe a cookie, as it contains sugar. And *no alcohol.* Contrary to popular belief, it doesn't help combat hypothermia, and it could hit you like a ton of bricks thanks to dehydration.

"Also, once you're feeling better, physical exertion will help you recover faster. You can start with simple exercises now. Flexing your fingers, moving your wrists, neck, that sort of thing. You said you can tense your muscles. Good. Do that. Give it a while before progressing to walking and calisthenics. And you!" Zander jabbed a finger in my direction. "You're in much better shape than she is, so keep an eye on her. Anything happens—and I mean *anything*—you come running. In fact, scratch that. I'll leave a man posted in the hallway outside in case of emergency. Get him if you need him."

I nodded. "You have my word."

Zander snorted. "Alright. Take care of yourselves then. And for the love of the gods, don't go diving overboard again! You nearly gave me a heart attack."

Zander walked off. The door banged shut behind him, and all was quiet except for the spark and pop of the logs in the fire.

I set my mug down and eyed Shay. "How are you doing? Honestly. You don't have to sugarcoat it for me. You know I'm here for you."

She met my eyes with her piercing azure pools. "I wasn't leading Zander on. I feel much better. Truly."

"I'm glad to hear that," I said. "But before we go on, let me add my own voice to Zander's. Please don't *ever* do that again."

"Fall into an ice cold ocean? I'll try my best."

"Try to die on me," I said, dropping my eyes to the floor. "When I saw that scrape on the deck and the scrap of cloth stuck in the railing, and when I dove in and spotted your dress and you floating in the water, I... Well, I..."

I couldn't finish the thought, so I trailed off, letting the fire's merry crackle eat my words.

"Jake?"

I lifted my head. "Yes?"

Shay's hair had now almost dried. It framed her face in haphazard, disorderly curls, cascading past her cheeks and onto the thick brown cotton of her blanket. She smiled, and whatever frost still stuck to my skin melted. "Thank you. For saving my life."

I couldn't help but smile back. "Well, I guess we're even now."

Shay lifted an eyebrow. "Even? How do you figure that?"

"Well, you saved me from that werewolf and from those brain-hungry zombies, which put me down oh-two, but I've since rescued you from the clutches of a vicious gang of smugglers and pulled you out of the ocean, so by my count we're even."

Shay smirked. "Oh. Well, I'd thought those first two were more joint efforts, but I'll go ahead and take credit. Although when framed that way, your rescues seem rather pedestrian as compared to mine."

"I play the hands I'm dealt," I said. "And no, that's not an intentional poker metaphor. But I don't mind if you get the fearsome creatures and I get the rest. As long as you're here. As long as you're safe. That's all I care about."

"You risked everything for me."

I smiled. "It's what partners do."

"Come on, Jake," said Shay. "Diving into the ocean after me? Putting your life on the line without hesitation? It's more than what partners do. You and I both know it. So thank you."

Shay set her mug down near the fire and leaned over to kiss me. As she did so, her blanket began to fall open, revealing the length of her arm and her shoulder and more.

"I... Uh... Shay? Your blanket."

Shay's mouth parted, and I felt her hot breath on my face. "I know, Jake."

I leaned forward and met her kiss, tasting the sea salt on her lips and rejoicing in their warmth and softness. Shay's tongue flicked out, brushing against the tip of my own and sending a surge of desire through me. Her blanket fell away. The flickering flames sent shadows dancing over her body, illuminating the supple curve of her breasts, the wave of her hips, and the long, smooth lines of her thighs.

Shay sucked on my lower lip and pulled away. She eyed me hungrily.

"Shay..."

"What?" she said. "Zander said we should engage in physical activity. I'm following the doctor's orders."

She slid her hands into my blanket, pushing it back over my shoulders. Her hands slid down my chest, then down my abdomen before she ran them over the hair of my thighs. I felt myself harden.

I planted my hands on her hips, my fingers gripping her tight and my thumbs trailing along the crease of her thighs down into the space between her legs. I ran my eyes over her smooth, naked form, her perked nipples and flat stomach, enjoying every inch. Despite the hypothermia, heat rolled off her.

"You're...sure you're not still confused? The doc said that can happen with hypothermia."

Shay leaned in and kissed the side of my neck, moving up toward my earlobe. Her voice came hot and breathy. "What do you want me to do? Solve math problems? Recite a passage from one of your silly mystery novels? *I want this, Daggers.*"

I felt a surge of desire flow through me. I couldn't hold it back any longer. "Good enough for me."

I wrapped an arm around her midsection and slid the other under her thigh, my fingers pressed hard against her smooth skin. Shay wrapped her legs around me and hooked her arms over my neck as I picked her up. Slowly I laid her back against the rug, then pressed my body up into her own. She welcomed me, and together, we sunk into the warm embrace of the fur.

32

heard a knock, somewhere distant in the far off reaches of my mind, followed by a muffled call. Steck's. "Mr. and Mrs. Waters?"

I cracked an eyelid. Bright sunshine filtered through the porthole windows, filling the living room with light. The fire had long since died, but its warmth still filled the room, along with the sooty scents it left behind.

I shifted and turned my head, laying eyes on my partner beside me. She lay with her breasts and stomach pressed into the thick fur of the rug, asleep with her head cradled against her crossed arms. The light played off her bare skin, illuminating the curve of her shoulder blades, the dip of her lower back, and the pleasant bump of her buttocks. I'd rested my eyes on it on more than one occasion but always with a dress or a pair of slacks to hide it. Sprung from behind those walls of fabric, it was rounder and fuller than I'd expected. I yearned to reach out and grab ahold of it, but the knocking continued.

I rose, grabbing one of the discarded blankets from nearby. I wrapped it around my waist before heading to the door.

I cracked it. Steck stood just outside as I'd guessed based on the voice.

"Ah, Mr. Waters. There you..." His voice trailed off and his lips puckered as he took note of my state of undress.

"What's up, Steck?" I probably should've lowered my voice in the event of nearby prying ears, but I figured that ship had more or less sailed.

Steck blinked. "Oh. Uh...I was just stopping by to check on you two. Make sure you were feeling all right and that you'd be ready for the start of the tournament."

"Poker. Right. I'd almost forgotten about that. What time is it?"

"Half past seven, roughly."

"And the tournament starts at...?"

"Eight, theoretically," said Steck. "Although I might be able to have the crew push it back by thirty minutes."

"Try for an hour," I said, tugging on my blanket to make sure it stayed in place. "And to assuage your fears, Shay and I are fine. More than fine. But could you send up some room service? I don't know about Shay, but I'm *famished*, and I'm not sure we'll have time to visit the dining room."

"Sure," said Steck. "No problem."

"One more thing before you go. How bad is it?"

"How bad is what?"

"Everything," I said. "The rumors. The gossip. Our covers. I can't remember everything due to the hypothermia, but I'm pretty sure we all let the veil slip last night."

Steck shrugged. "You're the hot topic of conversation. Everyone's heard about the rescue, but nobody seems to know what happened. As to your names? I'm not sure, really."

"Right. We'll hope for the best. Thanks."

I closed the door and returned to the living room. Shay had stirred, but she hadn't risen. She still lay on the rug belly down, propped up on her elbows with her knees bent and her feet kicked up into the air.

"Good morning, sunshine," I said.

She brushed back a lock of hair that had strayed into her face. "Who was that?"

"Steck, checking to make sure we're still alive."

Shay glanced at the grandfather clock. "Is it seven thirty already?"

"Hard to believe, isn't it?" I said. "I didn't think we went to bed that late."

"Went to bed is a bit of a misnomer seeing as we never made it past the rug," said Shay. "And while we may have turned in early, I'm not sure when either of us actually fell asleep. We got distracted. *Over and over* again."

"There's no shame in that," I said. "Or in sleeping in. I've made a habit of it. I think we both needed it. We had a lot of rigorous physical activity yesterday."

Shay smiled. "You mean you saving me from the ocean?"

"Yeah...let's go with that."

Shay gave me a nod. "What happened to your chest?"

I looked down and found a bruise blossoming from my ribs, on my right side near my sternum. "This? It must've happened during my fight down in the engine room. Didn't even notice it until now. Honestly I thought if anything it would be the knee to the face that would leave a mark. How's my cheek?"

Shay blinked and shook her head. "Wait, *what?* Fight? *Engine room?*"

Right. Shay still didn't know. We'd never really found an opportune moment to talk about it, although to be fair, we hadn't talked about much of anything. Most of our communication over the past ten hours had come in the form of grunts, moans, sighs of relief, and the occasional ecstasy-induced expletive.

I sat down next to her on the rug. "Yeah, we might want to talk about what happened last night. After you went to find Zander, Steck popped by claiming he'd followed Wanda into the engine room. Instead of *continuing* to follow her, he came to get me, and we hustled back down there together. I thought I caught a glimpse of her, but it turned out to be someone else, someone who attacked me in the dark. I have no idea who. Someone big and strong and who'd been drinking. I managed to lay into them with a length of rebar and drive them off, but we didn't catch them.

"It wasn't until after Steck and I returned to the room that I noticed your absence, so I took Steck and headed to Zander's office. When he said you'd never showed, I went looking for you. Thankfully I stopped by the lounge where I met the bartender you befriended, because if I hadn't I probably never would've found you in time."

"So...you disobeyed my orders to stay in the room," said Shay.

"Only because I had no other choice. We needed to track Wanda. And speaking of bruises and people who didn't do what they claimed they were going to do..." I nodded at Shay's right hip.

Shay glanced at the spot which featured a purple splotch. "Huh. Well, apparently you're not the only one who didn't realize they were sporting a nice shiner."

"The firelight was uneven," I said. "And I know I was more focused on other parts of your body. You want to tell me your side of the story?"

"Right. Well, I *did* set out with the intention of seeking out Zander and bringing him back, but it didn't take long for me to realize I was being followed. If I'd thought you were truly in danger from the drugs you'd been given, I would've ignored it and soldiered on, but since you'd insisted you were feeling better, I tried to out the tail. I headed into the lounge, had the bartender mix me a drink, and scoped out the crowd for any anomalies."

"Speaking of which," I said. "You opted for a drink, knowing the one I'd *just consumed* had been spiked?"

Shay lifted an eyebrow. "Come on, Daggers. This was an entirely different bartender, in a different part of the ship. I watched him make it. I wasn't about to be caught off guard. That said though, my strategy didn't particularly work. After fifteen or twenty minutes and a few sips of my drink, I got the impression I'd imagined it all, so I left, but not before trying one more tactic to unearth the identity of my tail."

"You headed outside to the deserted deck."

Shay nodded. "As soon as I got out there, I got that creepy feeling of being watched again. I walked along the deck slowly, keeping my eyes peeled, when all of a sudden, I suffered a...*brain freeze,* for lack of a better term."

"So someone *did* spike your drink."

Shay shook her head. "I'm telling you, it wasn't that. Not that I know what being drugged feels like. To my knowledge, I've never been. And to be fair, the symptoms I suffered were somewhat similar to those you described. Headache, dizziness, confusion. But the symptoms came on strong, and incredibly fast. Way faster than a drug onset. One moment I was fine and the next I felt myself doubling over with sharp needle-like pains driving into my skull. And as soon as they came they were gone."

"So what happened?" I said.

"That one moment was enough. Someone blasted me in the side while I swooned—and before you ask, I have no idea who. I didn't get a look at them, not even a poor one. I smacked my hip on the railing and tipped over. I remember falling and a blossom of pain as I hit the water, and that's about it. The next thing I recall was seeing you in that boat and being rushed back into our room."

"So to recap," I said, "someone tried to murder each of us, possibly the same person, possibly not. We can't know since neither one of us got a good glimpse of our attacker. There was more than enough time for my assailant to come after you on the boat deck, but I suspect it was two different people if you're right about the tail. The question is, why come after us?"

"Well, *you're* still in the poker tournament."

"Right, but you're not, which can only mean the attackers targeted us for personal reasons. They must know we're cops, and they're trying to eliminate us before we figure out who's behind it all."

"But who is *they*?"

I didn't have a good answer to that, so I let my silence speak for me.

Shay, being the bright gal she was, picked up on my non-answer. "So...how do you want to play this?"

"I don't think I have a choice," I said. "I have to keep going in the tournament. Since both of our assailants managed to strike without revealing their identities, we don't have enough evidence to go after anyone at the moment, and whatever happens today could provide valuable clues. Besides, we still haven't seen evidence of the fraud Steck initially was worried about—unless you count my spiked drink."

"Fair enough," said Shay. "I suppose that means we should get dressed."

"We?"

"Well, yes. For one thing, I need to be clothed to perform the sorts of regular tasks I do on a day to day basis. For another, I plan on attending the rest of the poker tournament. I'm the one with the exceptional observations skills, in case you'd forgotten, and after someone tossed me in the ocean last night, I don't particularly want to let my knight in shining armor out of my sight."

Shay sat up on her knees. She tossed her hair and drew her fingers through it, trying to disentangle the knots that had set up residence. The position gave me a wonderful view of her breasts and stomach. The creamy skin of her thighs pressed together, hinting at what lay between them.

I glanced at the clock. "I wonder how long it'll take Steck to get food and bring it up here. What do you think? Fifteen minutes? Twenty?"

Shay glanced at me. "Worked up an appetite last night, did you?"

"Well, yes," I said. "And I never ate dinner, either. But that wasn't why I was concerned about the time."

"The poker tournament, then?"

I shook my head.

Shay's eyebrows rose and her lips puckered as she understood my meaning. "Oh. Well, then. I guess I'm down for seconds. Or fourths, or fifths, or whatever we're on now. It all depends on how quick you can be."

"Trust me woman, that won't be a problem. No man in the history of time has ever turned down sex due to time constraints."

Shay tugged my blanket from my waist. "Well. I see you're ready to go." She wrapped her arms around my neck. "And, to answer your previous question honestly, I figure we have at least ten minutes. So you don't have to be *that* fast."

I pressed Steele back into the thick fur of the rug. I had less control over the speed of the process than she gave me credit for, but I'd do my best.

33

"**L**adies and gentlemen," said Patty. "If you could all please take your seats? It's time to begin."

Shay fixed my tie, gave me a smile and a wink, and turned toward one of the high stakes room's corner tables. Her backside wiggled as she walked, sending the pink and black pleats of her skirt swaying and my mind drifting. I'd thought an early morning romp would clear my mind of distractions and prepare me for poker. I was wrong.

The crowd in the gallery clapped as I took my seat next to Wanda, once again dressed in a black turtleneck, slacks, and shades and giving no indication of having undergone anything out of the ordinary last night, whether that be a trek though an engine room or an assault on a police officer. Theo was there, casually attired in a cream-colored dress shirt with the top two buttons undone, as was Ghorza in a voluminous indigo dress that gave her the appearance of a giant blueberry. She'd once more donned her floppy hat and glasses, but to what end, I couldn't tell. She certainly didn't appear to be hung over as she'd been on the first morning of play. Vlad helped her into her chair, which gave me pause, but then she yawned and stretched, pulling her arms over her head as she did so. Either she had an inordinate threshold for pain, or she wasn't the one who I'd blasted in the ribs with a steel bar twelve hours prior.

Johann, his thugs, and Jimmy were all missing, but despite having been eliminated, Orrin *had* arrived. He'd seated himself in one of the far corners like Shay, but unlike her he'd already helped himself to a drink. His jaw was set and his face drawn, even more so than usual. He hadn't looked inclined to chat, and I hadn't approached him.

Of course, no one had been particularly chatty this morning. Theo at least had asked after Shay's and my wellbeing, but no one else had. Given the uproar our deep sea dip had caused, I couldn't imagine it was due to ignorance.

Patty dealt the cards, and we began play. A hand became a half dozen, and then a score. I found myself playing with confidence, looser than I had before. The numbers from Steck's system came to me intuitively, and I won several hands on bluffs I never would've made the day before. Perhaps the physical and emotional release of my night with Shay had relaxed me, or perhaps the game simply seemed easier now that I'd played it while drugged and on the verge of collapse. Either way, I forced myself to pare my tactics, else someone caught onto my new gumption.

Theo continued his approach, remaining as garrulous as ever, and it worked. He won several hands over

Wanda, who despite her usual silent, icy chill had an aura of vulnerability about her. It went beyond her below average play. She seemed to be fraying at the edges. A flick of the fingers here. A twist of the lips there. No motion that she performed regularly enough for me to catch wind of a trend, but there was more action coming from her than before by a wide margin. She even ordered a drink.

I abstained. When lunch approached and a waiter brought appetizers to the table, I only touched those items others tasted first. I ordered a water, and when it came, I drank it slowly, even though I knew Shay had kept her eyes on its preparation and would've warned me if anything was amiss.

As we played, I couldn't help but speculate. Was my attacker, and Shay's, sitting by my elbows at the table? My own assault I could forgive, but if and when I discovered who'd nearly killed Shay, I might have a hard time keeping my fingers away from the soft flesh of their neck. Fortunately for the other players at the table, I had a hard time convincing myself any of them were responsible. Certainly, I didn't think any of them had come after *me*. The more I saw of Ghorza, the more certain I became she wasn't suffering any ill effects from a ferocious rib injury, and both Wanda and Theo were too small and weak to have inflicted any pain on me in the dark of the engine room. Orrin might've been able to, but he was too short. Given the trajectory of my swing, I would've hit him in the head rather than the ribs, and his face wasn't bruised in the least. He did seem nervous, though, as I glanced back at him during a pause in the action.

The morning turned into afternoon, and on we played. The crowd ebbed and flowed. My pile of chips stayed roughly even, Wanda's dipped, and Theo's and Ghorza's grew. Theo talked. Wanda didn't. Ghorza acted aloof. And then I noticed something. Something innocuous. Probably nothing, but then again, maybe not.

On a hand in which Theo, Wanda, and Ghorza all played to the flop, Theo clenched his jaw a little on the raise. It wasn't much. Maybe I'd imagined it, but the muscular clench went against the gnome's carefree persona. Certainly I hadn't noticed it before.

He won the hand after raising and forcing Wanda and Ghorza out, but later he did it again, and when pressed into a showdown with Ghorza, he lost the hand, and not with a particularly good set of cards.

Could it be...*a tell?*

Theo was smart. He knew as well as I did Wanda wouldn't last long, and then it would be a three way game between him, me, and Ghorza. Could he be introducing a fake, intentional tell to throw the rest of us off? I couldn't put the ruse past him, but then again, the more logical explanation—that the pressure of the game was finally breaking through his persona—made more sense. And poker, largely, was a game of percentages.

Either way, I'd only have one chance to use the knowledge to my advantage, and I needed to make sure I didn't waste my shot.

We played a few more hands. Wanda won a much needed pot, though it didn't do much to change her overall fortunes. I had the waiter refill my glass, but I didn't drink. Patty collected the cards, shuffled them, and dealt everyone a pair.

Theo was up first. "Oh, come on, man. Patty, you're killing me. When am I going to get something good?" He tossed forth his small blind.

Wanda said nothing as she tossed forth her big blind.

I glanced at my cards. Pocket kings, same as I'd had when I ousted Shay and Orrin. One of the best possible starting hands.

I matched Wanda's bet, not wanting to scare anyone off, and Ghorza did the same.

Theo snorted. "You all are so rude. Here I am with a bad hand, and you're forcing me to raise." He pushed forth enough chips to match the bet.

"I thought your hand was terrible," I said with a smile.

Theo smiled back. "It is, but I don't want to hurt Patty's feelings. Any more than I already have, that is."

Patty flopped three cards over on the table. The king of clubs, jack of clubs, and ten of diamonds.

Theo blinked and rubbed his eyes. "Whoa. Well. That makes things interesting, doesn't it?"

It did. The king gave me a high three of a kind right off the bat, but the jack and ten also set up the possibility of someone beating me with a straight, or with a flush should the cards fall right. Either way, it was a hand begging to be played.

Theo glanced at Wanda's chip pile. "Patty, how much does this creature of the night have?"

"Ten thousand, three hundred crowns worth left, Mr. Hornshoe," said Patty.

"Perfect. That's how much I'm putting in, then." Theo sectioned off the appropriate number of chips. As he pushed them across the table, his jaw clenched.

Gotcha, Theo.

Wanda sighed. Her head dipped, and though I couldn't see through her shades, I could tell she was eyeing her chips. She spoke—finally!—in a thin, reedy voice. "Very well. I'm all in, I suppose."

Given Theo's chip pile of about fifty thousand crowns, he might bluff, but Wanda didn't have that luxury. She must have something. Did she already have the straight?

My pocket kings were too good. I had to play. "Fine. I match."

Ghorza blew air through her lips. She ran her tongue over a tusk, collected herself, and spoke, something she hadn't done much of today. "Well, this pot is getting rich rather fast. Let's make it even more interesting."

Ghorza pushed forth ten thousand, three hundred crowns worth of her own chips.

Patty flipped another card.

Bam. The king of spades. I wanted to jump up and dance, pumping my fist through the air, but through some superhuman force of effort I kept calm.

"Well," said Theo. "This continues to get more...*interesting*." He stared at the cards, tapping his fingers on the table. He stared some more and kept right on tapping.

"You do realize the game goes on, even though Wanda reached her max bid, right?" I said.

Theo glared at me. "Don't get smart with me, Thomas. That's my role at this table. I know how to play the game, I'm just figuring how best to milk you on this hand."

He pushed forth fifteen thousand crowns worth of chips, again clenching his jaw as he did so.

The tell didn't matter anymore. He wouldn't beat my hand. The only question was whether I should check and try to squeeze more out of him on the river or impose my will now.

Subtlety had never been my strong suit. I grinned. "I'm all in."

An electricity had already been building in the crowd, but several gasps followed my play. I heard Orrin whistle, and Shay inhaled sharply.

The big orc woman sighed again. Sweat beaded on her brow. "Oh, my. Vlad? Fan me, please."

The elven manservant walked over and did as he was asked. Ghorza took several deep breaths, eying the cards, her chips, and me in series. She had the most chips of any of us, but only by five or six thousand crowns.

"So," I said after a pause. "What'll it be?"

Ghorza removed her hat and glasses, setting them to the side. She picked up her drink, a mint, lime, and rum cocktail, and took a long draught. She nodded. "Very well. I match."

It took all I had not to grin maniacally.

"Oh, come on, man..." Theo frowned and shook his head. "I hate you all. Yes. I'm in, too." He flipped his cards, revealing a pair of jacks, giving him a full house.

Wanda swore and turned over her own cards. A pair of tens, also giving her a full house, but a lesser one to Theo's. I thought I heard Orrin groan.

I dallied. "Ghorza?"

The orc woman flipped her cards. An ace and a queen, giving her a lowly straight.

I tossed my pair of kings into the middle of the table. Theo cursed and slammed a fist on the table. The crowd twittered. Ghorza held her breath.

Patty flipped the last card onto the table. The ten of clubs. Theo's eyes widened. Wanda gasped, but the fourth ten wouldn't help her beat my four kings. I started to reach for the enormous pile of chips.

"Royal straight over four of a kind and two full houses," said Patty, her voice as calm as a still pool. "Game and match to Miss Skeez."

Wait...*royal flush*? I glanced at Ghorza's cards. The ace and queen—*of clubs*. The king and jack in the flop had also been clubs. The first ten hadn't. But the second?

I slumped in my chair, and my jaw hit my chest. I stared at the table, my arms hanging limply at my sides.

Ghorza wiped her face with a kerchief, took another long drink of her mojito, and waved at Vlad to fan her harder. She looked more relieved than joyous.

Wanda left her chair and stormed out. Orrin followed her. Theo popped out from his chair, came over to me, and slapped me on the shoulder. "Poker's a bitch, isn't she? Want to grab a drink?"

I shook my head. "Uh...no. Thanks."

"Suit yourself."

He headed to the bar. I just sat there, feeling numb and wondering what had happened.

34

I sat at one of the high stakes room's corner tables with Shay, nursing a whiskey sour. Everyone, including the crowd in the gallery, had cleared out—except for the bartender, who sensed his professional skills might be needed given the way I'd flamed out on the last hand.

I shook my head. "I was so close, Shay. Over a hundred and fifty thousand crowns, after accounting for what was removed following Verona's death. All lost on the flip of a card."

"It wouldn't have been our money to keep," said Shay. "You know that, right?"

"Logically? Yes. But it's still brutal on a psychological level. I can't even imagine how I'd feel if I had been playing with my own money."

Shay took a sip of her wine. "And if the winnings had been yours to keep? What would you do with it?"

"I'd blow it all on dope and hookers, same as anyone else."

"Seriously, Daggers."

I scratched my head. "I'm not sure."

"Would you quit your job?"

I shook my head. "Nah. Then I wouldn't get to see you anymore. Or Quinto and Rodgers, for that matter. Heck, even Cairny's fun in her own quirky way. Besides, I like what I do, even if I don't like it every moment of every day. I'd be bored to tears stuck at home with nothing to do."

"So, then?" said Shay. "There has to be something."

I gave it some thought. "I might move into a nicer apartment. One that's never served as a de facto cat halfway house. But I wouldn't splurge on fancy food or clothes. Neither's my style, as you already know. And I wouldn't travel much, either. It would keep me away from work for too long. I don't know. I might invest some of it. Put it aside for Tommy in case he decides to go to a fancy college like you did."

"*Investments? College funds?* Way to live life on the edge."

"It's what you get for shacking up with a man of my maturity level."

Shay snickered. "Apparently that level is higher than I initially suspected. Basically, you're telling me you wouldn't change much of anything. So what are you upset about?"

"I already told you, it's not logical."

I heard the swish of fabric and turned to find Steck entering through the drapes that covered the front door. He motioned for the bartender to leave before crossing over to join us.

I tipped my glass to him. "Give my apologies to the department. Although I'd appreciate if we keep my loss on the down low. I'd rather not feel my fellow detective's wrath when we get our bonuses at the end of the year."

Shay lifted an eyebrow. "We get bonuses?"

"It's a joke."

Steck waved it off. "Don't worry about it. I didn't expect you to win. Not that I doubted either of you, but with the lack of preparation and the odds generally stacked against us, I didn't have high hopes. But that's not what I'm here to talk about."

It was my turn to lift an eyebrow. "Please tell me there hasn't been another killing."

"There hasn't," said Steck. "At least not that I know of. But that doesn't mean I'm not at my wit's end. We've had two disparate individuals murdered, two attempted murders on police officers, and yet despite all that—" He frowned and flicked his hands at the poker table.

"No fraud," said Shay. "At least nothing obvious."

"Exactly," said Steck. "You don't know because we brought you in at the last minute, but our sources were solid. One of the participants was bound to try *something* during this tournament, make a move to win this thing through dishonorable means. And yet nobody did!"

"Whoa, whoa," I said, holding up my hands. "Slow your horses. Shay and I might not have noticed anyone cheating at cards, but that's a far cry from saying this tournament was *honorably won*. Two people are dead. Shay and I are alive only because of our wits, quick reactions, and apparently, an unnatural cold tolerance. Someone spiked my drink. I suspect they did the same to Jimmy on the first day. Perhaps Ghorza, too, although I'm not as sure about her. It may not be fraud, but I'd call that a serious damn conspiracy."

"Sorry," said Steck, hanging his head. "You're right of course. I misspoke. It's just not at all what I expected when I organized this sting."

"You expected a more traditional con," I said. "Like where someone miraculously gets dealt the one and only card that could win them the game on the last play of the tournament."

"You think Ghorza cheated?" asked Shay.

"She was one of our original suspects," I said. "And what are the chances she would score a straight flush on the river? I haven't done the math, but I'm sure it was miniscule. But it's more than that. Ghorza, Wanda, Theo, and I *all* had fantastic hands that final round. It's almost as if someone *wanted* us to all go in at the same time."

"Wait," said Steck. "Are you suggesting the dealer, Patty, orchestrated this?"

"Someone spiked my drink yesterday," I said, "so she wouldn't be the first of the ship's crew to turn traitor."

Steck held up his hands. "*Really?* I mean...okay, look guys. I'm feeling extremely out of my element here, so I'm going to follow your lead. Tell me how you want to handle this, and I'll help any way I can."

Steele gave me a nod. "Daggers."

Nice of her to let me be the man and make the decisions—though I knew perfectly well she was capable of doing it herself. "First things first. The tournament is over, so there's no point in us staying undercover any longer. Captain Heatherfield and Boatswain Olaugh said they were behind our investigation a hundred percent, and I plan on holding them to that. Steck. I want you to gather any information you can on Patty and our bartender that just left. If there's any suspicion, or any connections to our players, I want to know. Meanwhile, Steele and I are going to pay a visit to Ghorza. See if she has any suspicious equipment or chemicals in her room. Depending on how that goes, we might be paying a few more of our competitors visits. Johann, mainly."

"You got it," said Steck. "I'll see what I can do."

I got the location of Ghorza's stateroom from him before he left. I eyed my drink, but chose not to tip the rest of it back.

"Ready?" I asked.

Shay nodded. "Let's do this."

Together, we headed out through the casino and up to the promenade deck. Ghorza's quarters were on the opposite side of the ship as ours, room one fifty nine. I patted my sport coat as we approached, wishing I had my badge with me now that I'd officially ditched my cover. Daisy's presence would've provided me an additional comfort.

It's possible Shay noticed me caressing my coat and read between the lines. "Any particular way you want to approach this? Do you want to come out as cops right away, or hold off on that until we need it?"

"Well, I was thinking—" I paused, my ears perking. "Hear that?"

Shay tilted her head. "Yes. Yelling. Is that...*Ghorza?*"

We rushed forward to find the door to her stateroom open. I burst into the living room where I found a bucking beast with three backs.

Jimmy had his hands wrapped around Ghorza's neck, choking and shaking her and shouting barely intelligible, rage-filled threats. Ghorza fought back, gripping the big man's shirt, pushing and trying to loosen his grip to little avail. Her face resembled her dress in its hue. Meanwhile, Vlad clung from Jimmy's back, holding him in a headlock and hanging on for dear life as Jimmy pitched about wildly. The broken glass remains of a coffee table littered the floor, and blood seeped from a nasty cut in Jimmy's arm.

I darted forth and lashed out with a kick, catching Jimmy in the back of the knee. I followed it with a punch aimed at Jimmy's head, but the big man buckled and twisted and I ended up catching Vlad in the side of the face. The elf grunted and lost his grip, falling to the floor with a thud.

Jimmy pushed Ghorza away, sending her tumbling over one of the room's loveseats, before swinging a wild roundhouse punch my way. He wobbled as he threw it, possibly from lack of oxygen.

I made him pay. I ducked under it, letting the punch sail over me. When Jimmy twisted back toward me, my fist greeted him solidly in the underside of his jaw.

Teeth clacked. Pain shot through my knuckles. Jimmy crumpled and crashed to the floor.

Ghorza groaned and gasped as she lifted herself from behind the couch she'd knocked over.

Vlad similarly rose slowly, holding the side of his head and stretching his jaw. "Gods. What the hell...?"

"Sorry about your face," I said. "I was aiming for this guy."

I crossed to Jimmy. His current less-than-cognizant condition allowed me some investigative liberties. I lifted his shirt.

"Bingo. Shay. Come check this out."

My partner stepped around the broken glass and took a gander. She whistled. "Looks painful."

A wicked purple and yellow bruise stretched across Jimmy's ribs, right at the height where a length of rebar swung from my hands might've impacted him.

35

I cracked the door and walked into the cell. My feet clattered off the smooth metal floor, the sound echoing off the bare walls before finding its exit through the bars at the front. Jimmy sat on a bench affixed to the wall, his hands cuffed and resting in his lap. He looked up at my approach. Other than a scrape across his temple and his bandaged arm, he didn't look much worse for wear, but his shirt hid the damage I'd done to him yesterday.

"Howdy, Jimmy," I said. "Feeling any better?"

The big man had remained unconscious while we'd transported him to the brig. I wasn't sure how much he remembered.

"Sod off," he growled.

"Now, now, Jimmy," said Shay, joining me. "That's really no way to talk to officers of the law."

Jimmy's brows furrowed. "You're *cops?*"

"More than that," I said. "Detectives—Jake Daggers and Shay Steele. Yes, I know Steele here with her disarming smile and sultry beauty doesn't look it, especially not in that dress, but she's one of the best investigators in the city. And me? Well, with a face like mine, I'm surprised you didn't suspect anything, but I'll take the compliment. If nothing else, it makes me feel better about my undercover skills."

"Fine. Whatever," said Jimmy. "What do you want?"

"We were hoping we could chat," said Shay.

Jimmy snorted. He stared at the floor. "Yeah? Well, keep hoping."

"It might be in your best interests, Jimmy," I said. "If we chat, perhaps you can shed light on the events of the past few days. If not...well, then Shay and I are forced to come to our own conclusions. You're not particularly going to like them."

"I'm afraid I don't know what you're talking about," said Jimmy.

"Why don't you break it down for him, Detective Steele."

Shay nodded. "First off, we caught you red-handed attacking Ghorza in her stateroom. That alone gets you an aggravated assault charge, although depending on how we prosecute it, we might be able to elevate it to attempted murder. And you might as well make those charges double, because based on Detective Daggers' testimony, we know it was you who attacked him in the ship's engine room last night. Of course, none of those charges hold a candle to *actual* murder, and, well...let's just say a guy your size could've snapped Verona's neck like a twig. The fact that you were snooping around in the engine room will help convince a jury you're the snooping sort. The kind of guy who pokes around people's baggage in a luggage compartment and wouldn't hesitate to drive a knife into one of Johann's thugs' backs."

Jimmy's head snapped up. "Wait, what? *Luggage compartment? Thugs?* What the heck are you talking about? I did *not* murder anyone in a baggage hold."

"So you're admitting to killing Verona, then," I said.

"What? No! I did *not* say that. I mean, I admit I attacked Ghorza. At least...I think I did."

"You *think?*" I said. "What the hell do you mean you *think* you did?"

"I...well..." Jimmy shook his head and averted his eyes. "I mean...look, I just—"

"Spit it out, man!"

"I don't remember, okay!" shouted Jimmy, spittle flying from his lips. "There? Are you happy? I don't know!"

"Oh, come off it. You weren't that drunk." I breathed in deeply to confirm my own suspicions, but I didn't get any whiff of alcohol from him. I didn't remember smelling any on his breath during our fight in Ghorza's quarters, either.

"I didn't black out from drinking," said Jimmy. "At least...not from the booze."

"Maybe you should elaborate on that," said Shay.

Jimmy shook his head again. "As if you'd believe me."

Shay glanced at me. "We might."

"It's...well...gods this sounds crazy." Jimmy sighed. "I think somebody drugged me. More than once. Look, it's no secret I enjoy a few stiff drinks every now and then. I've probably had more than my fair share over the last few days, but I know how liquor hits me. And messing with my mind? Making me sweat and setting my head on fire? Playing with my memories? Nuh-uh. That's something else. Someone's been feeding me something. I don't know who, and I don't know what, but they have."

I returned Shay's glance. "Jimmy, I'm not normally the type to buy into stories about magical fairies and alien encounters, but in this instance, I believe you. Not only because it matches the hints you dropped when we chatted in the lounge a couple nights back, but because someone spiked my drink yesterday afternoon, too. I think I experienced some of the same symptoms as you. But here's one of our problems. That evening two nights back when we met in the lounge? That's the night Verona was killed. And you went missing right around the time she was murdered."

"What?" said Jimmy. "You can't be serious. I didn't kill her!"

"If you expect us to believe that, then you'd better start talking," said Shay. "We saw you at the opera that night, seated next to Ghorza. You had a fight and left. What were you arguing about?"

"The same thing we are," said Jimmy. "I thought I'd been drugged before I got kicked out of the poker tournament. I'd seen Ghorza that morning, looking like she'd been trampled by a horse. I wanted to see if she'd been drugged, too. I danced around the issue, 'cause I didn't want to tip her off that I knew, but she got sore with me and I left."

"Where'd you go?" I asked.

"Down to the lounge. I got a drink from the bartender. Probably wasn't the best idea, seeing as I still wasn't feeling too good at that point, and darn it if that drink wasn't spiked, too."

"You blacked out?" asked Shay.

Jimmy nodded and pointed at me. "Next thing I remember, you showed up. I tried to play it cool, but I honestly had no idea what was going on."

"Why didn't you mention anything?" I asked.

"Why would I?" said Jimmy. "I didn't know you were cops. And like I said, I was out of it. I was trying my best to stay upright."

I did some mental math. "From the point you left the opera to the point I met you in the lounge was maybe an hour and a half. Plenty of time for you to head down to the pool and kill Verona."

"What?" said Jimmy. "I'm telling you, I didn't kill her. I blacked out in the lounge. I couldn't have gone anywhere. I must've been there the whole time."

"*Must've?*" I said. "So you're saying you don't remember if you stayed there or not?"

Jimmy started to stammer. "Well...no. But...look, I know how you cops think. You think I had an opportunity to kill her. But I had no reason to want her dead."

Shay snorted. "Verona knocked you out of the poker tournament, Jimmy. A tournament with a twenty thousand crown buy in. You must've been pretty angry about that."

"Angry, yes. At myself. For playing like a fool. I told your pal here the same thing in the lounge. And yeah, I was pissed about losing the money, but killing Verona wouldn't have helped me in that regard. It's not like she had my money with her. The ship held that, in escrow, right? I'm assuming they still do."

"Anger alone can be a pretty good motivator," said Shay.

Jimmy waved a hand. "Oh, come on. I know I come across as tough, but that's just my persona. I don't lash out in anger."

"*Seriously?*" I said. "You expect me to believe that? You attacked me without warning in the engine room, and you tried to choke out Ghorza in a fit of rage. And those aren't guesses. We *know* you did it. There's not even a shadow of a doubt in the latter case. Motive is irrelevant, if still a point of curiosity."

Jimmy stared at the floor again. "I... I..."

"Admit it, Jimmy," I said. "You're a loose cannon. A raging menace. You have a serious drinking problem. Verona, an old, snooty elf spinster, took you for a ride for more coin than most people see in their entire lives, and it pissed you off. You whacked her out of spite, didn't you? Is that why you murdered Johann's man, too? Unadulterated rage?"

Jimmy shook his head and gritted his teeth. "No. *No way.* I may not remember everything that's happened over the last couple days, but I know myself. I'm not a killer. I was angry, yes, but I didn't murder Verona, or anyone else for that matter. And I'm sure as *hell* not going to admit to anything I have no memory of, not when all you have to go on is speculation."

"You're sure that's how you want to play this?" asked Shay.

Jimmy nodded, still refusing to make eye contact. "Yes. Now get me a lawyer. I still get one at sea, right?"

"You'll get one," I grumbled. "But you might have to wait a while. In the meantime, enjoy your stay."

I motioned to Shay. We exited the cell, past the brig door, and into the waiting area outside. Our sailor friend James was there, more to watch Jimmy than for any other reason. I waved for him to head back in.

"Jimmy's right, you know," said Shay.

"About what?" I asked.

"His motives."

I frowned. "What are you talking about? You're the one who pointed out Verona knocked him from the tourney."

"Yes, but we need to look beyond Verona," said Shay. "We're assuming he killed her, because he had the strength, motive, and opportunity to do so—assuming his story about being in the lounge all evening doesn't check out. But what about his attack on you? Or his attack on Ghorza? What are his motives for going after either of you?"

"Well, Ghorza won the tournament."

"And his plan was what? To strangle the cash out of her? Ghorza hadn't received her money from the ship's escrow account yet, though she may have by now. And Jimmy got knocked out two days ago. If anger were his motivation, why go after Ghorza? And why go after you last night? Of all the competitors, you actually showed him some compassion."

I rubbed my chin and chewed on my thoughts.

"There's more than that, though," said Shay. "You pressed Jimmy about Lumpty's murder, but Jimmy, along with Theo and Verona, were the only ones who couldn't have murdered him. The waitstaff confirmed their presence in the bar area. And what about Wanda?

She's the one Steck initially tracked to the engine room."

"You need to stop bringing up important points of information, because the more you do, the less certain I become that Jimmy was involved in anything but the attack on Ghorza. I'm even doubting if he's the one I hit with the rebar."

Steele knew I was joking, but she still gave me time to process my thoughts. For a minute, anyway. "What's the other problem you hinted to Jimmy about?"

"Pardon?"

"While talking to Jimmy about Verona's murder, you mentioned we had a number of problems. You only mentioned Jimmy's lack of an alibi for the time of her death."

I sighed. "Right. Well, the problem I had in mind is more one for us than him."

"Being?"

"Being that people who are drugged don't behave the way we're supposing Jimmy did," I said. "Suffer from dizziness and sweating and headaches like I did? Check. Black out so they can be taken advantage of? Check. Get sloppy and aggressive and get into fights if provoked? Check. But lurk around, tracking people, and murdering them in secluded areas? No check. Anti-check. X. What-ever the opposite of a check is."

"It could be Jimmy is simply lying about the drugs," said Shay.

"Except we didn't volunteer that possibility. He offered it himself. And it matches the behavior I observed out of him as he got knocked from the tournament and when I talked to him in the lounge."

Shay crossed her arms and frowned. "So what do you want to do?"

I smiled. "Same thing we always do. Keep investigating until we're convinced we know the truth beyond a shadow of a doubt. We'll start in Jimmy's stateroom. If we can find the knife he used to kill Lumpty, I'll change my tone. And we should send word to Steck. We need to check Jimmy's story about being in the lounge all evening two nights ago against the waitstaff's accounts."

"I'm sure he'll love the extra work," said Shay.

"It's the curse of being a cop." I waved toward the exit. "Come on. Let's go."

36

I closed a dresser drawer and threw up my hands. "Well, I give up. There's nothing here."

Shay stepped from Jimmy's bathroom. His stateroom largely mirrored our own, except his had only a single bedroom and the living area was smaller and less ornate.

"Agreed," said Shay. "I didn't find any knives or weapons of any kind. No drugs, either, unless you include the booze—and that doesn't really count because it's all gone." She shook an empty bottle at me as evidence.

"None of which means anything," I said. "He wouldn't have drugged himself, and if he did murder Lumpty, he could've thrown the knife overboard or into a maintenance hatch. Therefore, we keep digging."

"So where should we place the next hole?"

"I was thinking I'd get your input," I said. "I'm not the only one with ideas worth paying attention to."

Shay smiled. "I know, but I'm willing to let you take the reins more often than not. With that said, though, I think either Wanda or Johann should be our next targets for interrogation."

I pursed my lips. "The nice thing about being on a ship is the suspects can't disappear on you. Why don't we start with Johann? He clearly suspected Verona's death, he was in the general vicinity of the pool the night she was murdered, and he knew about his own man's demise."

"Works for me."

We headed back to the promenade deck and in the direction of Johann's stateroom. Before heading to Jimmy's, we'd rendezvoused with Steck. To his credit, he'd stayed true to his word and hadn't balked at the additional task of talking to the waitstaff again. While there, he'd given us a list of all our competitor's room numbers, and we'd liberated the skeleton key from his clutches. Steck hadn't been sure if Boatswain Olaugh would approve of the transfer, but he and his captain had thrown us their full support, so I didn't see why he wouldn't.

We reached Johann's room. I knocked on the door. After a moment, it cracked open.

Humpty stood in the gap. "Yes?"

"We're looking for Mr. Preiss," I said. "And chance he's in?"

"It depends. Who's calling?"

I took a gamble. "Tell him detectives Daggers and Steele are here."

The tough's eyebrows furrowed. "I'll check."

He closed the door. Shay glanced at me. "Sure that was wise?"

I shrugged. "The man hasn't been particularly chatty when he thought us simply his competitors. His mood only soured after Verona and Lumpty's deaths. The threat of the law might loosen his lips."

We stood there tapping our toes for a minute. The door reopened. Humpty again. "This way, please."

We followed him to a living room much like our own but more opulent. More filigrees on the furniture's arms and legs, more crystal in the bar, more flowers on the hearth, and more gold inlay on the decorations. More of everything. Apparently the police department hadn't spent quite as much on our undercover operation as it could've.

Johann stood in front of one of the sofa chairs, dressed as always in an impeccably tailored three piece suit. "So. Detectives Daggers and Steele, is it? I must admit I'm surprised by your visit, although I'm even more surprised by the information you related to my man. I'd suspected you hadn't been entirely honest about your relationship to the rest of us, but *detectives*? Tell me, in what capacity do you function? Private? Municipal?"

"We're with the NWPD," said Shay. "5th Street Precinct."

"And your specialty...?"

"Homicide," said Shay.

Johann's jaw hardened. "So...*you knew*? That someone would be killed? And you did *nothing*?"

"No," I said. "It's complicated, but suffice it to say we weren't here in our capacity as homicide detectives. We came to investigate a fraud that was supposed to take place during the poker competition. The fact that anyone died during our time aboard was simply an...unlucky coincidence."

Johann's face fell. "Ah. I see. So you heard the rumors."

"You heard them, too?" asked Shay.

"Everyone heard them." Johann waved at the sofa. "Please, have a seat. Both of you. I'm assuming you have questions for me, so let's have at it. I'll do whatever I can to help."

"*You will?*" I helped myself to a free spot on the couch, and Shay sat next to me.

"Well, of course. What? You expected me to stonewall you? Why?"

"Well..."

Johann eyed me and took note of the look on my face. "Oh. I see. You thought me a suspect. Well, I imagine you think everyone guilty until proven innocent, but I assure you, I want this solved as much as you do. I was very fond of my man Ignatius. I considered him not just a bodyguard, but a friend. And as for Verona... I suppose if you're here, you can tell me what actually happened to her?"

Shay cleared her throat. "She was murdered, in the ship's pool area. Someone broke her neck. We found her floating in the water."

Johann's face darkened. "And you don't know who did it?"

"We have our suspicions," I said. "But for now, no."

Johann ground his teeth together. "The *bastards*. How dare they, whoever it was?"

"You seem surprisingly bent out of shape about Verona's death," I said.

"Well of course I am, you idiot," he barked. "I loved her."

I glanced at Shay. She looked as surprised as I felt.

Johann took a deep breath and let it out slowly. "My apologies. You're here to help. I shouldn't have exploded like that. I'm just...having a hard time dealing with the news."

"Mr. Preiss, I'll admit, you've caught us off guard," I said. "Perhaps you could fill us in? Specifically, could you tell us everything you know about the night Verona died?"

The old man nodded. "Certainly. I'll try to keep it brief. Verona and I...well, we go a long way back. Some thirty years ago we dated. At the time I suspected I would some day wed her, but I was too busy establishing my business. I spent too much time on it and not enough on her. Verona forgave me for it as best she could, but one day I lost a large sum of money on—of all things—a gamble. She left me shortly thereafter. I suspected it was because she didn't want to marry a pauper, but over the years I realized perhaps she took more offense to my reaction to the loss than the loss itself. Perhaps it was a combination of factors.

"Regardless, we parted ways, and the loss struck me deeply. I'd see her at social events here and there, sharing the occasional word, but we never had much time to ourselves. Until now. And seeing her here? Well, the encounter sparked feelings that had lain dormant for decades.

"Honestly, I didn't think she still harbored any feelings for me, but I'm an old man and not as inhibited as I used to be. Following the end of the first day of poker and my own elimination, I approached Verona and asked her to dinner. She hesitated, thinking my request was in some way related to my loss, but I assured her it wasn't and she accepted. We ate, drank, and had a merry time, connecting on a deep, human level—I think, in part, *because* of my elimination from the tourney. Due to it, Verona knew my interest in her was genuine. Anyway, after dinner we walked the ship, which was largely empty due to the opera, before our feet eventually carried us to the pool."

"So you were there that night?" said Shay.

Johann nodded. "It seemed a secluded enough place, and though neither of us harbored any delusions of youthful indiscretions, I think we both wished for our discussions to remain private. But it wasn't long after we'd arrived, while reminiscing about a party we'd attended long past, that a twinkle sparked in Verona's eye. She excused herself but told me to remain. I waited anxiously. Fifteen minutes later she returned wearing a brooch, one with an emerald at its center."

I'd almost forgotten about it. "Right. We found it on her but weren't sure where it had come from."

Johann smiled. "I gave it to her. Not that night of course. Years before, at the party we'd been discussing. I thought she'd kept it for its beauty, but Verona assured me she'd held on to it for more than aesthetic reasons. And so we continued to chat, each of us warming to the other. An electricity crackled around us, and I—again, being an uninhibited old man—told her to say put while I retrieved something of my own. I went up to my room, looked for it, and couldn't find it, so I asked one of my men where it was. They suggested it might've gotten lost and placed in the luggage down in the hold. I was forced to track down a porter, have him bring up the bags in question, and then, once I'd retrieved my item, I headed back down to the pool, hoping Verona hadn't become irritated by my delay. And that's when I chanced across the two of you."

"And this item...?" said Shay.

Johann reached into his jacket pocket. From it, he produced a small box wrapped in black felt. He flicked it open. Something small and round gleamed within.

"A ring," said Johann. "The one I'd bought so many moons ago when I'd intended to ask Verona to marry me. I never got rid of it, and knowing she'd be a competitor...well, I decided to bring it. I don't know if I would've asked her to marry me there in the pool room. Probably not. But I wanted to show her she wasn't the only one to hold onto such mementos."

Shay sighed, a pained expression of the sort women give while reading romance novels. If I wasn't so jaded, I might've acknowledged that the sniffle in my nose might've not been from allergies.

Johann snapped the box shut. "And now, this memento has become something else. A reminder that if I hadn't packed it away, resulting in my tardiness, Verona might still be alive. It's a...bitter pill to swallow."

"Don't blame yourself," I said. "That sort of thinking only punishes the victims. But if we could continue...? When we met, you said you were meeting an old friend. Someone you weren't sure was aboard?"

"Yes. Verona," said Johann. "Admittedly, it was a rather metaphorical way of putting things, but I thought the woman I'd loved had been lost to drink and the steady march of time. She hadn't. At least...she hadn't to me when I uttered those words."

Shay cleared her throat. "And after you met us...you headed back to the pool?"

Johann nodded again. "I found a crewman guarding the door. He refused to let me in. Said the space was being cleaned. At first I despaired, thinking Verona had slipped out on me, but as I gave it more thought over the course of the night, I began to suspect the worst. Clearly, I already knew Ignatius had gone missing. To be honest, I suspected the two of you after that odd meeting near the pool."

I glanced at Steele, not wanting to reveal what, or who, had been bundled on the linen cart. Maybe Johann already knew and didn't want to mention it.

"Speaking of your man Lumpty—er, Ignatius," I said, "let's talk about him. The night he went missing, you suspected he'd been killed, of course."

"I think I made my opinion of that clear yesterday morning," said Johann. "He *is* dead, is he not?"

Shay nodded. "Stabbed in the back in the ship's hold. Speaking of which, I don't suppose you'd know what he was doing down there?"

Johann cleared his throat and sat a little straighter. "Ah. Yes. Well, clearly you were aware of the rumors regarding this poker tournament. So was I, as I already made clear. My men are very *protective* of me, and of their own employment, so they took it upon themselves to investigate all of you, my competitors."

"Investigate how?" I said.

"Again, I wouldn't know," said Johann. "But they might've looked into your personal property to see if any of you were in possession of equipment that would allow you to cheat at cards or have documents tying you to a conspiracy. Again, all performed entirely of their own volition."

"Of course," I said. "And this all occurred the first night aboard the *Prodigious?*"

"Theoretically, if it occurred, it would've occurred then," said Johann.

I glanced at Steele. "Well, that explains who broke into our apartment."

"The first time, anyway," said Shay.

I turned back to Johann. "And your men. Were they assigned—I mean, did they *voluntarily choose* to investigate the possessions of specific parties?"

"They did."

"Who did Ignatius investigate?"

"To my knowledge," said Johann, "he'd taken it upon himself to look into the dealings of Miss Skeez, Mr. Hornshoe, and Miss Lang."

"Miss Lang?" I asked.

"Wanda."

Wanda. Of course. "And I don't suppose your men took it upon themselves to sift through our belongings multiple times?"

Johann eyed me with curiosity. "No. Just the once."

"What are you thinking, Daggers?" said Shay.

I gave my partner a smile. "I think it's high time we talk to the person responsible for the *second* break-in of our stateroom."

37

knocked on Wanda's door again and waited. Still no response.

"Guess she's not in," said Steele.

"Good thing we have this." I dug around in my pocket and produced Olaugh's skeleton key. I flourished it before sliding it into the lock and turning.

I walked into Wanda's stateroom, a smaller, one bedroom unit much like Jimmy's. Unlike Jimmy's, Wanda stood smack dab in the middle of hers. She eyed us—literally! She'd finally removed her glasses, revealing dark brown irises that were almost as hard to read as the rest of her.

"Excuse me," she said. "What the *hell* do you think you're doing?"

My experience at the door hadn't prepared me for her presence, but I could sling dialogue off the cuff with the best of them. "Couldn't be bothered to answer the door, huh, Wanda? Still brooding over your poker loss, I assume. It's alright. I know how it feels, except I had *my* victory snatched by the jaws of defeat and you sort of puttered and died. Not sure which is worse."

"That wasn't an invitation to chat," replied Wanda in her reedy voice. "And you still didn't answer my question."

"We're just returning the favor," I said. "Isn't that right, Steele?"

Shay nodded and smiled. "We're normally big on privacy, but we're also big on retribution. Plus we're at sea, so that irons out some of the thornier issues at play."

Wanda's eyes narrowed and she took a small step to the side. "Who are you?"

"Jake Daggers and Shay Steele," I said. "We fibbed about our names. I'd say we lied about our professions, but I don't think I ever told you what it is we do for a living. In case you're curious, my tax returns don't list 'professional playboy' under the occupation slot. Rather, there's something far more *murdery* listed there."

That made Wanda freeze. "Ok, look. I don't know who you're working for or what your beef with me is, but whoever it is you're after, it's not me. I played a clean game, and I didn't hurt anyone. For the love of the gods, don't kill me!"

"Kill you?" I said. "Who do you think we are? *Hitmen?* As if I'd list that on my tax return. Please. We're homicide detectives with the NWPD."

"What? *Police?*" Wanda blinked, but she recovered quickly. "In that case, I have even less to say to you than I did before."

"Do you, now?" said Shay.

My partner sidled up next to me and slid her hand into my jacket's breast pocket. I was about to ask her if this was really an appropriate time to get handsy when she pulled it back, my kerchief held between her fingers. She crossed to the bar and, using the handkerchief, plucked a used glass from a tray.

Shay stepped back with glass in hand. She held it up to the light. "You know, I'm not trained in forensics, but I'm competent enough to take a set of prints. And smart enough to dust for them after our quarters are broken into."

It was a bluff, but Wanda didn't know that.

The woman in black held up her hands. "Okay, look. Yes, I did break into your quarters, but I didn't take anything, alright. Is that what you want to know?"

"We want to know everything," I said. "Start talking."

"Why should I?" said Wanda. "And how do I know you're even cops? You could be bullshitting me for all I know."

"You want proof?" I said. "We left our badges ashore, but we could drag Boatswain Olaugh down here if we need to. And as for your motivation to help, I think we'd be willing to drop the B and E charge against you if you talk. That's assuming you're not guilty of stabbing anyone in the back."

"Whoa," said Wanda. "Cool it with the murder accusations."

"Then start flapping your gums in a constructive manner," I said. "You can start with why you broke into Steele's and my room."

"I broke in because you were stalking me like a creeper," said Wanda, "and I wanted to know what you and your lady friend's game was—which I only now discovered."

"You heard the rumors," said Shay.

"Of course I did," said Wanda. "Who didn't? And the two of you, coming in as a pair? That was suspicious enough to pique everyone's interest, even before you tried to follow me at lunch that first day."

"Orrin told me much the same thing before we started," I told Shay.

Wanda flinched at the dwarf's mention but didn't offer anything. I trained my eyes on her. "Well. Keep talking."

"What about?"

"Where were you the first night we were all aboard the ship?" I asked. "When all the rest of us were at the mixer and in the ballroom?"

"I was...meeting with someone."

"Who? Orrin?"

Wanda blinked. "Yeah. How'd you know?"

Orrin hadn't been at the mixer. Her flinch had given me the idea, but I didn't go into detail. "What did you discuss?"

"If you must know, we hashed out an alliance."

"An *alliance*?" I said. "Of what sort?"

"Of the same sort he expected you two to have," said Wanda. "He approached me that first night on account of my skill and play style, or so he said, asking if I'd heard the rumors about an impending scam. He thought you two might be up to something, being a couple and all. He proposed fighting fire with fire. I didn't like the idea of a partnership, but he presented a convincing argument. So we agreed not to go to battle over the same pots, and should one of us win, we'd split the earnings."

"And would you have?" I asked. "If you'd won?"

"Are you really questioning my integrity?" asked Wanda.

"Yes, but I suppose the answer doesn't matter." I turned to Steele. "What do you think?"

She shrugged. "Orrin was in the high stakes room this morning, same as me. He seemed pretty upset when Ghorza won. An alliance with Wanda would explain that."

Eyes back on Wanda. "Would Orrin confirm what you just told us?"

"Well I sure as hell hope so."

"Did you break into anyone else's apartment?"

Wanda chewed on her lip. "Assuming I did..."

"No B and E charges, I promise. Just tell me."

"Yes," she said. "Verona's and Theo's, the night of the opera. I didn't find anything. I would've kept going the next day, but the news of Verona's death threw me for a loop."

"And what were you doing in the engine room?" I asked.

"Trying to shake my tails," she said.

"*Tails?*" said Shay.

"That's right," said Wanda. "Jimmy, plus some member of the ship's crew. Not sure who, but I'd seen him hanging around the high stakes room."

"That's Steck," said Shay. "He's with us. You're sure the other was Jimmy?"

"Please," said Wanda. "That moose is hard to mistake."

"Well, so much for Jimmy's testimony," said Shay. "Daggers?"

I chewed on my thoughts. Wanda's story *sounded* good, but for all I knew, she was lying through her teeth. If she'd told the truth about Orrin then surely he'd corroborate her tale, but that didn't mean much either. Both had been unaccounted for during the time of Lumpty's death. That said, I didn't suspect Wanda of throwing Jimmy under the rickshaw. Too much of the evidence pointed toward him attacking me in the engine room. But did he murder Verona, or was it someone else? Orrin couldn't have done it. He'd been at the opera. And I didn't suspect Wanda had the strength to do so.

I leveled a finger at Wanda. "I don't know what your game is, but trust me, Steele and I are getting to the bottom of this. We're the best homicide detectives New Welwic has to offer, and if you think you can get away with murder on our watch—"

"Again with the murder accusations," said Wanda. "I'm telling you, I didn't kill anyone! I'm a poker player, pure and simple. I have no reason to want anyone dead."

"Maybe," I said. "Someone sure did."

"Daggers?"

I glanced at Shay. "Yes?"

"What about Ghorza?"

"What about her?" I asked.

"Besides Wanda, Ignatius was investigating *her* the night of his murder. She and Jimmy had a fight during the opera, which Jimmy claimed was over something mundane, but afterwards he tried to choke her. *And* she won the tournament, which all evidence suggested would be rigged in some capacity."

I scratched my head. *Ghorza.* Of course, Ghorza. We'd even headed to her stateroom following the conclusion of the poker tournament, assuming she might be guilty of the expected fraud, only to find Jimmy attacking her. Upon discovering the welt on his ribs, I'd been so sure he'd been the murderer that I'd completely forgotten to follow up with the orc woman. All told, the timing of the fight seemed a little convenient. It couldn't have been *staged,* could it?

I gave Steele a nod. "You're right. Let's go. Wanda? Stay here until we sort this out, otherwise all promises of B and E immunity are off the table."

Steele and I headed back into the hallway, crossed to the other side of the promenade deck, and made our way to Ghorza's room. This time, we weren't alerted ahead of time by crashes or yells of dismay, but something almost as sinister waited for us.

A door ajar.

I clenched my jaw and pushed on through, adrenaline rushing through my veins as I anticipated a fight or the presence of yet another body. I got the latter.

"Ghorza!"

The big orc woman lay on the floor, her arms sprawled out at her sides. I rushed over to her and squatted down beside her. I didn't see any blood, nor any wounds, but that didn't mean a lot.

"You've got to be kidding me," I said as Shay joined me. "Here I was sure that—"

Ghorza startled, reaching out and grabbing me with two hands. Her eyes fluttered. "What the...? I... Where...? Vlad?"

I nearly jumped out of my shoes. It made me feel better that Shay did, too.

"Ghorza!" said Shay. "You're alive!"

The woman kept babbling, incoherent. Her grip on me loosened, and her eyes, though open, remained unfocused.

A heavy chest on the far side of the living room caught my eye. Its ornate, banded top had been propped open. I could see bare wood within.

"Shay?"

She caught my glance. "That looks like a ship's chest. The sort where money from the poker tournament would've been held."

Would've. It was gone.

Ghorza kept babbling. "Vlad...? Where...?"

I glanced into the bedrooms. The elven manservant was nowhere to be found.

The truth hit me like a ton of bricks. "Gods, how could we be so stupid."

"Pardon?" said Shay.

"The con," I said. "It wasn't a fraud. It was a *robbery*. And based on Ghorza's condition, I'll give you one guess as to who was behind it."

I think Shay knew exactly who I was talking about, but before she could answer me, her voice was drowned by a resounding ship's horn.

38

The blare lasted a good five to six seconds. When the sound finally died, I turned to Steele. "I wonder what that was all about."

"Well, it was a single prolonged blast," she said. "It could be a warning signal."

"I meant that rhetorically," I said. "Seriously, you know what ships' horns mean?"

"The books I read tend to contain more than an assortment of dopey, tired mystery plots."

"So, what?" I said. "We're about to hit an iceberg?"

"We could also be nearing shore," said Shay. "Long blasts can signify approaching or leaving a dock. Remember the blast when we departed?"

I didn't, if I was being honest, but I'd had my brain scrambled by the sight of Shay in a tight red dress. I stood and crossed to one of the room's portholes. Sure enough, an assortment of warehouses, factories, cranes, and shipping containers rose up from the edge of the shore, not more than a few hundred meters away. The dock district sprawled behind it, as well as the rest of New Welwic's eastern side.

"We're back?" I said. "How can we have returned already?"

"We were never that far from the city," said Shay. "A few hours travel at most. You have to remember, this trip was largely a promotional stunt to advertise the poker tournament. The ship's real maiden journey will immediately follow this one. Maybe upon hearing word of the tournament's conclusion, the captain decided to turn the ship toward the harbor."

"But...we've had murders," I said. "Two of them. And we're not done investigating them. We can't let people off the ship. The captain couldn't possibly be so stupid as to want to let our killer go. He agreed to help us, in any way possible."

"Maybe he heard we had Jimmy in custody and thought the problem solved."

"Why would he think that?" I said. "We never sent word to Olaugh that our investigation was over."

"I don't know, Daggers," said Shay, exasperated. "I'm just trying to play devil's advocate. For all I know, Olaugh didn't even inform the captain of what was going on."

"Oh please," I said. "As if someone of the Boatswain's caliber would simply forget to mention..."

I trailed off, and my brows scrunched of their own accord. *Forget.* Could it be? I glanced at Ghorza, still delusional and without the will or way to lift herself off the floor.

"*Daggers?*"

I glanced at Shay. "Yes?"

"Were you planning on finishing that thought?"

"I was," I said. "But before I could, it sparked a new one. Jimmy. Jimmy suffered memory lapses, and though I doubt large parts of his story, I believe him about those. Ghorza here is barely conscious. And then there's Boatswain Olaugh."

"What about him?"

"What's the common thread between the three of them?"

Shay blinked. "I don't know. Olaugh doesn't have a drinking problem, does he?"

"Not that I know of," I said. "But keep that in mind for later. Something else."

"They're all...*large?*"

"Not exactly what I was going for, but close enough," I said. "They're all low breeds, or partially, anyway."

Shay's face darkened, and she frowned. "Come on, Daggers. I know you can be a bit of a jerk sometimes, but I've never known you to be a bigot."

"I'm serious," I said. "You can use whatever politically correct term you want, but Ghorza's a full-blooded orc. Olaugh is at best a half-orc, and by all physical indications, Jimmy is half-troll."

Ghorza moaned at mention of her name, but she didn't move beyond rolling her head.

Shay crossed her arms. "And?"

"They're not known for being the sharpest tools in the shed," I said.

Shay threw up her hands. "I can't believe this! I slept with a bigot."

"No," I said. "That's not what I'm getting at. What I'm trying to say is—*what if my drink wasn't spiked?*"

"Huh? Now you've really lost me."

"You may not be clairvoyant, but you know magic," I said. "You studied it for years. The psychic disciplines, specifically. So tell me, what can different sorts of mediums do? See into the past? Control objects with their minds? Influence people's thoughts?"

"Sure," said Shay. "Psychics, telekinetics, and telepaths, respectively."

"And how does telepathy work, exactly?"

Shay's eyebrows knit together. "Hold on. You're not suggesting—"

I jabbed a finger in her direction. "Does mental acuity affect one's ability to be mind controlled, or doesn't it?"

Shay sighed. "According to the texts I've read, yes. People who are less intelligent, or less psychically disciplined, are more susceptible to mental manipulation than others. As far as how telepathy works, it's more of an art than a science. The strengths of the telepath and the target are both important, but so is the technique. Successful telepaths often incorporate elements of hypnotism into their magic. Verbal suggestions, trigger words and phrases, even repetitive, calming visual cues. And substances that dull the mind can potentially make the subject more susceptible to manipulation."

"Like, for example, *alcohol*?"

"Yes. Like alcohol," said Shay. "But are you *honestly* suggesting a telepath was mind controlling Jimmy, or Ghorza, during their episodes?"

"Is it that outlandish?" I said. "If you accept my hypothesis of race-dependent mental resistance to the psychic arts—and the fact that you haven't already vehemently argued against it makes me think you've come across the same hypothesis before—then it makes a lot of sense, especially once you consider the contribution of alcohol. Jimmy was drinking heavily before his exit from the poker tourney, and throughout the past few days. Ghorza showed her fondness for liquor before the tournament began. Remember her hangover? And what about my own experience? I thought my drink had been spiked, but what if my drinking had simply provided a convenient moment for a psychic assault? My symptoms weren't exactly what I would've expected from a drug. And then there was your own mental lapse, right before you were pushed over the ship's edge."

Shay chewed on her lip. "I did have a drink right before I exited to the deck."

"But you're a half-elf," I said. "And, if I'm being honest, you're exceptionally smart. Even with a bit of alcohol in your system, the best a psychic attack could do is momentarily stun you—just long enough for someone to assault you."

Ghorza continued to mutter and ask for her manservant.

Shay glanced at the woman. "And you think Vlad is behind this?"

"We ignored him because he wasn't in the game," I said, "but he was always there. Always at Ghorza's back. Always close enough to initiate a psychic attack. He could've mind-controlled Jimmy into attacking Verona, who proved herself a serious competitor and, because of her elven heritage, immune to his telepathy. We didn't account for him the first night. He was tall enough to have delivered the downward knife blow into Lumpty's back, and he could've sent Jimmy after me in the engine room while tailing and ultimately attacking you on the deck."

"So Jimmy's attack on Ghorza earlier today...?"

"A distraction," I said. "A way to ensure we'd find Jimmy in the act and pin the murders on him. And Ghorza's been little more than a pawn the entire time. Think about it. Our initial intel suggested Ghorza was one of three prime suspects. Steck was right. *Almost.*"

"I don't know, Daggers," said Shay. "I find it hard to believe Vlad could mind control Ghorza so effectively and for so long. But—"

The ship's horn blared again. I glanced out the windows. The shore neared.

"But what?" I asked.

"Nothing," said Shay, her eyes following my own. "We need to find Vlad, and soon. Before we dock. Everything else can wait."

39

Shay and I headed out onto the *Prodigious's* deck and toward the front where the gangway extended, thinking Ghorza's condition, her missing cash, and the timing of the ship's horn couldn't all be coincidental. Unfortunately, we weren't the only ones who'd heard the blare of the horn and noticed our approach into New Welwic. A crowd of at least two or three hundred gathered near the ship's exit, milling and chatting, some with bags and some without.

I stopped shy of it.

Shay tipped her head toward the crowd. "Want to split up? Might give us a better chance of finding him."

I shook my head. "Finding Vlad isn't as important as making sure he stays on the ship, and to ensure that, we need to get the crew on our side. You hurry to the bridge. Get the captain, or Olaugh if he's lucid. Steck, too, if he's nearby. Bring them back with help. I'll work my way toward the gangplank. Hopefully, there'll be a couple crewmen there. Either I can convince them to help me, or I'll figure out a way to stall them until you arrive with the cavalry."

Shay nodded and ran off, and I waded into the crowd. They stretched across almost the full width of the *Prodigious's* deck. Those lucky enough to have found a spot at the railing rested their elbows while those behind them peeked over their shoulders on tiptoes. They chatted and smoked, and I caught snippets of conversation, from relationship quibbles to remarks on the weather, but more often than not unadulterated awe at the size of the ship. Even after having been aboard her for three days, I was still amazed myself, but I forced my eyes and attention inward, not on the roofs over which we towered.

Where could Vlad be? He was tall. He should stand out, at least over a goodly portion of the humans and dwarves in the audience. What had the man been wearing? Blast it, I couldn't remember. He blended into the background—by design, I was sure. Of course, he couldn't be alone, not truly. Given the sheer weight of the poker earnings, the man couldn't have squirreled them all away in a backpack or duffel bag. He must have a trolley with him, one of the shiny brass ones with the red velvet trim. The sun shone despite the season, and I scanned my eyes over the crowd, looking for a coppery shine. I didn't see one.

I felt a shudder, and the ship's horn sounded yet again, deafeningly loud now that I'd reached the open air.

Cursing the speed with which we seemed to have moved, I pushed my way toward the gangway, mumbling apologies as I shoved people out of my way.

Within a moment I'd spotted them: two crewmen in navy and white wrestling with the fixings of a huge ladder, and a third, busy holding back the impatient crowd.

I stepped toward them and paused. To their side stood a tall, thin man in a light brown overcoat. His pointed ears gave proof to his heritage, and though I spotted him in profile, I recognized him.

He turned and saw me just as I did him.

"Vlad!" I sprang toward him.

He returned the favor, springing toward me with outstretched arms.

The movement caught me off guard. I twisted and spun, lifting an arm to knock away Vlad's incoming one. We grappled in midair, each of us failing to find purchase before slipping past one another and trading spots.

I turned back to face him. Vlad pivoted and reached into his coat.

I was too old of a hat to overlook the movement. I danced to the side as Vlad's arm whipped out. A silvery gleam sparkled in his hand before shooting out, impaling itself in the wooden railing behind me with a thrum.

"He's got a knife!" I yelled.

The crowd around me had already pulled back, but at my shout they gasped and pressed into one another, suddenly fearful.

Vlad reached for his jacket again. I dove for his legs, scrummage-style, but the lithe elf jumped over me, landing back on the side of the boat by the railing. I rolled, hoping the movement would buy me a few seconds and keep me from getting speared by another flying dagger.

Crack!

Vlad howled as one of the sailors whacked him over the shoulders with a boat hook. The knife he'd already palmed clattered to the deck, and he stumbled.

I gathered my feet and rushed him, slamming into him with all the force my two hundred pound body could muster in an eight foot run up.

It was enough. I plastered Vlad against the deck, pinning his arms against his back to keep him from drawing any more knives.

"The gig is up, Vlad," I said, my heart beating strongly in my chest and my breath coming heavy. "We know all about your con and the mind control, so don't get any fancy ideas or I'll knock you senseless before you can do any more damage."

"Help!" shouted Vlad. "Someone help me! Get this man off me! He's crazy!"

"It's alright," I called out. "I'm a police officer. Now tell me, Vlad. Where's the money? What did you do with it?"

"He's a liar!" called Vlad. "Help! Please!"

The crowd held its distance. The sailors looked at each other in confusion. The one with the boat hook hefted his weapon.

"Now hold on there," I said. "I have a badge. It's just—"

"Move back! Everyone!" Boatswain Olaugh's voice boomed through the crowd, stilling the crewmen. When I looked up, I found him, Steele, Steck, and a pair of additional sailors rushing up the deck.

Vlad blinked and saw them, too. "Wait... The boatswain? You really *are* cops?"

"What?" I said. "You think we dragged Jimmy off just for funzies? Now tell me, where's the money?"

I looked around me. There wasn't a shiny brass and felt trolley nearby. No duffel bag or trunk. Where'd he stashed the crowns?

"No," said Vlad, though the conviction in his voice had faded. "This can't be right. I was sure you and that Steele woman were frauds. But...look, you've got to let me go. If you're being honest, we're on the same side!"

"Right," I said. "Tell it to the jury. Steele? Do you have any cuffs, or rope?"

"Oh, come on, man," said Vlad. "You can't be serious!"

A twinge zipped through my body, and my brain fluttered, wracked by a sudden, fleeting pang of confusion. *Come on, man.* That wasn't Vlad's line. It belonged to someone else.

Theo.

He'd uttered it over and over. When we first met. Before Johann's exit. Before Jimmy's exit. During the hand where I ousted Orrin and Shay when I'd suffered my drug-like symptoms. In the final hand where Ghorza prevailed. What was it Shay had said about telepaths? How they incorporated elements of hypnotism? Like trigger words and phrases?

I recalled Theo's face during that final showdown. That tensing of his jaw, that grimace as he'd pushed in his chips. I'd thought it a tell. A false one, perhaps, as it had turned out to be given his excellent starting hand, but a tell nonetheless. But what if I'd been wrong? What it if wasn't a tell? What if his shoulder were simply sore and had started to bother him as the day went on?

Theo stood about three and a half feet tall. His shoulder reached to Shay's hip. Right where her bruise was.

40

"It's not Vlad," I said. "It's Theo."

"Excuse me?" said Shay.

I stood, pulling Vlad off the ground and handing him to Olaugh. "I said it's not Vlad. Theo's our guy. He's the one behind the mind control."

"And you're sure of this because...?"

I gave her the condensed study guide explanation.

Shay nodded in response. "Theo did use that phrase a lot. And I noticed the grimace, too. He's small, but I was woozy and off balance. He could've knocked me overboard."

"So...should I let this guy go?" asked Olaugh.

"Are you kidding?" I said. "He tried to knife me. I'd be bleeding out on your deck if not for the guy with the boat hook. By the way, how are you feeling? Woozy? Disoriented?"

"Olaugh wasn't mind controlled," said Shay. "There was a miscommunication with the navigator. He didn't know about Jimmy or the con or anything else."

"Oh. Never mind then." I turned to our captive. "Listen up, Vlad. You said we're on the same side. Prove it. Tell me everything that's happened over the last thirty minutes. How is it we found Ghorza on the floor of her stateroom, and what are you doing here at the gangway?"

"If I do, will you let me go?"

"Not right away," I said. "But if you help us find Theo and unravel this mess, I might consider dropping the assault charges."

"Fine," he said. "About an hour ago, the ship's crew arrived with the poker winnings. Ghorza and I both had a drink to celebrate. Ten or fifteen minutes later, Ghorza took a seat, saying she felt a bit faint. I asked if she needed anything. She said it might be hunger and asked if I could grab her a bite to eat, so I went to the ship's kitchen and put in an order for room service. When I returned, I found her alive but unresponsive on the floor of our room. The money was gone. I ran into the hallway to see if I could find who'd taken it, but I hadn't been searching for more than a couple minutes when I heard the ship's horn. I assumed the thief would be heading for the exits."

"We must've just missed him," I said to Shay. Then to Vlad: "And? Why'd you attack me, then?"

"You jumped me first. What was I supposed to do?"

"Fair enough," I said. "But you knew we were cops."

"No," said Vlad. "You'd *claimed* to be cops, but neither of you had a badge and neither were dressed to fit the part. You're still not. You dragged Jimmy off before Ghorza and I could get any explanation. For all I knew, you two were in cahoots with him."

I glanced at the knife still sticking from the railing. "What can you tell me about Johann's man, Ignatius?"

Vlad blinked. "Who?"

Shay caught my drift. "Daggers, we'll have time for that later. Right now we need to focus on Theo."

"Right." I glanced into the crowd. It wouldn't be easy to see the little guy among the trees, but if Vlad couldn't manage the winnings without a cart, then what chance did Theo have? Unfortunately, I still couldn't spot a gleam of shiny brass anywhere. The sailors hadn't finished attaching the gangway to the ship, however, allowing no one to disembark, so at least we had that going for us.

"He's not here," I said. "We'd spot his trolley, if not him. Olaugh. Is there any other way off this ship?"

The big boatswain shook his head. "There's an attachment for a gangway on the port side, but there's nothing there at the moment. It would lead right into the Earl. Other than that, the only way off the ship is the way you two tested at sea."

"And I don't think Theo's jumping overboard with a sack of coins twice his own body weight," I said. "Which means he must've stashed the treasure somewhere aboard the ship. Where?"

Olaugh shrugged. "There's countless choices. The *Prodigious* is monstrous."

Shay shook her head. "I don't know, Daggers. If you're right about Theo—and I admit you make a convincing argument—then he would've known someone, at the very least Vlad, would find Ghorza and the missing cash. His only chance to get away would be to leave the ship before we could organize efforts to stop him."

"Maybe he didn't think we'd act so quickly," I said. "Or perhaps I was wrong, and he didn't suspect you and me of running with the law."

"Please," said Shay. "If he didn't think we'd act quickly, he'd be here, waiting to disembark. He must've known you and I were police officers. Why else would he attack us? He'd have to have some other...reason..."

She trailed off. Her brows knitted together.

"What is it?" I asked.

"You and Verona were both in-game threats," said Shay. "You were attacked after ending the day winning big hands. But I wasn't. A threat, that is. Neither was Ignatius. Something else ties the two of us together as targets."

Steck spoke, possibly because he didn't want to be forgotten. "Theo was one of the parties with luggage in the hold."

"Exactly," said Shay. "Theo must've had Ignatius murdered because of what he found, or what Theo feared he'd find there. And me?" Her eyes widened, and she grabbed my arm. "We need to get to the other side of the ship. Now!"

"What?" I said. "Why?"

"Theo didn't attack me on the deck because of *who* I was. He attacked me because of *where* I was."

I recalled the scrape on the deck and the scrap of cloth in the railing, wedged into the wood between the two... "*Lifeboats!* He's taking a lifeboat!"

We rushed off across the deck, me and Shay leading the way, Steck and Olaugh, with Vlad gripped in his meaty hands, in the middle, and the sailors bringing up the rear. Our feet clattered off the wooden planks as we reached the prow and rounded the bridge, then headed back down the port side. Given the sheer size of the *Prodigious*, it took a minute before we reached the area where Shay had been knocked overboard. I pulled air through my nose in deep draughts, blaming my fight with Vlad for my elevated heart rate.

"There!" Shay pointed. I spotted the scrape on the deck from the evening prior, and next to it, past the ship's edge, was a gap where one of the lifeboats should've been.

I gripped the railing and cast my gaze into the water. Despite the glare of the late afternoon sun off the water, it didn't take me long to catch sight of my quarry. There, not three hundred feet from the *Prodigious's* hull, floated a wide rowboat, and in it, a diminutive gnome. Theo sat at the oars, struggling with their size, and opposite him were two mustard yellow suitcases that seemed somehow familiar. Perhaps I'd noticed them in the hold the night of Lumpty's murder.

I heard a whump and a whack. Olaugh grunted. I turned to find the big boatswain staggering back, a hand over his stomach. Vlad stood by himself, his hands suddenly free. In one of them I spotted a steely flash.

I acted instinctively, throwing myself in front of Shay. Vlad jumped—but not toward us. He dove onto one of the spare lifeboats. His hand darted to and fro, snicker-snack. A rope whipped up and slapped the railing. Another spun through a pulley, producing a creaky whine, and Vlad dropped from sight.

I recovered quickly, pulling myself to the railing for a view. The lifeboat whose ropes Vlad had cut crashed into the river's brackish waters with a mighty splash. Vlad himself, clinging to one of the ropes still supported by a pulley near us, flew through the air, the wind billowing his hair. He landed lightly on his feet in the bottom of the rowboat like a seasoned stunt professional from one of the fight scenes in *The Pirates of St. Gustifere.*

"Hey! Quick! A boat! After him!" I shouted and pointed, incapable of stringing together more than two words at a time.

The sailors were ahead of me, already loosening the restraints on another of the boats. Olaugh jumped to their side, the front of his shirt clean and blood-free. Apparently, Vlad had merely punched him and not used his blade.

Olaugh jumped into the boat. I followed him, then turned toward the ship. "Shay?"

"Go," she said. "I'll keep an eye on things from here. Call for help. Organize efforts to track them both down."

I nodded. Olaugh gave the men an order. The pulleys creaked and the boat dropped.

Out in the ocean, Vlad worked the oars of his boat furiously. Theo wasn't oblivious to the action. He'd noticed the elf, and presumably us. He, too, cranked on his boat's oars, but his strength and reach limited him.

We hit the water. Olaugh grabbed the paddles and pulled.

In front of us, Vlad had abandoned his propulsion efforts. He stood in the small rowboat's prow. The low sunlight glittered off his hand. His arm whipped forward, and the gleam flew.

I couldn't hear the knife land over the lapping of the water and the steady whistle of the sea breeze, but I heard the scream it elicited from Theo. I stood and squinted, expecting to find the knife protruding from the gnome's chest, already dreading the interrogations to come wherein I'd try to shed light on the murder of our presumed telepath by the man who minutes ago I'd been sure had been behind the mind control efforts himself.

Theo continued to howl. He hunched over in his boat, and I caught sight of the knife. It protruded from the craft's lip, pinning the gnome's hand to the wood.

Vlad sat back down in his boat, and rather than make a break for it, he headed in Theo's direction at a more leisurely pace.

Olaugh and I caught up to Theo a mere moment after Vlad arrived.

The elven manservant straddled the edge of the two boats, keeping the craft together with his legs. Theo clenched his jaw, muttering though his teeth.

"Son of a...Vlad. You—argh!—piece of..."

Vlad gave Olaugh a nod. "Sorry about the shot to your midsection. I had unfinished business to attend to."

I glanced at Theo, then the bags that tipped the rowboat's aft toward the water's edge, then back at Vlad. "You didn't run."

"Or even swim," he said.

I scowled. That should've been my line. "You could've, you know. You might've even gotten away."

"And to what end?" said Vlad. "I told you, we're on the same side. I simply needed to deliver a little personal justice to Theo on behalf of my mistress. Something I didn't think you and your boys in blue would have the stomach for."

I snorted. On *my* side? I doubted that, but for the first time since setting foot on the *Prodigious,* I'd finally have a chance to find out the good old fashioned way— with a clenched fist and a deep scowl in a poorly lit room on dry land.

41

I emerged from the interrogation room, a sheet of paper rolled up in my right hand. I tapped it on my left palm and chewed my lip a bit before heading back up the precinct stairs into the pit.

I found Shay seated on the corner of her desk, still looking magnificent in her black and pink dress. Steck stood nearby, chatting with her. He hadn't changed either, but somehow his porter's uniform seemed more out of place in the station's depths than did Shay's cocktail attire.

"There you are," said Shay. "Thought we'd lost you."

"Don't give me that," I said. "I was able to conduct almost four interrogations in the time it took you two to do one. That gives me an eightfold per capita efficiency advantage. Someone should award me a medal."

"*Four?*" said Shay. "What are you talking about?"

"While you guys questioned Theo, I took on Ghorza and Vlad, one after the other."

"And while interrogating them, you forgot the most fundamental elements of math?" said Shay.

"Very funny," I said. "I finished talking to the pair and came back out here to find you still hadn't finished with the gnome. But even though *you* decided to take your time, not everyone on our staff did."

I handed Shay the sheet.

"What's this?" she asked.

"Preliminary CSU report," I said. "Our team found traces of blood on one of Vlad's knives. They matched it to Ignatius."

Shay's lips puckered. "I see. And you took this information back with you for round two?"

"Sure did."

"What did Ghorza and Vlad have to say about it?"

"Ghorza—who gave me a similar story as Jimmy regarding memory lapses and difficulty concentrating over parts of the voyage—claimed not to know anything about Ignatius, his murder, or the knife used to kill him," I said. "Of course, she also all but admitted she has no recollection of the events of that first night after arriving in the lounge and tipping back a few cocktails. Vlad similarly told me he had no knowledge of Ignatius. He vehemently denied ever meeting the man, much less killing him. He also claimed Ghorza couldn't have killed the man because she'd been in his care the entire time.

"Once I came back with the CSU report, Ghorza's story didn't change, though I could see doubt creep into her face. Vlad's story, on the other hand, changed dramatically. He took credit for the murder, saying he'd crept into the luggage hold and murdered the man while Ghorza was indisposed from drink."

"So Vlad's the killer, then," said Steck.

I shook my head. "I doubt it."

Shay tilted her head. "No?"

"He couldn't answer basic questions I posed him about Ignatius's murder and the condition of the hold," I said. "Besides, he didn't run when he had the chance."

"So why would he admit to the murder?" asked Steck.

"Because, despite my initial assumption to the contrary, he cares deeply for Ghorza," I said. "He's more than her manservant. I don't know what, exactly—a lover, a friend, a confidant—but I suspect he admitted to the murder to protect Ghorza. She must've snuck out on him that first night, and he didn't know where she'd gone. Perhaps he'd noticed one of his knives missing. Either way, he knew enough to connect the pieces when I related the CSU data. And he knew if he came forth, she'd be in the clear."

Shay whistled. "And they say chivalry's dead. No pun intended."

"So, how did the chat with Theo go?" I asked.

"Not as good as you might've hoped," said Shay. "I don't know if it's the recently stitched up hole in his hand or his incarceration, but he's become markedly less talkative over the past few hours."

"So he admitted to nothing," I said.

"Basically," said Shay.

"It wasn't for Detective Steele's lack of trying, though," said Steck. "She was like a badger, attacking him with everything she had. I've never seen anything like it."

"Probably because you don't participate in many homicide interrogations," I said. "Normally, I play the bad cop role, but Steele's come a long way. Although I have to take exception to your metaphor. As fierce as they are, badgers are black and white, not black and pink."

Shay shook her head at the joke, but she still smiled.

"Seriously," I said, "you didn't get *anything* out of him?"

"Not really," said Shay. "But we have a strong case against him. The motives all fit. He went after Ignatius after the man broke into Theo's room and after he discovered his custom strongbox luggage in the hold. He targeted you and Verona after both of you proved yourselves to be serious competitors for the winnings. And he went after me when he thought I was aware of his getaway plan. The people he targeted via mind control all fit a certain...*racial profile,* much as I hate to admit it. Well, except for us, but those telepathy attempts weren't successful. Less so with me than you, but hey—who's keeping score? The only thing we're really missing is proof Theo's capable of the charges leveled against him, so we'll need to bring in a forensics mage to administer tests. But if the mage determines he's a psychic, we'll be able to convict."

I frowned. "I guess that'll have to suffice. I hate it when the victims refuse to talk. Makes the conclusion of the case so much less satisfying."

Shay shrugged. "So...what do you think is going to happen to Ghorza and Jimmy? And Vlad?"

"Well, the law's a little slippery when it comes to cases like this," I said. "If we can prove beyond a reasonable doubt Theo was behind it all, that would mostly exonerate Jimmy and Ghorza. Murder, after all, must be premeditated, and if neither of the two were aware of their actions, they can't be held responsible, though either one might face lesser charges like manslaughter. There might also be civil suits. And while Vlad would go free, and while I'll keep my promise not to file assault charges against him, he's still facing numerous misdemeanor weapons charges for his knives—charges that might be elevated to felony charges given the use of one of those weapons in a murder. So it's not exactly what I'd call a happy ending."

A familiar crisp, light-hearted voice rang out. "Daggers! Steele! You're back."

I turned to find Rodgers and Quinto approaching.

"And looking snazzier than ever," added Quinto in his deep rumble.

"Thanks," I said. "Steele doesn't look too shabby either."

"I..." Quinto shook his head. "Never mind."

"So how'd it go?" asked Rogers. "You catch your conman?"

"Eventually," said Shay. "After being assaulted, drugged, or close enough, nearly dying of hypothermia, and having two people turn up dead along the way."

Rodgers and Quinto exchanged glances.

"Okay..." said Quinto. "After a teaser like that, you *have* to tell us everything."

"You sure? It's getting late." I glanced out the windows bordering the Captain's office, where only the barest glimmer of light trickled over the edge of the horizon on in.

"Oh, we're not missing this," said Rodgers.

The pair gathered chairs and settled in. Before we started, Steck thanked us for our help and excused himself, ostensibly to take care of paperwork, but I couldn't blame the guy if he headed straight home to bed.

From there, Shay and I regaled Quinto and Rodgers with our adventures. We spared no expense in the telling, except for the portion regarding our sexcapades— although I think our fellow detectives noticed when Shay's and my stories mysteriously deviated following our rescue from the ocean that night. Eventually, after a fair amount of jaw exercise and two cups of coffee and tea Quinto was kind enough to fetch for Shay and me, we reached the conclusion of our tale.

"Wow," said Rodgers, leaning back in his chair. "Mind-control? *Seriously?* And here I thought *our* case had been the goofy one."

"Do tell," I said.

"It's not anywhere near as interesting as yours," said Quinto. "A case of mistaken identities. Someone turned up dead, except it turned out not to be them. Instead it was their twin, except no one knew they had a twin, yadda yadda. I think Rodgers and I could've found more enjoyment in the investigation if not for the tough sledding we've faced with regards to the Captain's absence."

Shay glanced at the bulldog's office which had darkened under the fading will of the sun. "Where is he, anyway?"

"Still stuck in meetings with the police chief and DA," said Rodgers. "He's been MIA for days. We barely see him, and when we do, it's to sign a few warrants and mutter apologies. It's...odd."

"The absence?" I said.

"No, the apologies," said Rodgers. "You'd think he'd be angry about the wasted time, but he's almost the opposite. Resigned."

I noticed movement at the front of the station. Someone walked in through the broad double doors. "Speak of the devil."

The bald, stone-faced ex-marine waltzed on in, heading toward his office. He shifted direction once he caught sight of us, coming to a stop in front of our desks. "Steele. Daggers. Good to have you back."

"Good to be back, sir," said Shay.

"Rodgers. Quinto." The Captain gave them a nod, setting his jowls to quivering. "I know it's late, but could you gather the troops? I have an announcement to make, and I think everyone who's still here will want to hear it."

Rodgers and Quinto gave each other curious looks.

"Uh...sure, Captain," said Rodgers. "Just a sec."

The pair exited, leaving us momentarily in the Captain's lone company.

"What's going on, Captain?" I asked.

"I'll get to that in a minute," he said. "First, I want to congratulate you. I heard about the case, and it sounds as if the two of you performed admirably under less than ideal circumstances. I don't have all the details, but I take it you've apprehended the person or persons responsible?"

"We have," said Shay, "although we'll need the help of a forensics mage to confirm everything."

I expected the old man to complain about the cost, but he didn't. "Certainly. You'll get it done, I'm sure. Now there's one other thing I wanted to tell you. Apparently, the owners of the *Prodigious* are quite pleased with how you handled things. Despite two people being murdered, your swift actions not only kept their deaths quiet but allowed for the conclusion of the tournament. As far as they're concerned, Miss Skeez won fair and square, and that's the narrative they'll present. They expect good business going forward, and as a thanks, they've donated a hefty sum to the police department coffers, with the stipulation that a chuck of it be given to the two of you in the way of bonuses."

"*Hefty?*" I said. "How hefty?"

"Don't get any delusions," said the Captain. "After making bets of twenty thousand crowns, it might not seem like much, but trust me, it's the largest single check you're liable to ever get unless the city completely overhauls its tax structure. I won't let you know how much for fear of you spreading the news and having all of us get trampled by an angry mob in a few moments. Just promise me you won't blow it all on booze and floozies."

"See?" I told Shay. "That's the universal male go to."

"Oh, I never doubted it," she said.

A few other detectives and beat cops joined us, and we went quiet. Within a minute or two, Rodgers and Quinto had rounded up everyone who remained in the precinct at the late hour—probably forty or fifty bodies. A low murmur ran though the assembly.

Someone in the back, maybe Ferndale by the sound of his voice, spoke up. "Hey, Captain, what's going on? Is something afoot?"

The Captain eyed Quinto. "This everyone?"

"Far as I can tell," he replied. "I didn't hit the restrooms, though."

"Good enough," the Captain barked. "Alright, everyone, listen up. Everyone knows I'm a man of few words—"

"Though loudly spoken," I heard someone mutter.

"—so I'll keep this brief. As I'm sure you've all noticed by now, I've been away from my desk for the better part of the last few days. I'm sure you've all heard the rumors, too. That I'm in hot water. That I'm being investigated for my involvement with a gang of smugglers known as the Wyverns. That I'm about to be summarily dismissed from my post as the head of this precinct."

Another murmur ran through the crowd. *Summarily dismissed?* What the heck had happened over the past few days? What sorts of rumors had I missed?

"Well, you shouldn't listen to rumors, or spread them," the Captain barked, silencing the masses. "You all should know better. I'm here to tell you that after extensive discussions with the DA and chief of police, I'm *not* being dismissed."

I heard several individuals around me sigh, and a puff of breath forced its way from my own lips.

"However...I've decided to step down of my own volition."

"What?"

"No!"

"Captain! You serious?"

"Quiet," the Captain barked at the crowd. "Of course I'm serious. And both the DA and the chief of police are on my side. But the fact of the matter is once the

Wyverns case goes to trial, my relationship to one of their members will become public knowledge. In the court of public opinion, it won't matter what that relationship was, merely that I had it. It could cast a pall over this precinct, and I refuse to let that happen. You all deserve better. And so I'm stepping down."

I felt an ache in my chest. *The Captain was leaving?* On some level, I'd expected it, especially after what he'd told me following the end of the Wyverns case, but that didn't mean I'd really been prepared for it.

The murmur started back up, but the Captain spoke over it. "After speaking with the DA and the chief of police, they've agreed to vet, nominate, and name a successor to my post in short order. Probably within a week or two, which considering the bureaucracy involved would be a minor miracle. I wish I could have a say in the matter, but if I did, my successor could be viewed as a pawn and might be dogged by the same accusations of corruption that might be aimed toward me if I'd chosen to stay. However, I have been granted the ability to name an *interim* captain, subject to certain provisions, to hold down this fort until new blood arrives."

Was it my imagination, or did the Captain give me a look as he said that?

"Now, let me reiterate this is an interim position *only*. My successor will be here shortly. In the meantime, I expect all of you to treat the interim captain with honor and respect, and to aid them in the day to day operation of our precinct. It'll be overwhelming at first, especially given none of you have been adequately prepared for the responsibility."

I was sure of it now. The Captain *had* glanced at me. Good gods, I couldn't believe it! Interim or not, being named a precinct captain was an enormous honor. A stepping stone for future career advancement.

"The person I've chosen is hard working, brilliant, and attentive to detail."

That was me!

"Their commitment to justice is unparalleled."

Also me!

"They're incorruptible—"

I was incorruptible!

"—and, as made very clear to me by my superiors, their relative inexperience means they have no ties to the old regime or organized crime that could be used against them."

Once again me! Except I wouldn't call a dozen years on the force 'relative inexperience,' and my ex-partner Griggs had been implicated in the Wyvern smuggling scandal, but still!

"Detective—"

My heart swelled with pride.

"—Shay Steele."

Silence reigned before being replaced with a smattering of applause. My jaw refused to work. It kept flopping open.

"Alright, that's it," said the Captain. "It's late, so go home, have a beer, and get some rest. And don't shed any tears over me. I get to keep my pension."

The crowd started to disperse, but a cloud hung over us all. Then again, maybe it was just me.

The Captain grabbed my arm, leaned in, and spoke softly in my ear. "Daggers, listen to me. I know about you two. Maybe you thought I didn't, but I know. This wasn't the best decision. It was the *only* decision. So do the right thing. Help her. She needs you. Now, and in the future. Don't screw this up."

The bulldog gave me a firm glance and a nod of his head before releasing my arm, then about-faced and headed toward the door.

I turned toward Steele. She stood there with a terrified expression on her face. Rodgers and Quinto hovered at her sides, congratulating her, but she couldn't find the words to respond.

I just stood there with my mouth open.

Captain Steele? No way.

TO BE CONTINUED...

ABOUT THE AUTHOR

Alex P. Berg is a mystery, fantasy, and science fiction author, a scientist, and a heavy metal aficionado. Connect with him at www.alexpberg.com. If you'd like to be notified when new books are released, please sign up for his mailing list on his website. You will only be contacted when new books come out, your address will never be shared, and you can unsubscribe at any time.

Word of mouth is critical to author success. If you enjoyed this novel, please consider leaving a positive review on Amazon. Even if it's only a line or two, it would be a *huge* help. Thanks!